I0671891

TV-Live—or Dead

Olyve Hallmark Abbott

Deadly Niche Press
Denton Texas

Deadly Niche Press
An imprint of AWOC.COM Publishing
P.O. Box 2819
Denton, TX 76202

Manufactured in the United States of America

ISBN: 978-0-937660-70-6

Acknowledgements

A live TV show will not perform on its own, neither will an author write a book alone. With that in consideration, I would like to extend my thanks to Lisa Wilson, who lent her first name to my lead character (and I may not give it back); to Dennis Beck, Robyn Conley, Andrew Weaver and Tanda Dickinson.

Joseph W. Gray, M.D., ophthalmologist, offered invaluable assistance, and to Nan Alexander, who has sailed the ocean blue.

Many thanks to Tom Sawyer, author and producer of *Murder, She Wrote*, my favorite mystery series, and who offered helpful comments for this book.

And of course, applause and thanks to my editor, Susan Case.

TV-Live—or Dead
Cast of Characters

Lisa Warren: Singer, dancer, actress, and amateur sleuth

Mel London: Star of "Mel London's Comedy Show"

Dulce Carter: Former star

Cassie Brennan: Dulce's understudy

Steven Drake: Talent contractor and assistant director

Brad Hunter: Director

Raymond Meyer: Second Banana

Gregory Hardin: Stage Manager

Donna Springston: Actress, dancer

Jenni Kantor: Lisa's roommate

Jerry Mindel: Choreographer

Vince Varcasia: Tenor

Douglas Sander: Detective

Nate Sherman: Producer

Audrey Sherman: Mrs. Nate Sherman

Marty London: Mrs. Mel London

Dr. and Mrs. William Springston: Donna's parents

Chapter One

I never dreamed my big break in show business would come by filling the shoes of a dead woman. But that's exactly what happened. All I knew was they asked me to take Dulce Carter's place Saturday night on the biggest, hottest live TV show of the sixties.

Nothing could have made me late for that appointment, short of a Fifth Avenue bus hitting me. I entered the building, pulse pounding and high heels clicking across the shiny marble floor. I rushed toward the elevator as the door began to close.

A man held it open for me. "What floor?" He sounded impatient.

"Three, please." I thanked him and then realized I stood right next to Mel London. He was more handsome in person than on screen. Perhaps in his early thirties, wavy blond hair, broad shoulders... and he wore "Green Irish Tweed." I love that scent.

The famous TV star didn't seem very cheerful for a comedian, but maybe comedians had bad days, too. I smiled at him, hoping to get one in return. He simply pressed the button again, harder this time.

My attention shifted to the elevator walls on which small posters advertised a couple of current Broadway shows. I really wanted to see Zero Mostel in *Fiddler on the Roof* as soon as I could scrape up money for a ticket.

I hadn't even signed a contract yet but could already feel the excitement. This was big-time, glamorous TV and I was part of it. When I exited the elevator, London didn't follow. I wondered about that as I entered a large rehearsal area of mirrored walls, hardwood floors and folding chairs.

Leotard-clad dancers stood at a portable coffee bar in the far corner, all talking at once but in hushed tones. No one seemed to be in authority, so I walked toward them, feeling like an intruder. Singing gave me confidence, but breaking into song just then didn't seem to fit the moment.

Quiet fell over the group as one of the girls glanced at me. Her expression taut, she snipped, "Are you sure you're in the right place?"

"Yes, I think so. I'm taking Dulce Carter's role until she's well."

The red-haired dancer's face paled. Her green eyes flashed. "What do you mean, 'until she's well'? Is this some kind of joke? Dulce's dead!"

"She's what?" I couldn't have heard her right.

The redhead almost shouted, "Can't you hear? She's dead!"

The full impact of what she said scarcely registered before a familiar voice interrupted, "Cassie, we'll talk about it later...."

"But Steven, I'm Dulce's understudy!" With a brisk turn, she stalked away.

I spun around, thankful to see Steven Drake, the person responsible for getting me the role on Mel London's Comedy Show—quite a coup for this Texas girl.

"Lisa, darling, there you are." He reached out and put his arm on my shoulder. "I hoped this would work out for you. You look lovely, as always."

Steven had entered the room with a man he introduced as Brad Hunter, the show's director. He appeared to be the neat, casual type, with a brown wave of hair that dipped on his forehead, an engaging smile, and mesmerizing blue eyes. His firm handshake reassured my confidence.

"Miss Warren, thank you for coming. You can understand we're all disturbed, but trite as it may sound, the 'show must go on.'"

He's thanking me? I've dreamed of this moment for half of my life.

"We wanted a new face," he continued. "Steven vouches for your talent and I think we can both vouch for your face."

I'm pretty sure I blushed, but at least I felt more at ease.

"So if you'll come to my office, we can go over your contract."

I noticed the dancers staring after us as they took their respective places at the exercise *barres*—except for the girl who had snapped at me earlier. She gulped her coffee, crushed the paper cup and threw it on the floor, ignoring the wastebasket. I thought she'd rather have thrown it at me.

Steven and I followed the director to his office, and what an office it was. I'd not seen anything like this back home. Milano chairs flanked a tufted black leather sofa, which sat in front of a floor-to-ceiling bookshelf. Mr. Hunter gestured for me to take my choice and walked around to the other side of his teakwood desk.

Still stunned from hearing of Dulce's death, I needed to sit down.

Colorful chrome-framed pictures of previous television shows hung on the walls, reminding me where I was. And Dulce Carter was the reason for my being here in the first place.

"Miss Warren..." Mr. Hunter paused. "Lisa... as you can tell, this week isn't normal. We have some catching up to do." He fingered through papers on his desk. "Here are your script and contract for one performance, but I don't see your rehearsal schedule. If you'll excuse me, I'll be just a few minutes."

He stopped as he headed toward the door, lightly touching my shoulder. "Lisa, I gather you didn't know of Dulce's death before you arrived?"

I didn't answer for a moment, taken in by those blue eyes. "Uhm, no, I didn't."

"I'm sorry. We should have told you."

After he left the room, I found it difficult to stay calm. "Steven, what's going on? The red-haired girl in there told me Dulce was dead. I thought she had laryngitis or something."

"No, she's dead all right," he answered, leaning forward. "And the red-haired dancer is Cassie Brennan."

"She looked mad enough to drown the well-known swan in the lake."

Steven's smile carried no humor. "With good cause. She's Dulce's understudy."

I did not understand this. "So why didn't she get the role?"

He shifted in his chair, and after hesitating replied, "That's a story for another day."

I wanted to know right then but would settle for later. "But how did Dulce die?" Since I would be taking her place, I not only wanted to know, I thought I deserved an answer.

"That's the point," Steven said. "They don't know. The cleaning woman left early yesterday because she didn't feel well. When she came in this morning to finish her work, she found Dulce slumped on her make-up table. She couldn't rouse her, ran out screaming for Hunter, and he called an ambulance. The attendant said it looked like a stroke."

"But she was so young."

Steven paused, drumming his fingernails on the arm of his chair. He shook his head and sighed. "They gave her oxygen, and her heart was beating when she arrived at the hospital. She came around, alert, but something must've happened."

"Why do you say that?"

"Because in a matter of minutes, she was gone."

I pried a little more, "Didn't the doctors come to some conclusion? Anything... ?"

"Nothing final. They checked every possibility and called it a heart attack. They'll do an autopsy. Unusual, though.... Dulce came in last week, cheerful that her annual checkup was perfect. Her exact word, 'perfect'."

"That doesn't make sense."

"I know, but our producer was at the hospital. He said Dulce tried to say something, and the words didn't come out. They just thought she needed rest." Steven reached for a pen and handed it to me. "You better sign that thing."

"Right." This contract meant I could stay in New York a little longer. As great as the opportunity was, I needed more than a one-time appearance on this show. My paycheck would cover expenses for a while, but after it ran out, I'd have a problem. I didn't want to ask my parents for money. They'd done enough for me already. I glanced through the paperwork and flourished my signature.

"Great," Steven said. "Congratulations."

I had to smile when he did. He had a dimple in his chin—like Kirk Douglas. 'Course, he had a dimple whether he smiled or not. "I'm thrilled with the role but sorry how I got it." I held my arms close to my chest. I didn't have a chill, just didn't want one. Then, a sharpness of sudden cold swept through me, a familiar sensation I hadn't felt since I came to New York—foreboding, and I didn't know why.

Mr. Hunter returned with the schedule. "Fine, Lisa," he said, exchanging it for the contract. "If you'll go up to the fourth floor, I'll be there shortly."

Steven unfolded his tall frame from his chair and opened the door for me.

"Thank you," I said to both of them and left the office. Out in the hall, I couldn't help hearing Mr. Hunter's harsh, louder-than-whisper voice. Steven gave a brusque response, but I couldn't decipher either man's words, and I really wanted to know. There was no time to hold up a glass to the door. I needed to hurry, or my job might disappear before it began.

Lucky for me, rehearsal hadn't started yet. Not as large as the first room, this one had the same mirrored walls and parquet floors. Five young men and two women occupied metal folding chairs in the center of the room, half-heartedly laughing. They directed their attention to the show's second banana, Raymond Meyer, who was apparently filling in the break time.

I could visualize him as a head cheerleader, with his enthusiasm. He had a boyish look about him... maybe could lose a few pounds. I surmised his rosy cheeks could be a weekend on the beach still holding on, or, one too many gin and tonics the night before. But who was I to judge him?

Raymond sat on the edge of his chair, "But I didn't tell you how the book began," he said. "Now listen to this, 'Bang! Bang!... Bang! Bang! Four shots ripped into my groin and I was off on the biggest adventure of my life.'" He stopped midst his own whoop of laughter.

"Mr. Meyer," a man said, while scribbling on a clipboard. "Please save your Max Shulman quotes for a more suitable time." He peered out at me over half-glasses. "Ah, someone new to our group." He motioned in my direction. "This young lady must be Dulce's replacement for Saturday. Lisa Warren, isn't it?"

I detected a sarcastic tone. "Yes, that's right. I'm Lisa Warren." Everyone turned to focus on me. I fought the urge to check for a run in my stocking.

He introduced himself as Gregory Hardin, stage manager—slender built, with reddish, curly hair. He surely had freckles when he was little. After completing introductions, he said, "Our cast members are from all over. Would you tell us where you're from?"

For an instant, I surveyed the cast before answering. "I'm from Texas." I expected a varied response. *Oh, no. Tell me someone didn't whistle.*

Cassie Brennan gave me a condescending smile. I thought any kind of smile would have to pain her. She was so obviously jealous; the word might as well have been scrawled across her forehead.

Raymond accompanied a grin with a half wink. He took a deep breath and came up with a mock-operatic voice, singing, "Deep in the Heart of Texas."

The stage manager shot him a sneering look, but somehow, I figured Raymond didn't care what he thought. He indicated an empty chair for me to sit in next to a young woman with silky blonde hair.

"Hi. My name's Donna." She crossed long legs and smiled.

I smiled back, recognizing her right off. I'd seen her on the show and already liked her. Besides, I felt the need for a friend in this room of strangers.

"Here, sit," she said, patting the metal chair. "Don't let anybody get to you, Lisa. They're all wound up right now. It'll take a while to get back on track."

"Thanks for the encouragement. I appreciate your welcome, because I'm not sure I was—welcome, I mean."

"Basically, we're somewhat of a happy family."

As for Raymond, I'd always enjoyed him on television, but his off-screen manner annoyed me, like I wouldn't want him to date my sister. In spite of his antics, tension filtered my way. It made me uncomfortable, in part, because of Gregory Hardin. I could sense he resented me from the moment I walked into the room.

Hardin waved toward the door. "Here comes our illustrious director. I'll move on."

Interest shifted to Brad Hunter. I perceived the respect the cast had for him—either that or awe. In a short time, I had both.

"All right," he began, "as much as we might want to take a week off to collect ourselves, I'm afraid our sponsors would disapprove. We have to get to work. This scene will be a review for all of you, but it's for Lisa's benefit. If possible, no scripts. Understood?"

Everyone but Raymond seemed to agree. I suspected he held immunity to such directions. I decided Mr. Hunter was a taskmaster and rightly so. If the show faileth, the director faileth. But with the best comedy writers in the business, the show couldn't lose.

"We'll cut it short today," he said, "but be prepared to stay late tomorrow. And one more thing.... Mel's having a hard time with Dulce's death. He called to say he wouldn't be in today. That's understandable. We've all lost a talented performer and friend."

If feet could shuffle nervously, I thought I heard a few. It made me wonder what the cast had really thought of Dulce. With three run-throughs of the scene, I had my dialogue and stage directions almost memorized. This session was for blocking only, so I didn't go over my song. I used the remaining time at the barre. The first leg stretch reminded me I hadn't been working out. When the wall clock ticked its way to five o'clock, this rehearsal day ended. I changed clothes and met Steven at the elevator. Donna and several of the cast crowded in.

"How did it go?" Steven asked.

"The rehearsal went fine—all of it. And these guys made me feel at home." The elevator groaned to a halt and seemed relieved when we exited.

"See you tomorrow," Donna called. "Oh, would you look at that? It's sprinkling and I forgot my bumbershoot. No problem, I'll throw myself in front of a cab. It'll have to stop."

I waved goodbye. As she hurried away, I realized I hadn't brought my umbrella, either. Gazing at the gunmetal gray sky, I chastised myself. A girl should always be prepared in New York. This city amazed me. Cabs and buses whizzed by, leaving exhaust fumes in their wake. Buildings touched the clouds. The people were always in such a rush that I wanted to stop them just to ask the importance of their destinations.

"How about I walk you home?" Steven offered... "Hey, Tex," he snapped his fingers. "You still with me?"

"Oh, I'm sorry. I was absorbing the panorama. Yes, I'd like you to walk me home."

He opened an umbrella large enough to protect three people. That thing could be a real eye-opener. We took a right toward Fifth Avenue.

"I have an idea," Steven said. "Let's go to Schrafft's. Hungry?"

"Sure am. Haven't had a dessert all day." We carved a path through a crowd of pedestrians and passed Bergdorf-Goodman. As we walked, I asked him if he had any new reports on Dulce.

"Matter of fact, we have. A detective brought in a couple guys around noon. They fingerprinted everything in her room, including petals on the roses. They pestered the crew and staff with a hundred questions."

"Why the police? I thought you said a heart attack."

"I did, but like I said, they weren't satisfied. Until they get the autopsy report, they're not taking any chances—not when a famous person dies from mysterious circumstances, or so they think."

We rushed along in the drizzle. Since the hour was early, no line had formed at the restaurant. The counterman greeted me with a pleasant nod. The hostess led us to a booth against the wall, one of those with cushiony seats that caused the table to be too high.

"You seem to know a lot about New York to have been in the city less than three weeks."

"This isn't my first time here, so Schrafft's is already a priority." I unfolded the napkin in my lap. "I think I'll have a hot fudge sundae with almonds." I kept my weight under a hundred-and-twelve, so what was an almond or two? I was still curious about Dulce. After we ordered, I asked Steven if he minded more questions about her.

A furrow in his brow indicated he might mind. "Have at it, but don't expect any answers."

"Dulce had such talent. Let's say, for instance, someone was responsible for her death, what possible reason could there be?"

He seemed thoughtful, as if he might have an answer. "If we knew why, we might have the who."

"I just wondered how well you knew her."

Steven drank his coffee black, yet stirred it anyway then pushed it aside. "You have to understand, Tex, I didn't know that much about Dulce's private life, except her ex-husband was jealous."

"In what way?"

"Well, he used to meet her after rehearsal, and we figured it was because he wanted to make sure she didn't leave with anyone else. Dulce wasn't friendly toward most of the cast. You can ask them."

"No, thanks. I don't intend to don an interview hat."

The waitress brought Steven's tri-cut sandwich and set what appeared to be a dish full of almonds before me. "Now who would know there are all those calories under all those calories?"

I turned toward the counterman and smiled. He tipped his white cap.

Steven reacted with a raised brow and focused on his corned beef on rye. "Dulce was a beautiful woman and even at thirty-five, kept a certain plastic surgeon in business. But back to your question. From what I've heard and observed, she dated several men."

"Men with the show?"

"The writers might have joined the gaga-over-Dulce crowd, but I doubt they had enough money for her tastes. And some directors would use their positions to win favors from a woman like Dulce. Can't think that's Hunter's way." He took a bite of sandwich and reached for the mustard. "Even our own tenor, Vince Varcasia, had those golden retriever eyes every time he got near her."

"Was she serious about him?"

"She knew he came from a wealthy Italian family and went out with him for a while. Everyone but Vince thought she led him on. Come to think of it, she broke a date with him Sunday night. He was not a happy Italian. But come on, I don't put any stock in this murder theory. Are you a private detective or something?"

"It's hereditary. Uncle Hamp is a police chief back in Texas. My aunt and their little daughter were in a bank during a holdup, and the robber shot my cousin. When Uncle Hamp tracked down the killer, he was a hero to the town, and I guess to me, too.... I'm sorry, Steven. I don't know why I'm telling you all this."

He reached out and rested his hand on mine. "But I want to know more about you."

I slipped my hand from beneath his. I was ready to change the subject. "It's, well, we're a close family."

"I can see how your interest came about."

"In the fifth grade, I set a trap for a kid swiping Mars candy bars from one of my father's grocery stores. Hey, if the $64,000 Question had a category on Nancy Drew, I might very well have won."

Steven laughed and I crunched my way through almonds. I pondered whether to eat all of them or scrape the remaining hot fudge in the bottom of the dish. Not both. I do have self-control.

Steven paid the check and we left, hoping the weather had cleared. Good, no rain, and the air smelled almost fresh, as much as it could in this big city. We strolled a few blocks to the Fine Arts Hotel. Steven turned my key in the door for me and said goodnight. I watched him walk down the steps of the brownstone.

I signed in at the front desk and noticed my roommate had beaten me home. Jenni was the greatest. Brainy, too. She took modeling assignments to help pay tuition at Interior Design School. I felt lucky to room with her. It cost me a chunk of money to live a week on the eastside at the Barbizon Hotel for Women. One afternoon I ran into a dancer friend from Dallas who told me about the Fine Arts Hotel—convenient, economical, and theater-oriented. It took all afternoon, but I moved that very day.

When I entered our room, Jenni greeted me. "Hi, how ya doing?" She blew a wisp of dark hair from her eyes and resumed her vigorous waist-bends. She already had a twenty-one-inch waist. My passion for chocolate gave me a two-inch advantage, or maybe disadvantage.

Without allowing me to answer, she said, "Roomie, did you hear about Dulce Carter? I'm totally shocked. I just heard it on the news."

I dropped my things on the bed and erupted into an explanation. "As a matter of fact, I do know...." With dramatic pause, I said, "As of today, I'm Dulce Carter's replacement." I posed one hand on my hip and flailed the other above my head.

She stopped exercising and screamed, "How? How?..."

"Okay. Here's what happened. I met this Steven Drake during the TV-Spectacular I just finished. I had a small part, but I did get to sing. Someone told me Steven was a talent contractor and surveys other shows for prospective talent for London's company. So I, uh, innocently instigated conversations at coffee breaks—just in case." For all my unblemished façade, I hovered between innocent and devious.

"Now that sounded pretty easy. Any strings attached to getting this break?"

"You mean did I get cozy with the producer? That theory's merely an on-going rumor whenever some girl lands a great role. And that's spelled r-o-l-e. Hey, I haven't even met the show's producer."

"Very well, I'm convinced," Jenni conceded. "But now, I have a nighttime shoot on top of the Empire State Building, of all places. I've got to shower, but I promise not to use all the hot water."

I followed her to the half-opened bathroom door. "Jenni, I'm not taking this lightly. Sure, I'm thrilled to have a fantastic break, but someone died for me to have it."

"I know, Roomie," she called out. "But you can't look at it that way. It just happened."

"I guess you're right, but still... "

When Jenni finished dressing, she could have easily stepped onto the cover of *Vogue*. "You're gorgeous, Jen. Be sure to have someone see you home."

"Don't worry about me. And Lisa, I'm really happy for you. It couldn't happen to a neater roommate." She grabbed her tote and dashed.

Jenni surely didn't have reference to my tidy habits, so I hoped she meant I was clever and gifted. Whichever, I was still in luck—plenty of hot water left. I let it cascade over my tired muscles and reviewed my busy day. When the water temperature shifted downward, I towel-dried my hair, put on my pajamas and crawled into bed.

I read over dialogue until my eyelids grew heavy. Putting the script aside, I wondered if Steven and Brad's earlier harsh words had anything to do with me. And this thing with Cassie. I could understand why the dancer resented me. Actually, her charm impressed me a little less than Brussels sprouts.

Something else kept tiptoeing through my mind—something that happened during the day—but I was too tired to remember. I closed my eyes and drifted off, thinking of Nancy Drew and her little blue roadster.

That Nancy, she could solve them all.

Chapter Two

My alarm clock sounded like a Sixth Avenue fire truck. I finally admitted morning had arrived and groped for the off-button. A fall chill crept through the large windows of our first floor room facing the hotel atrium. More of a courtyard, it contained a smatter of flowering shrubs. Beds of lavender and white periwinkles still gave their all, until a future frost would strike them down. I loved periwinkles. It was almost like bringing my mother's garden to New York.

Untangling myself from the covers, I reached for my robe which had slid to the floor during the night.

A sleepy-eyed Jenni made a move to get out of bed. "Hey, we both need to expedite this getting dressed thing. I have a class and I daresay my celebrity roommate has rehearsal."

"That I do, but breakfast first. I'm starved." I scanned a drawer for my stockings and dragged my flats from under the bed. Shoving aside clothes in our shared closet, I settled on a brown tweed skirt, beige blouse, and my favorite teal cardigan.

"You know, Roomie, I've been thinking," Jenni said. "Won't it be some sort of prescience for you to take Dulce's place?"

"Maybe so. But nothing I had anything to do with. And you can't fool me with your big words. I know a few things about paranormal." I took a quick look in the mirror and ran a brush through my hair. Grateful for my Choctaw heritage, which gifted me with a natural tan, I applied only lipstick and a touch of rouge. "Oh, oh, my tights," I stuffed rehearsal clothes in my exercise tote and glanced through my script while Jenni dressed.

When she finished, we hurried down to breakfast, one of two meals a day provided by the hotel. Room and board cost us only thirty-five dollars a week, so as long as we paid the rent, we ate. I'm thinking some philanthropist for the arts must have subsidized the cost.

We went through the buffet and carried our trays of scrambled eggs and hot biscuits toward a table at the window. Jenni stopped, "Oh, I didn't get marmalade. I'll be right back."

"They don't have any," I said.

"How do you know?"

I had no idea how I knew. "Uhm, they forgot to order it, I guess."

"You're anomalous, Roomie. But I like you anyway."

Sometimes I wonder how I know these things. It happened soon after I fell out the door of my dad's pickup when I was little. For months I seemed to be sensitive to occurrences before they happened, and then it all stopped until just recently.

We sat down and Jenni slathered butter on her biscuit. "I sure would like some marmalade. Say, Roomie... you know, I've never asked you. How did you happen to come to New York in the first place?"

"Ha! Pure luck. The musical director of the last show in summer stock I did, said if I wanted the same role in a TV-Spectacular he was doing, he'd save it for me. I jumped at it."

"You always wanted a career? I know I always wanted to be a designer."

"Sure did. I started voice lessons when I was ten. My music teacher in grade school told Mother I had *resonance*, not that I knew then what it meant. I reminisced a moment, but it was as clear as if it were today. "My parents paid for voice lessons all my life. I guess I felt I had to do something with it. Don't misunderstand, a musical career has been my goal for as long as I can remember. I want them to know their support paid off."

By that time the other girls were down for breakfast, and Jenni broke the news about my TV role. Immediate congratulations came forth, for which I showed enthused appreciation.

One of the girls had picked up the hotel paper in the entry. "Hey, look! Here it is."

I glanced at the front page. The late Dulce Carter stared back at me.

"Let me see," Jenni said, leaning over to read. "Well, what do you know? They call it *mysterious*. Do they think she committed suicide?"

"Why do you say suicide?"

Jenni shrugged, "The sibylline part, I guess."

"They said it was a heart attack, but whatever the cause, her death has sure shocked big production television."

"They waited a whole day for it to hit the papers," one of the girls said.

"I know, but her parents were in Europe and couldn't be located till late yesterday. The funeral's private, but they'll have a memorial later." I didn't have time to discuss it further. I finished eating and downed the last of my orange juice. "Time's awastin'. See you tonight."

I arrived few minutes early at rehearsal. The London Show used three floors, with a wall or two removed for rehearsal halls. It was perfect and within walking distance of the theater where the show aired. I stood at the callboard and checked for any new instructions.

Hardin approached me with his clipboard, a stage manager's badge of office. "Miss Warren, the police completed their investigation of Miss Carter's room. It's dressing room 2, and you may use it," he added. "You might as well until they make a final contractual agreement, with— whomever."

Is unaffable a word? I'll have to ask Jenni. "Thanks, I appreciate it." I glanced at my watch and decided to stash my exercise bag in Dulce's—that is, my dressing room. I reached for the doorknob. My hand felt as if I grasped ice cubes. A strong precognition, but what did it mean? The eerie sensation, along with a blast of anxiety, caused me to yank my hand away. I couldn't explain it, but I retreated.

"On stage, everyone!" Hardin called in a strident voice impossible to ignore. It was not an actual stage, merely an area marked off as such, and I took my place.

Comedy sketches alternating with dance sequences made up the show. Primarily a singer and actress, I'd learned to dance just for kicks. Later, I found kicks necessary. Some choreographers in summer stock exuded an "I'm right about everything" attitude. Jerry Mendel seemed different, which put me at ease.

"Okay, Lisa," Jerry said. "The scene takes place aboard ship. I know this is a lot like rubbing your head and patting your stomach, but try to think like Gene Kelly."

"If you say so, but dancing across the bow of a ship while sending metaphors with these flags isn't easy."

"That's semaphores, Lisa."

"Well," I quipped, "I don't want to be one of those girls sending mixed signals." I rehearsed the routine twice before the other dancers joined. Two more exhaustive run-throughs, and I welcomed a break.

This time I was determined to enter my dressing room. The knob still numbed my fingers, but I drew a deep breath and opened the door to the scent of faded sweetness. Limp red roses stood in a tall crystal vase and reminded me Dulce would never see their petals fall. I removed the roses, avoiding their thorns. *Uhm, thirteen. The florist must have made a mistake.* I dropped them in the wastebasket and wondered how many flowers Dulce had discarded there before.

Since we already had costume fittings, we didn't have to rehearse late after all. I splashed cool water on my face and watched the water swirl around the hand-painted flowers on the porcelain washbasin. Not your every-day dressing room. Dulce had a plushy chaise upholstered in magenta and blue, with at least six toss pillows. I reached into the cabinet for a towel and noticed a small white envelope on the floor. It must have dropped out with the towel. I picked it up just as a knock rattled the door.

"Tex? You in there? It's Steven."

I scooped up my bag and dropped the envelope inside. "I'm here," I answered as I opened the door for him.

"C'mon, I'll escort you to the big gaudy costume company. It's like the public library with no books—only row after row of fantastic costumes."

"Thanks. I might not find it by myself. How do we get there?"

"A bus would be faster than a cab. We can walk the rest of the way."

We arrived at the bus stop in time to see No. 5 approaching. Vince Varcasia and Gregory had exited the building together and then parted company. I glanced back to see Vince, with dark eyes blazing, marching toward the bus. Donna ran after him and they climbed on right behind us, seconds before the door closed.

Sitting across the aisle, I noticed a muscle twitching on one side of Vince's handsome face. I thought his jaw would crack if he didn't relax.

"How do you think it went?" Donna asked. When no one replied, she gazed upward. "I didn't direct that at anyone special. What did anybody think of the rehearsal?"

Vince remained silent.

"Since that was a blanket question," Steven said, "I'd say you're probably thinking lovable Raymond is wearing a little thin."

"He may be trying to keep up our spirits," I replied. "I know Dulce's death affects you all. Not me as much since I didn't know her, but that doesn't keep me from being concerned. After all, she's dead."

We chatted the next few blocks and Steven looked over at Vince. "Vinnie, you okay?"

"Nothing I can't handle." He forced an almost smile then stood to ring the bell cord. No. 5 halted at the next corner, and we continued along the sidewalk to the building, which housed the costumes. Once inside, we took the elevator where Donna guided me to the floor where the women's clothes were located.

I gasped. "This is some kind of warehouse. Steven was right. It's a clothes' library. Uhm, they must use the Dior Decimal System. I sure wouldn't want to be here in the dark, alone."

Mrs. Bjornson, costume mistress, reached for a notebook from the countertop. She adjusted her glasses to the lower part of her nose and turned to the correct date in the Mel London folder.

"Ja, Miss Springston. And you're Lisa Warren? Correckt?" Her tone was sharp and precise.

I nodded, thinking she might have directed boot camp in a former life. I watched the woman turn on her heel and double-time toward the labyrinth of lace, satin, and chintz. I glanced around, awestruck by so many costume racks, more than a maze of hedges in an English garden.

Mrs. Bjornson soon returned with dresses for Saturday's show. She held up a brilliant turquoise number. "You like it?" she asked.

"Yippee-yes," I said. "My favorite color." I slipped on the dress. It was long, just right in the hips, but too small across the bazoom. That term came from Jenni. It appealed to me more than bust or boobs, and we never said breasts in Texas. "It's beautiful. I love it, except—"

"Ja, ja, I can see," Bjornson retorted, reaching for straight pins embedded in a red-checked pincushion strapped to her wrist. "I know what I am doing." She tipped her head and peered over the rim of her glasses. "It will be perfeckt." Her abruptness faded when the corners of her mouth began to curve up. "Yippee-Ja, it will be perfeckt."

Her sense of humor surprised me, and I think she knew it. "Thank you so much, Mrs. Bjornson. I love it."

Vince finished early, so he and Steven returned to the studio. I couldn't imagine what Vince's problem was, but maybe something concerning Dulce. Donna and I caught the bus before the going-home crowds. I had hoped to practice my song before rehearsal the next day.

"Why don't you rent a piano room at Fischer's?" Donna asked. "It costs only pennies for a half-hour. I'll play for you."

"Would you, please? I didn't know they had rental pianos."

Fischer Music Store was a few doors down from the bus stop. I gave the fifty-cent fee to the cashier for a half-hour. The small room contained an upright piano, a bench, and little space for anything else. We rehearsed my solo twice, and I felt secure. It helped that I had sung "Baubles, Bangles, and Beads" dozens of times in summer stock. *More than Dulce?*

We didn't use the full practice time. On the way out, I said, "If it isn't too much of a detour, how about going to the Warwick for coffee? I'd like to talk to you. There's never any extra time during the day."

Donna agreed and we walked to the hotel. We sat at the drugstore counter, ordered coffee, and split a salad.

"This is an old hotel, but it's cozy." Donna stirred two parts cream into one part coffee. "If you time it right, a celebrity will come in sooner or later. Just last week I saw Rex Harrison. Now, what do you want to talk about?"

I glanced behind us to be sure no one could overhear. "First, the police are waiting for results from Dulce's autopsy. If Uncle Hamp thought for a minute she was murdered, he'd stay with it until he had an answer. It would take him longer to be satisfied, but he would be satisfied. Did that detective question you or any of the others?"

"I don't know about others," Donna said. "All they asked me was how well I knew Dulce, and if I had reason to believe anyone would kill her. I told them what I knew. Nothing. Dulce didn't pay much attention to the rest of us," she added, spearing lettuce with her fork." It's unbelievable she's gone."

Dead is like that, I thought.

"Lisa, who's Uncle Hamp?"

"Oh, of course you don't know." I gave her the rundown on my favorite uncle.

"I'm impressed. No wonder you're into a detecting mode."

"You know, Donna, there's something else, too. Cassie glares spikes through me when we pass each other in the hall, or wherever. Dissention is not good."

"Cassie's talented but vindictive. Make sure your back isn't turned when she's glaring."

"I'll remember that. So tell me more about Vince Varcasia and our self-important stage manager. Something about them is a half-bubble off plumb."

"Uh, I don't speak Texan. Anyway, I wouldn't take an oath, but consensus is Vinnie had it so bad for Dulce, he was a wreck."

"And?" I accepted a refill of coffee from the waitress.

"The 'and' is, Gregory needed oxygen brought in for himself. He couldn't stand it when Vinnie went out with Dulce." She glanced up at the Nu-Grape wall clock above the counter. "Hey, I've got to run. I have a couple stops to make on the way home." She grabbed a cookie from the dessert tray and handed me three dollars. "This should cover it, okay? See you tomorrow."

"But..."

Donna was already out the door. I sighed and paid the check. As I walked past the magazine racks, I was pretty sure I recognized Ethel Merman perusing the latest issue of *True Romances*.

Chapter Three

The next morning my dressing room resembled the aftermath of a Texas whirlwind. "What is going on here?" I said to no one. My table was upside down and its drawers pulled out. The contents of my make-up kit would never be the same, especially my compact with its smashed mirror.

A would-be thief lost out unless he had a market for sweaty leotards. Although there wasn't anything valuable here, I still needed to report the break-in. First, I had to get to rehearsal.

The early schedule called for line readings and set description. Mel and I had exchanged hellos at a distance but had not yet been introduced. Mr. Hunter saw to the formalities, and I took my place for the skit.

"Please, everyone. I don't need to tell you we're against the clock. Mark all directions and try to memorize them as you go. If possible, I'd like to take it through a third time with no scripts."

Raymond Meyer was not there for his cue. This man traveled in chronic late syndrome.

"All right, here's the scenario," Mr. Hunter said. "Mel and Donna are in the Oriental restaurant, waiting for Raymond and Cassie. Lisa walks in, and when she sees her husband, Mel, with another woman, she's angry enough to chew nails. Instead, she chews chopsticks. You won't have to worry about a splinter, Lisa. It's uncooked spaghetti. Okay, we'll run through this segment first."

Cassie waited at stage left and turned back every few seconds. Talk about an aura of impatience. Dialogue progressed and still no Raymond.

Brad called to the stage manager, "Gregory. Go get him."

At that second, Raymond slid into place, grabbed Cassie's hand and tucked it under his arm. Making his entrance, he said, "Sorry I'm late, Mel, ol' buddy. Just keep on rollin' them egg rolls."

The line wasn't in the script, but I supposed adlibbing might be a common practice. No, it shouldn't be, not in live TV where timing meant everything. Mel's face reddened.

"All right, all right," Mr. Hunter said, "we have a show to do."

By the third run-through, the scene played smoothly. Mel voiced only one comment to me. "Well, you made it through the scene. We'll see tomorrow if you can sing."

I couldn't deduce a compliment from that but thanked him anyway. Besides, he said it with a sparkle in his eye. We'd probably get along. I dashed off the set to catch up with Mr. Hunter before he left. He could decide what to do about my ransacked room. As I turned, a man stepped in front of me. Rude, I thought.

He showed me his badge and introduced himself. "Miss Warren, I'm Detective Douglas Sander. I'd like to speak with you a moment."

I guessed it was my turn to be interrogated now. "Yes, of course," I said.

The detective wore a navy suit and light blue shirt—well-dressed, but not well-mannered. He pulled a notepad from his pocket. "Miss Warren, my questions to you are a technicality since the autopsy report on Miss Carter isn't in. Is there somewhere we can talk in private?"

Without waiting for an answer, he headed for a corner window. "I'm merely covering all the bases. I'm sure you understand."

"Yes, but I don't see how I can help, Detective Sander."

"Why not let me decide that?" His dark eyebrows raised on the word *me*. "Miss Carter was stricken before nine o'clock in the morning. Your director tells me you took her place on the show almost immediately?"

"Yes, I did. Mr. London's office called me and—"

"Did Mel London, himself, call you?"

"Why, no. He wouldn't be the one." I felt my face flush, but I didn't mind if my irritation showed. "To be specific, Steven Drake discussed it with the director and the director called."

"I see. But something interests me here, Miss Warren. How long have you known Mr. Drake?"

"About three weeks. I met him during a network Spectacular."

"Don't big shows like this hold auditions? And you waltzed right in and took over a role?"

With great effort, I reined in my temper. "Steven Drake is a contractor, Detective. He's paid to scout new talent so a television show doesn't have to hold open auditions, as well as those for union members. That takes days." I hoped the facts satisfied him. "Now if you'll excuse me, my break's over."

Sander folded his notepad. "One thing more, Miss Warren. I've heard you're asking a lot of questions. I suggest you curb that curiosity and concentrate on your career."

I turned away, thinking the only thing I intended to curb was my dog—if I had a dog. I didn't tell him about my vandalizing visitor. I hurried to Mr. Hunter's office, but he was in a meeting. My music rehearsal couldn't wait.

Afterward, back in my room, I stared at the mess as if it would've straightened itself. I shoved my make-up into the kit and set the table upright before thinking I should've let it stay like I found it. I left the building, a little surprised to see Steven waiting for me.

"How about a movie?" he asked.

I had visions of going straight home. "That would be nice, Steven, but I'm in need of a nap, followed by a long soak, followed by another nap—all night." That sounded so good to me.

"It's still early. We could stop at Schrafft's, except I think the counterman has a crush on you. You can't tell me he puts twenty-two almonds on every pretty girl's sundae."

What a persuasive voice Steven had. "A movie might relax me at that." I hesitated then said, "Tell you what, I'll go to a movie and settle for popcorn and a soda. What shall we see?"

"There's a good re-run at Loews, *The Serialist.*"

We could have taken a cab to the Broadway theater, but a bus fumed to a halt right in front of us. We climbed aboard and as soon as we found seats, I told him about my room. "Steven, something alarming happened today. Mr. Hunter doesn't even know, but someone ransacked my dressing room before I came in this morning."

"They did what? Was anything taken?"

"Not that I know of, but the idea of someone being in there is scary."

"We'll take care of it. It was probably a one-time thing. At least, whoever did it learned you don't keep your jewels in your dressing room."

"What jewels? Maybe you're right, but that won't keep me from looking over my shoulder."

We got off the bus in the West Eighties and entered the palatial old movie house. Steven bought a large popcorn to share, two colas and a couple of candy bars. "I brought you a Mars Bar, for old time's sake."

"A meal fit for a queen," I said, as we settled into our seats. "These old theaters astound me."

The lobby's chandeliers are glorious, right out of *Phantom of the Opera*. When the intro music began, I whispered, "This music sounds weird for an art film."

"Who said 'art?' It's about murder."

I gasped when the title came on the screen: *The Serialist*. So much for articulation; I thought he said *Surrealist*. The portrayal of a deranged serial killer left nothing to the imagination.

When the film ended and we exited the theater, Steven said, "I'm sorry, Lisa. This movie was bad timing, with Dulce and all. Got rave reviews and I missed it the first time around."

"Forget it. It just surprised me. You know, like expecting a Mai Tai and getting gin."

We caught the bus and headed back down Broadway. The evening had turned cool by the time we exited, so we walked the remaining blocks at a fast pace.

When we reached the hotel, Steven said, "I'm really sorry about the film."

"Will you stop that? It's okay." Before he could respond, I said, "Oh, I forgot to tell you, Detective Sander caught up with me today."

"So he finally talked to you. What did he say?"

"Well, he inferred I was a busybody. He asked questions about auditions, how long I've known you, and who asked me to replace Dulce—that sort of thing. Then Jerry called for us."

Steven had been leaning against the steps' railing, concentrating on my recitation. "Look, Lisa. You have two reasons not to worry. Number one, you didn't have anything to do with Dulce's death, so don't take anything he said seriously."

"And the second?"

"Oh yes, the second is you didn't have anything to do with Dulce's death." He smiled. "Is that clear now? I'm glad you told me about your room. We'll see what Brad says. Now go take that nap." He kissed two of his fingers and lightly pressed them to my lips.

Uhm, that was sweet. "Thanks for the evening, Steven. I'll see you at rehearsal."

When I went inside I noticed the coffee urn still sitting on the dining room buffet, so I carried a small carafe up with me. I had finished my bath and dried my hair when Jenni bolted through the doorway. She dropped her sweater on the chair. "Hi, Roomie. You have the murder solved?"

"The murder investigation hasn't gone anywhere. Nobody's interested in that theory but *moi.* Someone searched my dressing room and then a detective questioned me—"

"Wow, they searched your room?" Jenni's eyes widened. "Did they leave a message scrawled in blood across your mirror?" She swirled letters in the air with her graceful hand. "But why would anyone question you?"

"I can't imagine about the searching, and the detective was just doing his job. He sounded as if he thought I killed Dulce to take over her role." I poured what was, by now, lukewarm coffee. "Want some of this?"

"No thanks. I have a late tryst with that intriguing magazine editor. He asked me out, and believe it or not, he isn't married. At least that's what he tells me." Jenni began sorting through her rendezvous clothes.

"I'll never get used to these New York hours." I moved her sweater and sat down to go over my lines. "Oh, drat, I have to wash my stuff."

"I can do yours first thing in the morning," Jenni said. "I have a bunch, too."

"Thanks, but I need it for rehearsal. Why not let me wash yours?"

"Nah. I haven't sorted it yet."

I gathered up my stuff and headed for the laundry room. It was either do laundry by hand, send it out, or share four washing machines with everybody in the hotel.

Surprise. Two machines sat empty. Dim overhead light did little to enhance wallpaper of cabbage roses on a pale green background. I shoved my clothes into the first machine, turned it on and watched water trickle forth. When it began its babbling mode, I sat down with my script in a folding chair—the kind we used in church when the sanctuary was crowded.

The machine eventually chugged to a halt, and I pulled out my wet clothes. If I didn't stay until my things dried and someone else needed the dryer, my leotards might wind up on the floor. As it happened, no one else came in, even though the other machines had stopped. I turned off the lights and left. Nine-twenty and I hadn't even had my first nap.

Thursday morning arrived, and everyone in rehearsal raced around at a frenetic pace. Thinking of the energy required for one live performance exhausted me. The company had its own set department, so by this time, plans were well under way. Dancers and singers rehearsed in their respective areas throughout the allotted floors. The entire operation suggested synchronization of a water ballet.

Nate Sherman, the producer, seemed visible in all places at all times. Without Sherman, the show couldn't go on. I still hadn't met him, but I noticed him during the activity. He had an important say on everything, including the show and the performers—and paychecks.

This was the big day for dialogue rehearsal. When I walked in, actors had already assembled onstage. Raymond stood in the wings, early for a change.

Mr. Hunter motioned for the cast to come closer. "People, I have a favor to ask of you. Dulce's family has invited me to attend her services at 1:30. There will be a memorial at a later date, but for now, would you mind working through until one o'clock and break for lunch then? I'll adjust your hours."

This presented no problem and we began the restaurant scene. The only hitch was the head writer changed several lines, right after I had the first version down pat.

"Don't worry about the changes, Lisa. It moves faster and has bigger laughs."

"Oh, I'm not worried, Mr. Hunter." So maybe I didn't understand why they couldn't do it the best way first.

"Call me Brad," he said in a matter-of-fact tone, after which, he directed his attention to the sound of Mel's voice.

Mel's temper flared. "Why didn't you wait until today to write the whole damn thing, so we wouldn't waste our time?"

I thought this outburst not in character for him, but his and Raymond's scene had undergone drastic changes from the original. Still, the new jokes were perfect, and I couldn't see his being so upset.

The writer, who normally never spoke a serious word, walked over to Mel. "Look, I know this week is hard on everyone, but I assure you the changes will work. That's what we're here for, to make it better." He patted Mel on the shoulder and added, "Thanks for understanding."

"I know.... Sorry." Mel settled down and said no more.

After we finished, Orville, the sandwich entrepreneur, appeared with his shiny food cart. He always wore a smile, and I judged he enjoyed a successful business. His cart contained a selection of everything from peanut butter and jelly to ham on rye—and bagels, always bagels.

I made a choice of the latter with cream cheese, chose a cold drink and headed toward my locker. Opening the door, I grabbed my exercise tote and made it to my room before I realized the tote wasn't mine. Although the same color, it had gold initials, "D.C." Out of all those lockers, I opened the wrong one—Dulce Carter's.

I set down the bag and wondered, but not for long, if I should see what was inside. I found the expected make-up and also a small, brass folding frame containing two pictures. One appeared to be a family grouping and the other showed a young couple. It took a moment to realize the woman was Dulce. I didn't recognize the man.

Further search produced a contact lens container and a bottle of lens wash. I had no reason to know she wore contacts, but many performers do. I don't know why I opened the box. I just did. It had space for two pairs. One space was empty, but brown lenses rested in the other one. I had a second glance at the photograph. Dulce's eyes were blue.

I decided to return the tote to the locker and tell Mr. Hunter about it later. Eating my bagel came first. Rehearsal second.

A choral sextet backed up my solo. The sequence began on a serious note. Then Mel made a grand entrance, singing in some unknown accent. It was one of those moments of collective slapstick hysteria where everyone struggled to maintain a straight face.

When we finished the scene, Mel turned toward me. "All right, kid, you really can do this, can't you?"

I would have valued his compliment more if my mind hadn't still been thinking about brown lenses on blue eyes.

Chapter Four

The next day I found our director in, of all places, his office. Sometimes I thought an office was merely a set so a man's secretary could say he just stepped out of it. I explained about the mess in my room. "I'm sorry, Mr. Hunter. I should have told you about it sooner."

"Call me Brad." He smiled and maintained a casual air as if he thought my upside-down room had no importance. After a slight pause, he added, "Anything missing?"

"Nothing, except my peace of mind. But, the place was a wreck. We had a tight rehearsal schedule, and you left before we finished. I didn't think waiting to tell you would matter."

He nodded. "It could have been a worker or an outside thief, but it's odd they didn't disturb anything else in the building." Pulling out a file drawer, he inserted several scripts. "Since he didn't take anything, don't let it concern you. I'll check into it."

"One more thing," I said. "I found Dulce's tote bag. Should I give it to the police?

"Do you know what was in it?"

"Not much, make-up and—"

We heard a light tap on the door, and when it opened, Bert, the errand boy, peered inside. I'd heard Bert entertained dramatic aspirations, but his southern accent would have to go before he had any theatrical success. It took me long enough to struggle through my Texas drawl.

"Excuse me, Mr. Hunter." He acknowledged me with a smile. "Mr. Sherman would like to see you, sir."

"Thanks, Bert. Tell him I'll be right there."

"Lisa, we know Detective Sander will be back. I'll mention the dressing room. Please, don't worry."

"If you say so." I wondered how he would react if it were his room. "Thank you, then. I'd better be on my way to rehearsal." I left his office and headed for the stairs. Hurrying up the steps two at a time and watching only my feet, I almost collided with a man on his way down.

"Hey there, don't break a leg before Saturday," he warned.

I recognized Nate Sherman at once. "Oh no, I'll wait until Saturday." *How clever a response was that?*

"You do know who I am, don't you, Miss Warren? I'm the producer of the show you're in."

"Yes, of course, Mr. Sherman."

Our producer stood about five-ten, exuded charm, and wore glasses. I would like to know the name of his dentist. He had perfect teeth.

He descended to the step in front of me and reached for my hand. "You see, Albert Franks, director of the spectacular you were in recently, is a friend. Without his and Steven's recommendations, we might not have agreed to sign you, Lisa."

"Oh, I had no idea. I'm grateful. Thank you."

"Well," he said, with a sigh. "I have to meet with our director for a moment." With that, he released my favorite hand and took off.

"Whew," I said under my breath. "What was that all about?" I made a mental note to ask Donna.

The entire cast met for the first time in the larger of the two rehearsal halls. We worked this run-through only for timing. Occasionally the director substituted a complete skit, but the dry run went well and needed only minor adjustments.

Afterward, Donna and I stopped Orville as he prepared to leave—just in time to buy sandwiches to eat on our way to the theater for orchestra rehearsal.

"You know, it wouldn't matter how many days we had before a performance, we'd still be rushed," Donna said.

We exited the building, and I reached into the small white sack, retrieving a Swiss cheese on rye. "Darn, I forgot the mustard. Oh, well... Say, Donna, what is this with Mr. Sherman?"

"What do you mean? Now, wait a minute, don't tell me." She stopped in the middle of the sidewalk and snapped her fingers. "Ha! I bet he squeezed your hand."

"Yes. Yes, he did. Does he, you know, mess around? But isn't he married?"

"Of course he's married," Donna replied. "And happily. You have to understand this cast has worked together for quite a while. As I mentioned before, we're sort of family, and Sherman tested your reaction."

"My reaction?"

"Yes, but he's all business. No hanky-panky, at least not that I know of. I doubt it will happen again."

"I'm not usually at a loss for words. So give me an 'A' for not squeezing back."

The sky had turned that gunmetal gray again and sprinkles fell on our way to the theater. We arrived ahead of hard rain. I opened the side door and we checked in.

The theater's thick walls apparently kept it cool. A dramatic production once aired on Wednesdays from the same theater. After a long run, it sank. So the London show elected to move into the bigger space. It had been empty three weeks, and a musty smell still permeated the building. But the aroma of fresh coffee, with the help of exhaust fans, was rapidly filtering it away.

After an extensive wait, I said, "If we don't start, we'll never finish. Is it always like this?"

"I'm afraid so. Everyone has so much to do. Orchestra members receive pay based on when they're supposed to begin, not when they do. You can bet the delay isn't on purpose."

We went around to the green room and heard additional notes on the show. This room really was painted green. Benches, a soft drink machine, water, and a short exercise barre provided necessities for the last few harrowing moments before a performance.

"Places for the Fair scene," the stage manager announced. "Dancers? Places, please."

Cassie jumped up from her seat and stood on her mark. She was a dancer first and actress second, but performed as both on the show.

I walked to the rear of the theater and sat down. I wanted to see how much talent Dulce's understudy had.

"Hello," came a voice from the row behind. "Haven't seen you all day. How is everything?"

I turned to see Steven. "Hi, things are good, thanks. But I'm still nervous about those meta... I mean, semaphores. I have two more chances, today and dress rehearsal tomorrow."

"Didn't I say you'll be fantastic?" Steven moved from his seat to the chair beside me.

"This is my first time to see Cassie dance," I said, directing my attention to the stage. She's good. We haven't spoken to each other except in rehearsal scenes since that first day she almost took a shot at me."

"I've noticed she's somewhat irked at you, but she'll simmer down after a while."

"Steven, let me ask you—I found Dulce's tote. I reached into my locker, only it wasn't my locker, and brought out her tote bag instead."

"Okay... so what do you need to ask me?"

Gregory Hardin's voice came through the megaphone, "Places for the Navy scene."

"Don't go away," I said, "I'll ask after we do this number."

The orchestra began "Popeye, the Sailor" music. I felt comfortable throughout the scene, semaphores and all. By the time we finished, Steven was talking to Brad, and then Mr. Sherman called both men over to him. I took a couple sips from the water fountain and reclaimed my seat.

In a few minutes, Steven returned. "Sherman congratulated me for discovering you. Says I'll probably get a raise. Now, what about Dulce's duffel bag, or whatever?"

"What color were her eyes?"

"Her eyes? What kind of question is that?"

Uhm, I thought a simple one. "I found contacts in her tote—brown ones. And in a picture, they were blue."

"Well, yes, they were blue. She had blue eyes and wanted brown ones. Thought they were sexy. She didn't want anyone to know she wore contacts."

"That was her business, but why the big secret?"

"Can't answer that. A whim, I guess."

"I'm sure you're right." I wasn't sure at all. I couldn't get answers I wanted.

The lights in the theater dimmed. "I better get back to the control booth," Steven said, "Hunter's signaling."

As soon as he left, Donna called to me. "Lisa, wait. Want to go hunt food with us?"

"I don't know. I'm on the outer rim of fatigue," I said, with a well-deserved stretch. "Is it time to eat... again?"

"That's what performers do. We act. We eat. We act and we eat."

"All right, you win. Where do you hunt for food?"

"Usually around the corner at the Theater Bar & Grill. One of the guys can see you home."

I gave it a three-second thought and decided to join them. As we left the theater, Gregory Hardin and Cassie whisked by us. A few yards down the sidewalk, Cassie stopped and turned back at me. "You sounded good," she clipped.

"Thanks. You're a super dancer." I meant it but didn't know if Cassie realized I did. On reflection, I think Gregory nudged her just after she complimented me.

"Well, Donna, at least we're speaking. We did speak, right?"

"I'm a witness. Ah, here we are. I told you it was close. The Theater Bar and Grill is waiting. Or is that *are* waiting?"

By this time most of the cast members had paraded into the popular eatery. Vince, Steven, and four of the dancers joined Donna and me at a table for six. Slim people could do that. Bowls of pretzels and popcorn served as centerpieces.

I noticed Gregory and Cassie slip off to a faraway small table. As they passed, I did not miss the sharp glare from Gregory to Vince.

The Grill's décor screamed theater. Old playbills adorned the walls. Autographed pictures from Helen Hayes to John Raitt and Frank Sinatra hung on the walls of the booths. Tiny thespian masks patterned the white tablecloths.

"This is theater, all right. I would think you had to show your union card to enter."

"It's comfortable," Donna said. "And Lisa, it's really nice of you to come with us regulars. I know I enjoy being here. You can see Mel and Raymond had better places to go."

"Like you said, it's 'comfortable.' Even if I'm here only a week, I want to know everybody better. It's a good thing they didn't ask for my right arm to be on this show. I would have given it."

A mustachioed young waiter made a prompt appearance. I figured he thought the mustache gave him more maturity. His uniform included a satin vest trimmed with the same masks as on the tablecloths. He took everyone's order, with surprised reaction to my desire for mere coffee.

"Do you mean," Steven said, "as a new New Yorker, you're not having a real drink?"

"I've been known to occasionally imbibe... Oh, waiter, double-cream, please?"

"Oh-ho. Double-cream, is it? That makes all the difference."

The group's discussion centered on the show, with critiques varying from well done to extra good, and what we could do to make it better.

Vince went out of his way to sit next to me, or maybe I imagined it. I realized what Steven meant by Vince's golden retriever eyes. They did get your attention. I also wondered if he knew I noticed the hostility between him and Gregory. "Where are you from, Vince?" *Such originality. Should've been a scriptwriter.*

"I'm from right here, or rather New Jersey. My family came from Italy."

The waiter returned, singing "Your Time Is My Time," while he rotated a large tray above his head. We all responded with gracious applause. He delivered the orders and said to me, "Your coffee, Mademoiselle." Taking everybody in with one glance, he announced, "And in lieu of tips, *s'il vous plais*, please extend your praises of my singing talent to your producer." He perfected a low histrionic bow and departed.

I stared in amazement at my coffee cup, with cream whipped into a thick frothy layer covering the top. "This is gorgeous. I don't know whether to spoon it or lap it." I returned my attention to Vince. "Steven tells me you have an exceptional voice. From the little I've heard so far, I agree. Is this your first work in New York?"

"My first television job, yes, but I want to sing opera. You know, Verdi, Puccini. I've studied opera all my life. My grandmother sang at *La Scala*."

"Ah, I'm impressed. Opera's my dream, too. Who knows? Perhaps our paths will cross at City Center, or even the Met."

After a silent moment, Vince said. "Lisa, I think you're doing a good job as Dulce's replacement. She... " His voice faltered. "She was quite a performer. I thought... "

I decided to jump right in, pianissimo, of course. "Were the two of you close? Or, I guess it's none of my business." Steven had told me, but I wanted to hear it from Vince.

"That's all right. I thought we could have been close. Dulce was a few years older, but she said it didn't matter. I'm afraid I didn't handle her rejection very well."

Maybe Dulce had him fooled. After all, she was an actress. Vince quaffed his gin and tonic and ordered another. I detected bitterness in his tone and changed the subject.

"Steven, will you pass the popcorn, please?"

"Sure thing." He handed over a bowl, which became lighter as it moved around the table."

Donna took a handful and gave the near-empty bowl to me.

"Thanks a lot. This is real sharing." I finished the six remaining kernels and drained my coffee.

"I don't know about you all, but I need to get up early in the morning."

Everyone agreed and after paying the happy faux-French waiter, we exited. As we started to cross the street, I suddenly stopped, as if something held me.

"Come on," Steven said, "light's green." He grabbed onto my arm, but I froze.

Donna had already stepped off the curb.

"Wait!" I blurted.

She turned back, startled. "What's wrong?"

At just that moment a car screeched by the stopped traffic, ran a red light and sped through the intersection. The car's fender brushed against Donna and knocked her to the ground. Vince pulled her to her feet, while the driver sped in and out of traffic until he vanished.

"Donna, are you all right?" She should be the breathless one, but I was as well.

Vince held on to her. "My God, that was close! But Lisa, how did you know?"

Steven put his arm around my shoulders. "You knew that car was coming? You were turned the other way."

"I don't... I... must have known." I didn't say more, but the occurrences were coming more often.

"That was really strange," Steven said.

"Donna, are you sure you're okay?" I asked.

"Yes, I'm fine. No harm done. Except my tote bag is a little distressed and I'm afraid I tore my sleeve. Other than that, I'm good. I do believe we have a clairvoi—or whatever, in our midst."

"That's clairvoyant," I said, "but it doesn't happen often." The incident made me lightheaded, but I soon bounced back to reality.

Steven took hold of my arm. "If you're both okay, there's an all-night yogurt shop across the street. Like some for dessert?"

Donna declined and I said, "You're kidding. I can't see eating yogurt in the daytime, let alone, midnight. You know they put nuts and honey on it so you'll mistake it for something good and not something just good *for* you."

After a brisk five-minute walk, we reached the steps of the brownstone, "Thanks, all. I'll see you tomorrow. And Donna, regarding your morning wake-up service, be sure the police can reach me if you're missing."

Jenni was already asleep, so I turned my bedside lamp on dim. After changing into my nightgown and climbing into bed, I brought out a small spiral tablet from the side table and looked for my pen. I went to get my purse but stopped short when Jenni turned over.

"Is that you, Roomie?"

"No, it's a burglar. Go back to sleep."

"Okay, whatever you say. G'night."

The depths of my purse didn't turn up the pen I knew was there this morning. I glanced back at the side table, and there it was, right by my tablet. *This is slowly getting on my nerves.* Again settled in bed, I opened the tablet to the first page and wrote:

Who had reason to kill Dulce Carter?

I changed it to *may* have had reason.

Gregory Hardin—Jealous because Vince dated Dulce. *If Hardin couldn't have Dulce, he killed her, planning to frame Vince. OR, he could have killed Dulce so Cassie could take over her role. If the latter was his plan, it didn't work.*

Vince Varcasia—Distraught because Dulce dumped him. *Men have killed for less.*

Writers?—Steven said they didn't have the dollars to interest Dulce.

Cassie?—Jealousy can do weird things to a woman, so I've heard. *I can't say from personal experience.*

The ex-husband—Him, I don't know. *Exes are under suspicion right alongside current spouses. That's what Uncle Hamp always said.*

Anybody at all. Even Steven or Brad.

So, I'm a list-maker. But I don't know everybody yet. I studied my list a minute then closed the tablet and laid it on the table. Plenty of additional space remained.

I set my own wake-up service, as in clock, for five a.m. and turned off the lamp... still wondering about the recent paranormal occurrences.

Chapter Five

I surveyed the doughnuts, twists, and maple nut rolls on the cart and critiqued each one as to buttery meltdown. "I wish I could relish the taste without eating one," I told the pushcart lady, who arrived at the theater Saturday mornings around six-thirty.

"I don't know about that, Miss. You could eat a dozen and they'd never show."

"Thanks, that's all I need to hear. I'll have a maple nut and a chocolate lattice, but please move on before I double my order."

Handing me the goodies, she returned my smile and maneuvered the cart along. I kept my eyes on the doughnuts until they were out of sight.

"How about coffee to go with your breakfast? Sure you won't need a tray?"

I glanced up to see a grinning Brad Hunter holding out a cup of coffee.

"How long have you been there?"

"Long enough to see you labor over a monumental decision."

"Can't help it. Sweets are my vice. I could take chocolate syrup intravenously, but I do eat my vegetables. Besides, I ran five blocks to the theater. And thank you for the coffee."

"Here," he said. "Sit down and balance your bakery while I hold the cup."

We sat in the back seats on the theater's lower floor used by audience overflow from the balcony. I savored a bite of maple nut. "Mr. Hunter, what—"

"Call me Brad."

"Okay, fine. When does rehearsal begin if we're called at seven?"

"Anywhere from now until eight. We want to make sure the company is here early. If we have Danish, our people don't have to breakfast at home, and the sandwich vendor will be around later. We want the cast accounted for all day in case we need to revise anything."

"That makes sense."

"Lisa, a memorial is scheduled for Dulce on Monday at three o'clock. It isn't necessary for you to attend, but I wanted you to know."

"Thank you for telling me. I'd like to go."

"Good. Now if you'll excuse me, I hear my name being called, whether in vain or otherwise."

The schedule on show day was rigid, with no allowance for sensitive feelings or strain. If the orchestra went overtime, those paychecks could soar. The day of the show was divided into five segments. First, we had a last check on costumes that were already in our dressing rooms.

Next, we blocked the entire show's scenes for the camera. It went well. After a break, we had a straight run-through for timing and smoothness. I soon learned laughter couldn't be estimated at rehearsal. Since the audience couldn't adjust to the time, the show had to adjust to the laughter—a precise point. I figured I'd get used to these technicalities.

The stage manager called for attention. "All right, people. Take one hour for lunch."

Donna rushed toward the cold drink machine. "Oh, wow! I can't take it anymore."

"And 'it' would be? I thought everything went great."

"Yeah, I know." Donna popped the cap of a cola and took two swallows. "That Cassie. She makes me look like I don't know what I'm doing. If I ever fall on stage, you can be sure that witch tripped me. What is her problem?"

"I'd be the one Cassie would trip, not you. Don't let her know she gets to you. C'mon, let's have a sandwich from the vendor." We grabbed the first thing we could put our hands on and were glad the company arranged for Orville to be here.

Donna continued with her semi-tirade. "I thought Gregory wanted Dulce out of the way so Cassie could take over. But I couldn't forget his jealousy when she dated Vince." Her face remained flushed. "You know, it wouldn't shock me if Cassie killed Dulce. I mean I wouldn't bet she did—just that it wouldn't shock me."

"Don't let her get to you. Say, we better get dressed." I wanted to get her off the subject. We downed our sandwiches on the way to the dressing room. "I have a question, Donna. Where's the stage?"

"Oh, that. They removed the original stage to allow space for the sets and the soundstage. The sloped floor's perfect for the orchestra's platform."

I already knew that most of the lower-floor seats in this formerly impressive movie theater were in storage to make room for the television equipment. "Amazing. But in summer stock, we had dress rehearsal the night before the show. Sort of makes me nervous not to have dress until right before show time."

Sandwiches eaten and costumes zipped, we hurried out to find the musicians tuning up while Mr. Hunter made an announcement. "Use crisp dialogue so your grandmothers on the back row can hear every word." He sounded like a professor giving double assignments.

"One more thing," he added. "Remember, our producer is here, and he signs your checks. Be sharp, on your toes. Ready in ten."

Nate Sherman would be watching, for sure. I had already learned he carried the most clout and was the one to keep Mel happy. But the big-time responsibility of the show's success was actually on Mel's shoulders. I didn't believe he'd have it any other way."

Dress rehearsal went great. Jerry Mindel changed a couple of steps in a dance routine, and the director gave a pep talk to the entire company. I didn't need motivation. I had been inspired for a week.

Steven came over to me, flashing a 500-watt smile. "You were wonderful out there. Lisa, you don't have any cuts in your sketches, so you're done till the show."

"Thanks," I said. "I do feel good about it. Would you tell me one thing? Why does Mel stay in the control booth during dress?"

"Because he's a perfectionist. The cast isn't fond of the idea, but Sherman lets him do it his way. Mel makes last-minute adjustments while his understudy takes over."

"I had no idea that would happen. I thought it might throw us off, but if that's what it takes in TV land, I'll adjust."

"You apparently didn't have any trouble," Steven said. "Going to eat before the show? If you'd like, I can bring in something."

"Thanks, but no. Never eat before a performance. I may meditate."

"I believe I'll have something. See you after a while. "

Steven left and I took advantage of the one-hour break. Back in my room, I set my alarm to allow for the additional half-hour for makeup, in case I dozed. It would be hard to doze. The room was freezing. I changed to my robe and lucky for me, I found a blanket in the closet and nestled down on the chaise. Comfort won over and I drifted off to sleep.

Surely only a few minutes had passed when I awoke, a roar in my ears, and my arms flailing. I gasped for breath. *What is it? Where am I?* I didn't have nightmares, but this had to be one. I was drowning, a dream I've never had, even though water has always scared me. My blouse dampened with perspiration, an absurd fact in this cold room. The alarm jangled. Puzzling about the dream, I stood for a moment, pulled myself together and headed to make-up.

Cassie was leaving. When I spoke, she answered with something unintelligible. I took her reply as civil and smiled.

Donna sat in one of the make-up chairs, having her shiny blonde hair combed. "Did you get some rest?" she asked.

"Not exactly," I said. "Did you and Cassie just now have words?"

"No, no. She was her normal gritchy self."

I sat in the next chair and the cosmetician began her artistry, except for artificial eyelashes.

"Why honey, you don't need artificials," she said, "It's a wonder your own don't get tangled when you close your eyes. Ah'm only goin' to apply liquid liner with this little brush here."

I guessed she migrated from Georgia.

My medium brown hair was thick and shoulder length and easy to style for whatever the role required. When she completed her magic, I returned to my room and slipped into my first costume.

A knock vibrated the door. "Ten minutes. Green room, please."

I glanced into the wall mirror one last time. "Now's my big chance." I drew in a deep breath. "Mom, Dad, wish me luck." They always hoped I would gain what they ventured. Seeing their daughter on the little screen would be a big screen event in my parents' eyes. I wished they could be here in person. They've done so much for me. *I better get out of here before I cry.*

Meanwhile, the orchestra began to play the show's theme. The audience responded with enthusiastic applause in accordance with the lighted signs overhead. Mel's understudy took the stage to warm up the crowd with his individual humor and sight gags. Nothing but the best for Mel London. I wanted that to include me.

At the five-minute call, I stepped out of the green room into the wings and joined Donna and Cassie for the restaurant scene.

I whispered to Donna, "What happens if the show runs short, or long, for that matter?"

"Well, right after the finale, Mel announces the guest for the next show. If we're long, he can speed up. If we're short, he can ad-lib forever."

"That's what I'm afraid of. Since he didn't do the dress rehearsal, what if he ad-libs so much I won't know my cues?"

"He did that once with Dulce. Everyone thought she forgot her lines. I figured she would quit on the spot if Sherman didn't fire him. He didn't fire him, of course."

"I guess not. He'd never find another Mel London... Listen. I love that intro," I said. "Uh-oh, here comes Mel."

London took his place in the wings, exuding confidence. "Okay, Donna, let's go," he said with a smile as he reached for Donna's arm. They sat at the restaurant table during the intervening commercial. Lights came on and the scene began. Raymond still hadn't shown up, just like at rehearsal.

I caught a glimpse of Cassie in the wings. There was no mistaking her agitation. I didn't have to lip-read to make out a clear "dammit." Then, I saw Raymond, breaking a slide with his foot. He was clowning, making Cassie furious.

In a minute or so I heard my cue. My solo, "Baubles, Bangles, and Beads," began as a serious musical number. That changed almost forthwith. I was emoting my heart out, when Mel made his entrance through hanging strands of thousands of brilliant beads. He became entangled like a moth in a spider's web. All the while, he sang "Stranger in Paradise," every note intentionally off key—not easy. I joined him in a duet, and while I gave him exaggerated nudges to sing on pitch, the strands of beads broke. The scene ended with Mel's execution of one hysterical pratfall after another, slipping on an avalanche of bouncing beads.

During the next commercial, the stagehands cleared the floor for the finale. A crew had constructed a magnificent prop ship, with all the trimmings except water, for one flashy ending.

I think I waved those little flags at the right time, but I'd have to watch the kinescope to be sure. After we finished, the audience continued to applaud while the cast took additional bows.

Mel turned to me. "All right, kid! You have a gift for comedy." He grasped my hand and we enjoyed one more curtain call.

His words meant a lot. I accepted all compliments, even half of one from Cassie. After all, Donna did say the cast was a happy family, which I still questioned.

I returned to my room to change. Warm with excitement from my first show, I opened the door. My emotional warmth vanished when the room's chill again overpowered me. I forgot to ask about some heat. It was still confusing to me that the rest of the theater stayed comfortably warm, and my room didn't.

Then I noticed the display of flowers. This time, the scent was sweet and fresh. I went first to the dozen yellow roses. The card read, "A great show... Steven." A colorful bouquet from my parents and sister sat on my dressing table, and another from Uncle Hamp. Next, an arrangement of irises, daisies—all old-fashioned flowers: "Congratulations to the new member of our cast... Brad. P.S.—Wait for me after the show?"

Long-stemmed red roses caught my attention. Uhm, no card. I figured it would turn up later, so I shed my sailor costume and threw on a robe. I set the make-up remover by the basin, removed the lid and then reached for a cleansing towel. When I turned back, fingers ready to plunge into the oily cream, the jar was gone.

Whoa! Am I losing it? I blinked and scanned the countertop. It wasn't there. But not four feet away, the closed jar sat on a table by the chaise. A surreal chill ran through me. I remembered taking off the lid because it was difficult to turn, and I certainly did not put it on the table.

The incident shook my nerves, but I couldn't stand there wringing my hands over it. Assembling courage, I grabbed that jar and slathered cream on my face. I would try to think of something else while I had my shower. It must have been a good idea, because my nerves calmed after warm water dashed over me.

I brushed my hair and settled my thoughts on Brad Hunter's invitation. I donned a gray silk Oleg Cassini dress with a triangular cutout in front, not too low if I stood up straight. Bergdorf's had this great sale right after I got paid for the TV Spectacular, so what could a girl do?

Paycheck well spent. My mother always said, "Simple elegance is best and be sure to watch your posture."

Before leaving my room, I peered among the stems of the red roses, thinking the card may have slipped through. I felt as if a cool misty web draped over me. I stepped back, with a tingle of dark uneasiness.

Chapter Six

A voice from outside the door broke the spell, if it was a spell, and the misty web vanished.

"What are you doing in there?" Steven called.

"Give me a minute." *Talk about punctual.* I drew in a deep breath, collected myself, sprayed on a touch of Bond Street, my favorite scent for fall, and opened the door. "Hi. I didn't mean to take so long."

Donna stood there with him. She balanced on one leg while she removed a black suede shoe and adjusted a small buckle. "Godfrey! Whoever invented ankle-straps ought to be sentenced to ten days in the Automat without any change."

"But the shoes are great," I told her.

"Don't you look great yourself." Steven said.

"Thanks, and also thank you for the flowers. I love yellow roses."

"Glad I made the right choice."

I noticed Brad approaching. Smiling, he asked, "Are you ready, Lisa?"

"Well, I told Steven and Donna I'd go with them, but... "

"We can all go in my car. First, I need to get something from my office. I'll meet you in front of the theater."

By the time Steven, Donna, and I reached the sidewalk, the crowd had thinned to a few stragglers who stood outside. Several theatergoers headed to the Grill, as they often did after a show, hoping to see the stars up close. They couldn't know the stars seldom went there after a performance.

Brad hurried out the front entrance. In private, I could refer to him as Brad, but somehow couldn't call him that to his face. He tipped the attendant who brought his car around and opened the front passenger door for me.

Donna patted Steven's arm. "Don't be concerned. He's just being polite."

"But I wanted to be polite."

I looked forward to the party and even fleetingly wondered if the murderer might be there. Would he, or maybe she, have a sign on his or her back?

We drove a couple of blocks and Brad asked, "Lisa, are you all right? You're rather quiet."

"Oh yes, I'm fine. If I'm tense, it must be the thrill of the show." I forced myself to relax. "Do the Shermans always host parties for the cast?"

"We don't have one after every show. You may think it's unfeeling to have one now, but Nate wanted to. He thought it might be good for all of us."

We drove east to Park Avenue and turned south for several blocks before stopping in front of an impressive dove-gray stone building. We exited the car and Brad handed the keys to a valet.

Atop the banisters sat two wondrous stone griffins, daring anyone to enter without permission. I braved their glares while a guard opened the door and checked our names off a list. High security, I thought.

Brad pressed the elevator button for the penthouse. "You'll like their apartment," he said.

As we neared our floor, faint orchestral music filtered down to us. The elevator came to a halt and we stepped into an exquisite marble foyer. I noticed the gorgeous Louis XVI entry table first, with fern-filled ceramic urns on either side.

Nate Sherman acknowledged us when we entered. "Come in, come in. We were beginning to wonder if we'd lost you. Lisa, come with me. I want you to meet my wife."

He led me through a crowd of people, many I did not know, and some I did, to one of two sets of French doors opening onto the terrace. "I believe she's out here," Mr. Sherman said. Audrey?"

A slender, attractive, and Oscar de la Renta-dressed woman of about forty turned from her conversation with three of the I-didn't-knows. She seemed to float as she walked toward us.

"Lisa Warren, this is my wife, Audrey Wells Sherman."

She flashed a faux-charming smile and said, "How do you do, Miss Warren. I must say you are a superb replacement for Dulce Carter." She turned to her husband and flicked an invisible speck from his lapel. "But she didn't find replacing Dulce too difficult, isn't that right, Nate?" She glanced back at me. "I expect you didn't even have to audition, did you, my dear?"

Nate Sherman tugged at his shirt collar. "She did a great job, sweetheart, and no, she did not audition. Steven Drake's word was good enough for Mel and me."

"I'm very happy to meet you, Mrs. Sherman, and thank you." I heard myself say the words, aware they were automatic. Being a polite individual, I searched for a sincere compliment. "I love your apartment... "

"Great party, Audrey, Nate."

Thanks to the thespian gods, it was Brad, a real knight to my rescue.

"Oh Brad," Audrey said. "We're glad you're here."

"Thank you. So am I." He put his arm around my shoulder. "Lisa, how about a drink?"

"Yes, please. I'd like wine. Wait, I'll go with you." I snatched the chance to distance myself from Audrey Sherman.

We strolled over to the bar that opened from both sides into the room large enough for a dance or a piano concert, and perfect for a cast party. I could see the jade-inlaid doors would conceal the bar when not in use. Brad selected wine from the bartender.

"Mr. Hunter, I wonder..."

Still holding my glass, he said, "If you call me Mr. Hunter once more, I'll have to ask Nate to take back this contract I have in my pocket."

"Contract? What are you talking about?"

"That's the reason I returned to my office. Nate forgot it when he left the studio."

"But..."

"No buts. You remember what I wrote on the card with my flowers? 'For the new member of the cast'?"

"Yes, I do, but I thought you meant for tonight's show."

Handing me the wine, he half-whispered, "I'll let you in on a secret. Mel and Nate gave you their stamp of approval Friday afternoon for the entire year. After that, we'll see what happens. No one can make a prediction until the end of the season."

"I never thought past tonight. I... I'm so thrilled I don't need a drink to feel dizzy." I could scarcely keep from pirouetting across the dance floor. "What can I say besides thank you for the contract, and the flowers?"

"Not another word. Let's eat."

During dinner, with everything on the buffet from caviar to *mousse au chocolat,* Nate Sherman announced I would be Dulce Carter's permanent replacement. The response was almost unanimous. Cassie hit the pads of her hands together, giving the impression of vigorous applause, when in reality, it made a faint thud.

Donna gave me a hug. Even Gregory exuded politeness. Amid offers of congratulations from other cast members, Vince Varcasia pushed through.

"Vince," Brad said, "would you take care of this young lady for a few minutes while I attend to some business with Nate?

"No need to ask."

"Don't let this Italian tenor steal you away," Brad added.

Grinning, Vince grabbed my arm and made a pretense of rushing toward the door. "Lisa, you wowed them tonight. Now, if you could only sing a big number."

"You mean like an aria from *Turandot*? Maybe, if I return as a guest performer one day. But I love comedy and Mel's talent for it. I'm so fortunate to be here."

"Nevertheless, would you sing a duet with me, even in the rehearsal room? Preferably Italian, preferably on key?

"The first opportunity we have. Now, I haven't had chocolate mousse yet."

"You have mousse. I'll have a King Alphonse. Why don't you sit here while I play waiter?"

I watched Vince as he walked away. A handsome Italian is so-o handsome. He soon returned with dessert. "I suspect this is a tad rich, and it's all yours," he said, sitting in the burgundy silk chair next to mine.

I sampled a taste. "Nothing can compare with it. I'll never eat plain chocolate again."

"I'll interpret that as a lie, but enjoy it anyway."

Thinking a moment, I tried to compose a question. *Don't compose. Ask.* "Vince, it's none of my business, and you don't have to answer, but were you in love with Dulce?"

The tenor stared into his glass as if reading tea leaves. "Even if it were your concern, I'm not sure I know the answer. I thought I was in love with her."

"If someone killed Dulce," I said, "have you given any thought to who might have done it? I mean, if Dulce led you on, wouldn't she have done the same to someone else?"

"Kill, as in murder?" He started, as if the idea never occurred to him. "I don't know who she was involved with, I was so wrapped up in my own adoration of her. When she died, I came to my senses and realized I had added another brass ring on her carousel. She had quite a collection."

"Vince, I'm sorry. I really am." I felt as if I had known Vince for months, not a few days. He could probably have any woman he wanted. Except Dulce.

A waiter stopped by with an offer of more wine. I could safely handle another, but only one. As he handed it to me, a voice reverberated above all the other conversations. "Ladees and gentlemen..." Raymond Meyer didn't need a microphone. He stood near an impressive ice-sculpted angel on the buffet table. "I want to propose a toast... a toast to a special someone."

"Do I perceive a formal recognition of our new star?" Vince whispered.

Raymond continued. "Quiet, everyone. We... ah... are neglecting the obvious acknowledgement of a person... very close to us."

I was struck by his expression, like he'd stayed too long under a high-intensity strobe light. With a glass in one hand and a bottle of scotch in the other, he poured amber liquid to the glass's rim and then wedged the bottle somewhere between the *salade nicoise* and chicken liver pâté.

"Vince, I believe Raymond's drunk and he isn't talking about me."

"Just notice this angel in front of you." Raymond placed one hand on the outspread wings of the ice sculpture, almost toppling it.

"Well, we had our own angel," he slurred, raising his glass. "A toast! To someone we loved. And if not, you didn't take time to care... to care about the real Dulce Carter." He broke into sobs and dropped the glass on the floor.

Gregory and Brad rounded the table and half-carried him from the room before he could fall across the buffet.

"Oh, Vince, not Raymond too," I gasped. *What kind of spell did Dulce weave?*

Nate Sherman stepped forward. "It's all right, everyone. The week's events have been a bit much for Mr. Meyer. He'll be fine." Sherman motioned to the orchestra to resume playing. He smiled broadly to the guests. "Please continue with your evening. You haven't consumed nearly enough food. And coffee is being served."

I wondered if sobriety tests were on the evening's schedule. This entire episode caught me by surprise, since nothing had indicated Raymond felt this way about Dulce. I needed to rotate my brain to see if I had missed something important.

Vince shook his head, clearly embarrassed for his friend. "I have no idea what all that was about with Raymond, but it's over." He offered his hand. "*Signorina*, may I have this dance?"

"*Grazie, signor,* I'd love to dance with you." I would ask no more Dulce questions, at least for the present. We walked toward the end of the room, passing original oil paintings that adorned the walls—Matisse, Monet, El Greco.

The orchestra played, "When I Fall in Love." We had almost finished the dance when Steven tapped Vince on the shoulder.

"May I cut in?"

"Oh, well, Drake, if you must." Before releasing me, he said, "Remember, Lisa, a duet."

As Steven took me in his arms, he said, "Congratulations on the contract. I thought they would ask you to hang around awhile. After all, that's what I'm paid for, to find the best."

The orchestra continued with "When Smoke Gets in Your Eyes," one of my favorites. I still needed to tell Steven about the flowers. "Steven, after the show, these roses..."

"Ah, yes, yellow roses for the 'yellow rose' of Texas. Glad you liked them, but you've already thanked me."

"That's not what I mean. I received red roses."

"I'm sure you did." He twirled me around once more. "You deserved them."

"Steven, will you please listen to me?"

His expression shifted to serious. "I'm sorry, Lisa. Of course I'll listen."

I was going to tell him about the flowers but heard a familiar voice. "Excuse me. I lost this young lady earlier to her fans," Brad interrupted. "I'm sure you'll share with a friend?"

"Some friend," Steven replied. "No one ever said I was generous. But only for a little while, you hear?"

"If you can find us!"

I laughed at the sparse humor. "Do you mind if we don't dance, Brad? I'm afraid I've had enough. It's been a long day." I noticed his left eyebrow arch when I called him by his first name.

"No, I don't mind at all. We can try a little sightseeing. The Shermans like to show off their apartment." Walking past the buffet and the bar, we found our way to the study. A gallery of photographs hung against smooth walnut-paneled walls.

"Look at this," I said. "Here's a picture of Mr. Sherman with Gary Moore. And this one—he's playing golf with Bob Hope. He's definitely been around."

"Nate's a friend to many people."

I paused in front of a photograph of Audrey accepting an award. "I just realized something. Mr. Sherman introduced his wife as Audrey Wells Sherman. She must be the author, Audrey Wells, right?"

"That's the one. Writes hot-selling romantic suspense. In that picture, she's receiving the Elmont Award."

"I've never read her, but I am impressed." I had seen the author's books in Brentano's window and in bookstores back home during the past five or six years. "As much as I read, my preference was bona fide mystery, like who dropped the bloody dagger in the hallway. Not much romance in that."

"With her success, Audrey adds gold to the Sherman coffers, for sure," Brad said. "I don't know if you've noticed, but she keeps a tight rein on her husband."

"No question. I've noticed."

"Now, shall we go out on the terrace? It will be a definite change of scenery."

"Great idea. Oh, what about Raymond? Is he going to be all right?"

"Sure, he'll be fine. Nate will see that he gets home after he sleeps it off."

As we passed through the crowd, Mel stopped us. "Lisa, you were grand. I know Monday's your day off, but can you meet me at the studio before Dulce's memorial service? I have a few ideas for sketches I think would work for us."

"Yes, I can do that. Ten? Eleven?"

"Make it eleven. See you then."

Mel turned and walked away without another word.

With no further interruption, we headed for the terrace. "I expected it to be cold out here, but it's warm for September. By now, even Texas can be chilly at night."

"I guess you haven't noticed the heat coming from above." Brad pointed high on the wall. Placed about every five feet were concrete "green men" faces. "What do you think of that?"

"They're blowing warm air! It's so quiet—unbelievable. What's next, a rocket ship?"

"Or 'Gene Autry and the Metropolis in the Center of the Earth,' or whatever they called that serial." I strolled over to the outer railing, with its pots of begonias and planter boxes of vibrant cyclamen. The begonias wouldn't last much longer, but for now, they were spectacular.

"What a beautiful view, Brad. The city looks as if all the stars have fallen on it, but they're still shining up there, aren't they?"

"They appear to be. Oh, look, one's falling." He stepped closer to me and pointed toward the western sky. "There, see?"

"You know what that means, don't you? My Choctaw grandmother said a falling star was a witch soaring through the sky, a premonition of bad luck."

"I've never heard that."

"I wonder if a star fell when Dulce died," I said.

"A star did fall—Dulce."

* * *

We wandered inside to say our good-byes and collect our group. The party was drawing to a close. Donna picked up her purse from a table and headed toward us. We spotted Steven over by the foyer, engaged in some sort of stiff confrontation with Gregory.

Brad walked toward them. "Ready to go, Steven?"

"Yes. Be right with you," he answered abruptly. "Gregory, we'll talk later."

"Sure. Later."

The only thing the scene lacked was Gregory grinding out a cigarette on the marble floor. Talk about tension.

We exited the building and the valet retrieved Brad's car. Brad offered to drive Steven to his apartment in the Village. "It's no trouble. Besides, there's little traffic."

"No, I wouldn't think of it. Just let me off at the subway. I'll be home in minutes."

"Very well. We'll drive Donna home first."

Brad let Donna off at her apartment. After she got inside, we drove Steven to the subway.

"Thanks, Brad. I appreciate it," he said. "Again, Tex, good show." He waved and disappeared down the steps.

We drove the short distance to my hotel. Brad swooped in and parked next to the curb, albeit illegal, and escorted me to the door. "Lisa, I'm afraid I've been a little dense. I think you were planning to go to the Sherman's with Steven. If that's so, I'm sorry."

"No, no. We didn't have real plans. Nothing other than the party."

"In that case, at least you know it was innocence on my part, even though short-sighted."

"Think nothing of it. And thanks for bringing me home." I reached into my purse for the key.

"All right, if you're sure." Brad took the key and held my hand a few seconds. He hesitated and then unlocked the door. "I'll see you Monday."

As he walked away, I couldn't help think of how comfortable it was to be with him. Yes, I thought the term was "warm demeanor."

On the way to my room, I immediately replayed the evening's events. Did I see the murderer at the party, or even dance with him? And Raymond—was his drunken toast

motivated by grief or guilt? Before I delved into that answer,
I had another question.

Chapter Seven

I hated to wake up my roommate. If it weren't so important, I'd have let her sleep. I turned on the lamp and crossed to her bed. Jiggling the mattress, I said. "I'm sorry, Jenni, but this can't wait."

Jenni stirred and sat upright. She pulled off a sleep mask, exposing a sprinkle of freckles across her nose. "What is it? Is there a fire?"

"No, nothing like that." I sat on the foot of the bed. "I have to ask you something."

"If it's about the show, you were wonderful." She brushed a strand of hair from her face. "Everybody in the place watched the television in the library."

"It isn't about the show. Do you remember seeing a tiny white envelope?" I made a small rectangle with my fingers. "Like a floral card?"

She stared at me as if I had told her Macy's would never have another parade. "What's so important about a floral card? And when would I have seen it?"

"It would've been about Wednesday. I think I put it in my exercise bag." By now I had begun to pace. "I may have dumped it with my clothes in the wash the night before. And you were going to wash Wednesday morning, remember?"

"Hmm, I do recall something in the dryer. I was going to toss it." She got out of bed, slid into her slippers and walked to the bathroom.

I ceased pacing and called after her. "Please remember. What do you think you could have done with it?"

Jenni wandered back, sipping a glass of water. "We ate pizza tonight and I can't get enough of this. Why is it so important?"

"Okay, listen. I received thirteen red roses after the show, with no card. Dulce had thirteen red roses in her dressing room when she died. It's her card I'm trying to find. At the time, I thought it was a baker's dozen, compliments of the florist." I dropped down in the chair, one leg folded beneath me. "And now I'm thinking there's some connection. Jenni, I'm scared." I resisted an impulse to bite my longest nail.

"Whoa, take it easy. Give me a minute." She paused, concentration covering her face. "I stuffed the envelope in my pocket."

I teetered on the edge of my chair. "Which pocket? I need to know who sent Dulce's roses. Please tell me you didn't throw it away."

"No, I don't think so. I forgot." Jenni rifled through the closet, stopping at everything with pockets. "This one! I wore this." She took a multi-striped shirt from its hanger. "Aha! Here it is, sort of."

I reached for the bedraggled envelope and removed the card. "Oh, no, the ink's smudged." I held it under the lamplight "Part of the message is clear: 'I'm sorry for everything. But I loved....' That's all I can make out. The signature's smudged, too. It's... oh, I can't read it."

I took off the lampshade and held the card above the light bulb, but the card was too thick. "I know, I'll trace it. My notepad paper should be thin enough." I turned the card over on the paper and scribbled hard with my pencil, all over the back of the card. "There!"

Jenni hovered over my shoulder. "Did it work? What does it say?"

"Drat! It worked on all but the smeared part, and that's still the same—smeared." *Talk about frustration.* I tossed it in the wastepaper basket.

Jenni took another sip of water and crawled into bed. "Don't be so worried, Roomie. The florist added an extra rose. He couldn't count. Now get some sleep."

"Oh, I'm not worried." I failed to sound nonchalant. I prepared for bed and pulled down the covers. After staring at shadows on the ceiling for a few minutes, I raised up and puffed my pillow. *The florist!* I popped out of bed and scrambled for the card. But the florist's name was frayed, leaving a pale blue ribbon trim on the edges. On second thought, maybe I was worried.

The morning sun made its way into the garden, with a single ray angling through the window. Surprised, I noticed a rainbow. I'd believe a unicorn in the garden, maybe, but a rainbow six floors from the rooftop? I scuffed across the carpet in my fuzzy slippers and sat on the window seat. Rain fell during the night and sparklets clung to the shrubbery.

Fossil the cat, pride and joy of Mrs. Jordan, the hotel director, snooped around the birdbath. No doubt she hoped to find feathered visitors nesting in the flowers. *Kitty, sparrows don't nest on the ground.* I wondered how little birds found their way into this refuge for shade and an occasional bath.

Mrs. Jordon's apartment was on the other side of the garden, and I had often seen her let the tortoiseshell feline out the window. Fossil had it made in her inside-outside world.

"Roomie? You up already?" a sleepy voice asked.

"Yes ma'am. 'Already's' here. It's 10:30."

"After your cast party last night, I figured you'd sleep till noon."

"I thought so too, but I get a headache after only two glasses of wine, red wine, and I knew better." I left my window seat and headed for an aspirin and my toothbrush. "I guess we missed breakfast. What say we mosey down to the Warwick for pecan bran muffins?"

"Can't. No place to sit. You know, remodeling. They're replacing the countertop, too." Jenni grinned. "I tell you, that Texas accent. 'Puh-con,' you say. You're an actress and still don't know it's a pea-can."

"Thash crude," I smurgled through toothpaste. "Okay, lesh go to Schrafft's." Within the half-hour, we signed out at the desk and were on our way past the museum.

"Here's a church on the corner, and we're not in it," I said.

"Since you're a Methodist and my last name's Kantor, we'd be in the wrong pew anyway."

"I agree, but we need to get in a good habit."

"You did not say that." She giggled. "C'mon, I'm hungry."

The line inside Schrafft's reached the door. While we waited, I remembered I hadn't told Jenni about my contract. "I have a surprise for you. Are you ready?" I paused for a moment of high drama. "They gave me a contract for the entire season."

"That's wonderful!" she squealed to me and everyone else in hearing distance. "Did you all hear that?"

"Shh!" You're creating a scene."

"A scene? Who cares? I am so glad you got the job. Now you can stay in New York. Do you have any idea how hard it is to find a good roommate?"

The dozen or so amused people standing in front of us were members of a tour group. Lucky for us, the hostess seated the entire bunch at once. She showed us to the next available table and announced the waitress would return for our orders in no time at all.

Jenni glanced toward the door, cleared her throat and turned back to me. "Uh, some dark and handsome guy over there keeps glancing this way. At you, not me."

"Are you sure?"

"Very."

I started to turn.

"Don't! He'll see you."

"From what you say, he already has." I struggled to keep from seeing for myself. "What's he doing now?"

"Here he comes." Jenni stirred her coffee to the sloshing point. "Okay, here he is," she said with lips almost closed.

Vince Varcasia stopped at our table. "Lisa? With all the restaurants in a city of eight million people, I find you in this one." He gave a glancing smile to Jenni.

I'd expected Vince even before he spoke because of the label my roommate had given him. "Hi, Vince. Sit down. Have breakfast with us."

"I've already eaten, but I'll join you ladies for coffee."

I made the introductions, all the while suspecting Jenni wished he had sat next to her. But now she could make eye contact. "You're a long way from home on a Sunday morning. What brings you up here?"

"Today's my Aunt Sophia's birthday and my uncle has reserved Cousin Rudolpho's restaurant for the occasion. His food is the best in Manhattan, although Aunt Sophia's is better. If you don't believe it, ask her. Every cousin I know will be there. Probably even some I don't."

Vince glowed with affection when he spoke of his family.

"Sounds like a great party. When is it?"

"About half-an-hour. From the bus window, I caught sight of you walking toward this place. I demanded the driver stop, and here I am."

Jenni grasped the next moment of silence. "Vince, I've watched Mel's show as long as it's been on. How long have you worked with it?"

"You could say I was in on the ground floor."

I had previously told Jenni about Vince and his interests. And now she was asking him the same things I'd already told her—the theater, his love of opera, and Italian food. My roommate always sought out intellectual challenges and there she went, making like her I.Q. measured two digits. She knew all about theater, as well as French, Spanish, and Italian cuisine but was clever enough to conceal it.

After lengthy conversation, Vince said, "Unfortunately, I must leave you two lovelies before Aunt Sophia's candles melt into the frosting." He signaled for the check. "Oh, are you going to Dulce's memorial tomorrow afternoon?"

"Yes, I decided to."

"I'll see you tomorrow then. Pleasure to meet you, Jenni."

We left the restaurant at almost one o'clock and watched Vince as he turned the corner. Or rather, Jenni watched. "Roomie, what's he really like?"

"From your interrogation, I think you found out about everything. I don't know him very well. He strikes me as being as nice as they come, although I've seen a hint of temper."

"I have an urge to brush up on my Italian. On second thought, Vince isn't on your list of suspects, is he?"

"I didn't say that. I just said I noticed his temperament. And, when it comes right down to it, everybody's on my list, except you, of course."

"Whoa! That's a list I'm glad not to be on. You're one determined roommate, Lisa Warren."

We wandered toward Bonwit Teller's. Grecian accessories dressed one front window. That is, except for a white marble statue, and she wasn't dressed at all. We were merely killing time. I hoped killing time didn't make me a bad person. Still, the "killing" bothered me. There I was, right back to Dulce Carter.

Jenni announced she needed to study, so we turned the corner toward the hotel. I recited my to-do list: telephone my parents, write my sister, take a nap, and shampoo my hair. At some point during these activities, we would both think about exercising. Anything to clear my mind of Dulce.

The next morning, I took my leisure getting ready but realized I'd taken too long and had to hurry to the studio. A grinning Mel London, already there, held open the elevator door. "Step right up, Miss. This car goes to any floor, day or night." This was an amazing change from the last time I stepped into an elevator with Mel.

He pressed the Up button. "Be sure to tell my wife we're alone in the building. A little jealousy never hurts."

My eyebrow raised involuntarily. "Then maybe I won't tell her." This was the first opportunity I'd had to let him know how much I enjoyed the show so I began, "Mel, working with you is more than I hoped for. I really do thank you."

"No groveling, child. Don't ever let a man know you're in awe of him. That can tear away your self-esteem."

Mel had such a youthful appearance, yet he called me a child. He must have read my résumé. The elevator stopped and he led the way to his office. "The writers should be along any minute, so we won't be alone, after all. Such ill fortune."

He opened the door to a room, over-powered by a large tweed couch that would be perfect for naps between rehearsals. "This isn't an office by normal standards, but I needed a cubby hole somewhere to call my own. Here, please," he said and indicated an overstuffed chair which had comfort written all over it. Mel sat behind a sleek modern office desk and offered me a cigarette from an ebony box.

"No thanks, I never succumbed to the habit."

"Smart. They're bad for you." He gestured across an array of papers. "As you see, my desk is full. We have great writers, but whenever I get an idea, it goes on any scrap of paper I can lay my hands on. If I don't write it down, I might forget how brilliant it is."

"Do they often use your ideas?" I had no knowledge of the true workings behind the scenes.

"Are you kidding? If I have a good feeling about one, they'll work it into a skit and we see if it flies. Some do. Some don't." He flicked a lighter and inhaled from a Lucky Strike.

I ignored the smoke circles he blew toward the ceiling and sat closer to the edge of my chair. "What kind of skits do you have in mind?"

"Okay, this is one." Coughing, he put out his cigarette, which was only an eighth smoked. "You understand we stray a little from the original operetta. The scene's from *The Chocolate Soldier*, the one where Lieutenant Bumerli, this Swiss mercenary, climbs into the upstairs window of Nadina's house. He's so exhausted from the chase; he falls into the heroine's bed. You're the heroine. I'm the soldier."

"My thoughts exactly."

"What I didn't mention is it takes place in an outdoor theater. You know, a show within a show. So it's a stormy night. The wind machines are blowing their circuits out."

"Don't tell me, the bed starts to move?"

"...so the bed starts to move. By now, you, Nadina, discover the sleeping soldier, but the wind's rolling the bed downstage. You try to stop it, except it's too heavy." Mel stopped to light another cigarette. "Bumerli realizes he's been discovered, jumps out of bed, not knowing it moved, and falls into the orchestra pit. This is when you sing "My Hero." You know, the 'Come come, I love you only, my life is lonely' thing. Then the chocolate guy climbs out of the orchestra pit, battered and torn, and you embrace. What do you think?"

"It's... I love it."

"I'll take that to mean demonstratively resplendent. The scene should be Three Stooges funny, with all the extras. Besides, my mother adores that song. Since you like it, I'll talk to the guys."

Mel spent the next hour going over possible skits from the eruption of Pompeii's Vesuvius, to the Perils of Pauline, to Pilgrim Fathers coming to America.

"Looks like the P's have it," he said. "All right, forget the Pilgrims and Plymouth Rock. That's a turkey."

"Mel, are you ever serious?"

"I'm always serious. He glanced at the clock on his desk. "Say, it's twelve-thirty. I'm going to meet my wife at the memorial service. Come with me. We'll find a cab."

Chapter Eight

Organ music filtered through the heavy oak doors as Mel and I entered an impressive church on the east side. Our timing could have been better, but at least the minister had not yet welcomed the gathered crowd.

I spotted a gloved hand gesturing toward Mel. It belonged to a woman dressed in a lapis suit and matching hat. "Over there on the right, Mel. Is that Marty?"

"Yes. Yes, that's Marty."

By the time we reached her, the strains of "How Great Thou Art" filled the sanctuary. In a whisper, Mel introduced us.

Show business personalities from television to Broadway occupied the pews. While obviously trying to appear casual, some of the people craned their necks to see who else was present.

The minister took his place, opened the service with greetings, and followed with a lengthy prayer. He spoke of the tragedy of losing someone so young. "But now, we will not mention the word 'tragedy' again during this service. We will center our thoughts on the celebration of Dulce Carter's talents, her giving nature, and loving heart."

I wondered if the minister and Raymond Meyer had compared notes, and then I felt guilty for wondering. The Shermans, Brad, and several cast members sat together a few rows in front of us. But, no Cassie or Gregory.

Across from us and two aisles down, a man pressed a handkerchief to his eyes. Mel told me he was B.J. Carter, Dulce's ex-husband. Four or five friends and relatives presented appropriate messages. One family member could not finish and needed assistance leaving the podium.

The choir director led the congregation in "Amazing Grace," whereupon the minister returned to deliver the last portion of a reverent service. The expressions of those attending shifted into neutral when Dulce's recording of "I Could Have Danced All Night" floated through the sound system. Hearing her voice caught me by surprise, but I guess she could dance all she wanted now.

I had located most of the cast, but still no sign of Cassie or Gregory. Did one of them kill Dulce? What could the murderer have gained? My obsessive theorizing stopped when the service concluded.

After everyone filed out of the church, Vince waved from a distance. Our group congregated on the sidewalk and exchanged comments. We all agreed Dulce would have approved of the service.

Marty London stood in the sun. Her brown hair glistened with gold highlights from beneath her stylish hat. She was perhaps more striking than beautiful, with a flawless complexion. She impressed me with her unpretentious charm.

Marty spoke first. "Lisa, I truly enjoyed Saturday's show. As soon as theatrical agents heard of Dulce's death, the phone began ringing. But Nate and Mel didn't agree with anyone they suggested to take her place. They preferred an unknown. So when Steven discovered you, their worries ended."

"Thank you. That's very kind." The comments coming from Mel's wife made me feel special. I still had to pinch myself to believe this fairy tale.

Mel took her arm in his. "That about wraps up our official critique. May we take you home, Lisa?"

I was about to answer when Donna came up behind us. "Marty, hello. Say, blue's definitely your color. Lovely memorial, didn't you think?" Without giving them a chance to answer, she continued. "I'd like to abscond with your friend here, if that's all right. We have places to go."

"I guess we can give her up," Mel said, "but only until tomorrow."

"Thanks for the lift, Mel. I look forward to seeing you again, Marty."

Donna tugged at my sleeve. "How about a walk in the park?" she asked. "We can talk about old times."

"Sure, our times are already a week old. They deserve to be talked about."

I hurried down the sidewalk with her, losing my hat in the process. "Let me catch my breath." I picked up the hat but didn't bother to put it on.

"Lisa, in no way do I want a walk in the park," Donna said. "Did you see Cassie?"

"No, as a matter of fact, I didn't see her, and I didn't see Gregory either."

"But Cassie was here. She sat two rows from me and kept glancing at her watch. I'm sure she was searching for him."

"I can't imagine Gregory would have missed the memorial."

"He didn't," Donna said. "He came in before the final prayer and they left together. I tell you, that pair is too close. Listen, I drove my car from the Island today. It's around the corner. My parents are expecting us for dinner."

"Oh, I don't know."

"It's settled then. I'll take you by your hotel and you can get your things. We'll be back tomorrow morning in plenty of time for rehearsal."

I felt pressed into an affirmative answer, but why not? We reached the convertible, and I climbed inside. Donna wheeled the car from its space, taking less than fifteen minutes to reach my hotel. "Bring your bathing suit," she called as I ran to the door.

I rushed in, packed my suit, a dress, and a gown in my overnight case and closed it. I opened it again and tossed in my rehearsal clothes since we might be back late. "Oops, not yet." I grabbed my toothbrush and closed the case once more.

Frowning, Jenni temporarily abandoned her knee-bends. "Why do I think you're planning a trip?"

"Don't frown, you'll disturb your freckles. Now where are my sunglasses?"

Jenni pointed across the room. "On the bureau. Hey, you'll never guess who asked me out to dinner?"

"Okay, I won't. Who?"

"Someone you know. Vince."

I expressed surprise I didn't feel. "Why, that mysterious Italian. He never said a word."

"And should he?" She laughed.

"Oh, no, no. That's great, but I've got to run. I'll be home tomorrow afternoon."

"Where will you be in the event Frank Sinatra calls?"

"At the Springstons' on Long Island. I think it's King's Point, but I'll leave it on the sign-out. Oh, and tell Frankie-boy to call again." I dashed out of the room and down the steps to get specifics from Donna.

"The rules of this place are strict," I told her. I went inside and jotted down my whereabouts so the hotel director and Jenni would know. In another three minutes, I leaned back on comfortable leather seats of the Mercedes. "This is really nice. Is it yours, I mean all yours?"

"It's mine all right. I keep track of the mileage in case my little brother sneaks it out for a spin." Donna shifted into drive. "My father paid for my first car, a light green Dodge convertible, but I bought the gas. He wanted me to understand responsibility. And now I do," she added, with a sigh. We turned on Sixth, almost missing the light.

"When I began working, I traded the Dodge in on my dream car," Donna continued. "It's a stretch of the paycheck, but I guard this baby with my life."

We turned left at the next corner and moved into a steady lane of traffic. They couldn't all be going to King's Point.

"Have you ever been out to the Island?" Donna asked.

"Once, last year, when I was at Juilliard. A friend's parents invited me to their home for Thanksgiving. We went on a hayride and..."

A car darted into our lane and crossed in front of us, swiping the left fender. Donna swerved and rammed into the vehicle to our right. I hit the passenger door, but Donna almost went over the steering wheel before bouncing back against the seat.

We shuddered to a halt. "Donna, are you all right?" I grabbed at my right shoulder.

"Yeah, I think so. Are you?"

"Uh-huh." I wasn't sure she believed me. I wasn't even sure I believed me.

Her next move was to climb out of the poor baby Mercedes—the one she guarded with her life. She expressed more concern about the damage to her car than to herself. It would need a fender lift for sure.

The driver who hit us jumped out and ran down the street. We caught a blurred glimpse of him but nothing more. A policeman on the corner viewed the entire scene and gave chase to the long-distance runner. Talk about a witness.

Three bystanders came over to see if we were injured. One gentleman opened my door and offered words of sympathy. The front fender had dug into the tire so the Mercedes needed towing. The policeman soon returned without a suspect. We pulled ourselves together and gave our account of the accident to the officer. He had seen for himself but wanted our version.

Donna turned her head from side to side, rubbing her neck. She turned back to me. "Lisa, are you really okay?"

"Yes, only shaken." I massaged my shoulder. A bruise would show up tomorrow. "Are you sure you're not hurt?"

"Not that I know of. What can I say?" Donna blurted. "I guess this takes away our weekend at King's Point. Sorry. I'll phone Dad to see what he wants me to do, but I'll still have to call a tow truck."

Donna exchanged information with the driver of the car we hit and went inside a shop where a couple of employees had gathered at the door to watch. She made her phone calls and returned.

We waited for what seemed hours. Come to think of it, we waited hours. When the tow truck finally arrived, Donna gave the necessary information to the driver and we hailed a cab.

"Again, I'm sorry about our weekend," Donna said, "but I still want to have the cast party. My parents have already agreed. Say, why don't you come on to my apartment? We can have dinner brought in. I owe you."

"You owe me nothing," I said. "Thanks for the invite, but I think I'll go back to the hotel and wait for tomorrow."

Chapter Nine

Tomorrow came and there I stood, gazing at myself in the rehearsal hall mirror, distressed by pink leotards and black half-leggings. Pink was my least favorite color but somebody out there considered it synonymous with female dancers.

I stretched one leg out on the exercise barre and tried to touch my foot with my head. My shoulder didn't hurt as much as I expected, so if I wanted sympathy, I probably wouldn't get it. After the tenth stretch, I heard footsteps coming toward me, or maybe it was crackling vertebrae.

"Lisa?" a voice called.

"Hi, Raymond. You're here early." This was a first for him. He flashed his trademark smile, one that allowed him to do commercials for a major toothpaste company which paid his rent until he hit big time television.

"I hoped to see you before everyone else came in," he said. "I owe you an apology."

"You owe me an apology? Whatever for?"

"It's about the other night at the Shermans'. I'm afraid I made a fool of myself and caused you discomfort." He smiled with the slightest hint of embarrassment.

"No, you didn't bother me, but it was obvious you were distressed." I paused, thinking of how to arrive at what I wanted to know. "Raymond, Dulce's death shocked everyone. She had friends and non-friends, and I'm thinking not everyone loved her."

Raymond strode over to the window and stared down at the street, as if counting taxi-drivers bluffing Tuesday morning pedestrians.

I followed him and sat on the windowsill so I could observe his reaction. "If you don't mind my asking, were you and Dulce close?

"At one time, yes, I thought we were. She certainly made me feel that way."

That still wasn't the answer I wanted, but I found the nerve to ask. "I mean... were you having an affair?"

"An affair?" He laughed—in no way a stage laugh. "That depends on the definition. She got to where she wouldn't give me the time of day. It called for a major rewrite to give me any part of a night. That didn't diminish how I felt about her. But she so infuriated me." Raymond slammed his fist down on the sill.

I'd never seen him angry before.

"I guess my little speech surprised everyone, although I scarcely remember it."

My question sounded awkward, or maybe the feeling came from his answer. "I stepped out of my business on that one. But I assumed you two had something going from the way you talked about her at the party.

"Only for a while, but our relationship was going, going, gone." His voice trailed off.

"Raymond, did you send red roses to Dulce? The ones in her dressing room when she died?"

"Roses? I don't know about roses she received that day. I sent her flowers in the past, but not in a long time. Say, I gotta go. Seriously, folks, I have a scene I can't be late for, Marx my words."

He headed for the stairs.

"Oh, Raymond," I called, "even if you did owe me an apology, which you don't, I would accept it." I also accepted what he told me as the truth—at least, for the time being.

With twenty minutes left before rehearsal, I returned to the barre to loosen the muscles. I didn't regret being blunt with him. How else could I add anything to my little spiral tablet? Asking questions, while trying not to come off like a busybody, wouldn't be easy. But it was more than Detective Sander had done.

After reviewing Monday's activities, beginning with my meeting with Mel, followed by Dulce's memorial service and a could-have-been serious accident, I was exhausted. No wonder I slept so well last night. But now I needed to think about Saturday's show. My routine involved a take-off on flamenco dancing. That should be fun, except I didn't know flamenco. I knew it included taps, a lot of ruffles, and dancers wore minimal pink. The spit curls, I would paint on.

I finished my exercises, took a sip of water at the fountain and headed to rehearsal. With the help of Jerry

Mindel, I felt ready to plunge into the famous gypsy dance—flamingo, as I called it in my childhood.

Jerry waited for me in the fourth floor rehearsal hall. He had choreographed summer stock, one Broadway show, and a couple off-Broadway before the offer of his present job. He worked with Mel for three years, and from all indications, enjoyed every minute of it.

"Lisa, are you ready? You have your taps?"

"Good morning. I'm ready except for my feet." I wondered if I should have known to bring taps, but no one told me. "I had no idea until a few minutes ago that I needed them."

Jerry slapped his forehead with the palm of his hand. "Geez, that's my fault. If we had followed our conventional wisdom, you would have known last week. The truth is, I forgot."

"Can't we do a flamenco soft shoe instead?" I might as well be facetious.

"That may have its place." He half-chuckled. "But the sketch is built around tap clicks with added sound. You and Raymond are dancing when Mel enters in a jealous rage. His line is something like, 'So you want to dance, do you? I'll just help you out.' Of course, you think he's drawing a gun, but he brings out this peashooter. He manipulates the thing, reloading over and over from a 'powder horn' of peas."

Skeptical me nodded in agreement. "Where does the sound come from?"

"That's the recording of a machine gun. The faster it goes, the faster you and Raymond dance, and the faster Mel reloads the peashooter. Trust me on this. It'll work."

"If you say so. I'm here to follow directions."

"Now that's nice to hear. I'm not one to speak unkindly of the departed, but as much talent as Dulce had, she always wanted to change routines. She would have fought for soft-shoes, not because she wanted them or even thought they would work, but because nobody else thought so." Jerry sighed. "Forget I said that. Hang on, I'll try to find you some shoes. What size?"

"Seven, or closest to." I did a quick mental review of what Jerry said. His comment colored another insight to Dulce's personality. I was still wondering if I could master this flamenco thing when he returned with a pair of tap shoes.

"These are from Cassie's locker. She won't mind." Jerry grinned as if reading my thoughts.

"Cassie's? Oh m'gosh. She may hit me."

"What she doesn't know... you know the rest. She won't be in for an hour and we'll be finished." He handed me the shoes.

"If I get one scratch on these... Why do they have to be so new?" After an hour's rehearsal, I felt at ease with the routine. Practicing on my own, I would have it by Thursday. I deposited Cassie's shoes back in their niche in her locker.

I'd never been a borrower. My best friend in high school borrowed my cashmere sweater and spilled fingernail polish on it. It was a pink sweater, so I couldn't have liked it much anyway. I climbed the stairs two at a time to the fourth floor.

"Here comes Annie now." Brad handed me a script and explained the first skit from *Annie, Get Your Gun,* with Buffalo Bill. "This one has the atmosphere of the Shootout at the OK Corral. Annie shoots an apple off a kid's head, the orchestra becomes confused and plays the 'William Tell Overture,' etcetera, etcetera. We'll read through this and see what happens. After lunch, Mel and Lisa will get acquainted with a scene from Mozart's *Magic Flute.*"

I memorized the Annie lines by lunch break, not a spectacular feat since there was more music than dialogue. The bow and arrow were authentic, all except the arrow's point. Props had substituted a Jell-O-like tip for the real thing. The kid had nothing to worry about, not with sharpshooter Annie Lisa.

Donna watched the run-through and said it went great. She called out as soon as Brad came off the set, "Wait up a minute, Brad. I need to ask you something."

"Ask me anything. I'm sure I can find an answer."

"I hope so. I'd like to invite the cast to come up to King's Point," she said. "What about Sunday while the weather is still good? This is the best fall we've had in years."

Brad nodded. "Great idea. The notice can go on the callboard. I hope that many guests won't inconvenience your parents."

"I'll call them, but they'll be ready for the maximum. We have a pool, plenty of food, the ocean, and a sailboat."

"That's what I call a brilliant invitation, and I expect everyone will agree. I love sailing." He checked the wall clock. "Speaking of food, what about lunch? I'm buying."

Donna shook her head. "Thanks, but I have a date." She turned to me. "Lisa, you're okay, right?"

"I'm fine, but I'm worried about your neck."

"I replenished the aspirin bottle and a little wine at lunch won't hurt," she said. "And what's more, I learned this morning the car that swerved in front of us had been stolen right off the street. We may never know who was responsible. They didn't catch the guy."

"What's the matter with your neck. What car? Clue me in to your conversation," Brad prodded.

Without giving all the details, I outlined our near-death experience.

"You're saying that magnificent car is wounded, but not you? Listen, if there's the slightest chance either of you is hurt, take time for X-rays...."

"No, we're all right, really," Donna replied, "and don't anybody hesitate to ask who my date is, but not right now. I'm in a hurry. And speaking of boats, he's a real dreamboat. Bye now." She took off in a flying rush and left us with a question mark.

"And now, Miss Warren," Brad said, "if you don't need medical attention, how about lunch?"

I hesitated. "I had planned to work on the flamenco routine, even without taps."

"No problem there. We can get lunch and eat in the park. You'll be back with time to spare." Brad escorted me to the elevator.

Good timing. Orville pushed his cart through the front door as the elevator doors opened. The vendor had grown tired of airplane jokes about his name—his mother's idea. It wouldn't have been so bad if his last name hadn't been Wright.

Brad caught his eye. "Orville, my friend, what's on the menu today?"

"You name it, Mr. Hunter. I got ham an' cheese on rye, pastrami, liverwurst, roast beef on a bun, bagels, and a jug of pickles."

We made our choices, including cold drinks. I opened my purse, but Brad said, "Put it away. This catered luncheon is on me." He paid Orville and handed him a generous tip, evoking a toothy smile.

Instead of having lunch on a bench in Central Park, Brad hailed a horse and carriage. "This ought to make you feel right at home. I don't want you to be homesick." Brad offered his arm as I stepped into the carriage.

"It might surprise you to know I haven't been this near a horse since I wore braids and visited my cousin's farm in Oklahoma."

Brad started to comment when the top-hatted driver turned around. "Where to?" he asked.

"Drive around in the park till we say stop." Brad smiled and gave a soda to the driver.

Nice, I thought.

He turned back to me. "I would like to have seen little Lisa on the farm. Missing at least one front tooth, and freckles?"

"You're about right," I said. "We even had a haystack, except we never found the needle."

"I'm sorry I missed out on that, but now for luncheon, Miss Warren." He handed me my sandwich and drink and placed a napkin on my knee. We ate in silence a few moments and then he asked, "Do you think anyone would mistake us for tourists?"

"Only if we gawk at the skyscrapers. In Dallas, it's the flying red horse atop the Magnolia Building." I turned my attention to food. "You know, you can buy big pickles like this for a nickel in my father's grocery stores, right out of the gallon jar on the meat counter."

"You're kidding. That's only five cents."

"Correct, a nickel is five cents." I had another bite and considered Brad was more or less captive with no phone to answer or anyone to interrupt. "Brad, I heard Detective Sander came back last week. Do you mind telling me what's happened?"

He shifted in his seat before coming up with an answer. "No, I don't mind. Sander said they've labeled Dulce's death a heart attack. They ruled out poison. With no trace of it, what can they do?"

"But why did he have to come in person to tell you that? Besides, Donna said he was there quite a while."

"Did she? I don't remember it being very long." He finished his pastrami sandwich and replaced the empty bottles and napkins in the bag. "Let's change the subject, shall we?"

His abrupt suggestion didn't surprise me, as he usually skirted the subject of Dulce. "Sure, I was only curious. Mainly, I wanted to know if the police thought it involved foul play in any way." So, for another subject, "What do you think of Donna's invitation to King's Point?"

"I'll tell you what I think. I'm really anticipating it. I know Donna lives close to me on the east side, but I thought her parents also lived there."

"They come and go and also use the apartment for small social functions. Believe me, I think the Springstons will make it a fine Sunday."

Brad checked his watch. "This has been lovely, but I'm afraid our hour is about over." He reached up to signal the driver to head back.

"It's been fun, Brad. When I was a kid, I took a carriage ride in Central Park. I think I've seen this driver before, or maybe he's a different driver with the same hat."

After I freshened up, I rushed back to rehearsal. Brad was already explaining the new skit. *Don't men ever need to rush?*

"In this scene you have the roles of birds, Papageno and Papagena, from *The Magic Flute*, which later has something to do with New York's Birdland. You don't need to laugh yet."

Mel's face froze. "It never entered my mind."

I wondered what the writers would have in store for us once they got their hands on this scene.

"I'll set it up for you," Brad continued. "Raymond plays the Prince. Donna is the Queen of the Night, except it's

'Nightie,' contrary to what Mozart intended. Mel is Papageno, attendant to the prince. I'm sparing you the story of the opera since we're satirizing only one scene. We're not dealing with the pathos of the Prince Tamino and his beloved. There's no humor there."

"But there is humor *some*where?"

"Trust me, Mel. The birdman is about to commit suicide, because he has never found a wife. In the nick of time, he finds a gorgeous bird-woman, Papagena. That's you, Lisa. Realizing they are two birds of a feather, they sing a song of courtship," he continued. "Great singing isn't required. Precise timing is. Okay, that's it in a nutshell."

"Eggshell. Now that would be funny," Mel said.

"Thanks for the bird's-eye view," I added to the already zany repartee.

"That's enough from you two. Writers, we have. Kurt's waiting for you in the music room and he'll take you through it. When you finish, come back for choreography. These birds dance."

That night I fell into bed and thought I wouldn't wake unless lightning struck the Fine Arts Hotel. My thoughts began to swirl. I heard myself chuckle at dancing birds and Mel shooting chickpeas from a peashooter. I also wondered if Raymond had told me the truth about what part he'd really had in Dulce's life—or death.

Chapter Ten

"Mel, you don't have to zing it like an opera zinger, but you must get timing correckt! Ve do it again." Kurt Scofeld played three measures and stopped. "Ven you come to das trill on *ringing*, exaggerate it. Now! Ve do it."

After Mel struggled through, Kurt informed him he would play "*dei* glockenspiel." Mel's expression defined incredulous. "Couldn't I just play dei harmonica?"

"Ha! Not yourself do you play. You pretend, while another plays. Three spirits bring in lovely Papagena and you begin your duet. I play it through for you."

"Short and jovial Kurt Scofeld knew as much about pop music as he did opera. After going over the duet three times, Mel and I thanked Kurt and left to work on the choreography. Jerry put us through the paces of a wild bird dance that would make Mozart climb out of his grave. Mel sang the notes he could reach and spoke those he couldn't, while I sang my role legit.

The choreography sapped our cumulative energy, leaving us in a state of hysteria. I wondered how grown people could be so giddy.

Mel pulled out a chair for me and fished his cigarette case from his pocket. He offered me one, but I waved it off.

"Oh, yes, you never took up the habit." He lit up and inhaled. "You know, that scene is probably the most difficult I've ever done, but don't tell a soul. I'm supposed to be infallible. I've tricked them, of course."

I had shared alone time with Mel that day in his office and he was always "on." For the first moment since joining the cast, I felt comfortable with his normal personality. I figured this was the time to ask why he was in the elevator the first day I came to rehearsal.

With a tad of courage, I asked, "Mel, would you mind if I asked you a question?"

"A question?" He reached for an ashtray from the piano and crushed out his cigarette. He never finished one without lighting another. "No, of course not. Ask."

"My first day at rehearsals, you called Brad to tell him you couldn't come in." Mel's expression didn't change. "But I remember standing in the elevator with you that day." *I may have just accused Mel London of lying. Had I lost my mind?*

"That's your question?"

Apprehensive, I said, "Yes... that's it."

He answered in a smooth, matter-of-fact voice. "I did come to the building. But once I entered the elevator on my way to rehearsal, I had this sudden sick feeling. I was too unnerved about Dulce to rehearse." He hesitated with a shrug. "So, you got out of the elevator. I went back to my office, picked up some scripts and went home. Does that take care of your detective work for the day?"

Rather than crawling under my chair and pretending this conversation never happened, I said, "I'm more than a little embarrassed. Forgive me, but Brad made a point of saying you wouldn't be there and I had seen you."

"Forget it, kid. It's no problem. Now, if you'll excuse me, I have an appointment with a couple of writers."

That may have been stupid of me, but I had to know if he lied. So he didn't lie. He told Brad he couldn't handle rehearsal, and he couldn't. I headed for the callboard to check the schedule. We had costume fittings at four o'clock.

I waved to Donna and Raymond, who were beginning their routine. "Donna, I'll wait for you and we'll go see Mrs. Bjornson. If I'm not out here when you finish, come get me. Okay?"

"Right," she answered.

I headed to my dressing room and stretched out on the chaise. Would this place ever get warm? I stared at the ceiling and wondered if I had time to open the little door in my mind. I stored things there for future reference, including sad thoughts I didn't want to think about at the time. A thought crept out—the one about my ransacked dressing room. Mel had a plausible explanation, and I think I believed him. But if Mel didn't search my room, who did?

"Lisa? Wake up! Sergeant Bjornson's waiting." Donna stood at the door, peering inside.

I jumped to my feet and out I went. "Gee, I didn't even sleep, only rested. But I'm ready to get feather-fitted now." I joined her and shut the door. As an afterthought, I locked it.

We raced down to the elevator. Outside the building, a crisp wind pushed against us. "I hope this isn't a harbinger of a cold weekend," Donna said. "We need gentle breezes for our cast party, not a hurricane."

"As long as it doesn't rain. I do want to go sailing, in spite of my dread of the water. Are you certain your parents don't mind?" I could see No. 5 coming up Fifth Avenue. "There it is. We can make it."

We ran the short distance to the corner and climbed aboard, finding places midway in the bus. Donna slid to the window while six other riders squabbled over the remaining three seats.

"You asked if my parents mind? To tell you the truth, they're anticipating it. Dad's ordered steaks and Mom's planning everything else. It's all set, except for the guest list."

"I didn't see the notice on the callboard."

Donna slapped her hand to her forehead. "I can't believe me." She opened her bag and drew out a sheet of paper. "Here it is in big black and white. I forgot to tack it on the board. No matter. One day won't hurt—I hope."

"If a single day made a difference, they probably couldn't come in the first place," I added. For the remaining few blocks, we discussed the party and speculated on who might attend.

As soon as we entered the Costume Company, Mrs. Bjornson's stern presence greeted us. "Ah, I wondered when you would be here. You are the only ones left to be fitted." She eyed me from top to toe. "Uh-oh. Just as I remembered. We will have a problem with the feathers." She removed the show's file from the top of her desk and soon became lost amid the racks.

"This is the most foreboding place," I said. We walked over to the mirrored area used for marking alterations.

The sergeant soon returned and handed Donna a glossy black gown trimmed in sparkles and royal blue velvet. "And this is for your head," she proudly announced.

Donna hung the dress on a single rack and reached for the oversized headdress, her hands dipping from its weight. "It's beautiful, but they'll have to widen the camera lens for this one."

Mrs. Bjornson removed the cover from my Papagena costume. "Ah, Mr. London's fit him. For you, I think they have sent an eagle's costume to clothe a canary. I am afraid it will not fly, Miss Warren, but I will fix it." She helped me step into the mass of green and yellow feathers that covered my arms and legs and dragged past my feet. I sneezed. I knew I would.

She placed the feathered chapeau on my head. "Tsk, tsk, it will never do. This bird must molt," she said with intense expression.

"Mrs. Bjornson, you are too funny, but you're right. I can't dance in this. And what's more, I can't see." I pushed up the feathers that covered my eyes.

The wardrobe mistress, pincushion on her wrist, secured the proposed seams with large safety pins. She held onto the heavy costume while I removed it. I almost toppled over in the process. "Now we will try on your others, and I hope there will be no problem." After the fittings, Mrs. Bjornson wrote her notes in the folder and prepared to leave for the day.

The rows of racks amazed me. I made a mental note not to come up to this gloomy place alone. You could get lost. On our bus ride back, again lucky to find seats, Donna asked, "Did you talk to Brad about Detective Sander?"

"As a matter of fact, I did." I sighed in frustration. "Sander said Dulce's case was about closed. They labeled the cause of death as 'coronary occlusion'. There was a note that read: 'Contributing factors unknown.'"

"What do you mean, 'unknown'?"

"I mean there's either a secondary cause or there isn't. This indicates something else may have contributed, but they didn't know what."

"I've never seen a death certificate. Is a secondary cause always listed?"

"Not always. I once read a copy of a death certificate in my uncle's office. The woman fell down the stairs and broke her neck. An added factor was alcohol. If she hadn't been drinking, she might not have fallen in the first place, but the fall broke her neck."

"So what are you saying?"

"Do you think I know what I'm saying?" I decided to pay attention to where we were, or I'd miss my stop. "Anyway, Dulce may have died of a coronary, but something else might have contributed to it."

"I see what you mean. It is a little odd."

"I'm still not satisfied. Brad suggested a thief could have wrecked my room. I can't imagine why." We sat in silence for a couple of blocks. I reasoned Mel could have searched for the floral card, regardless of what he said. "Oh m'gosh."

"Oh your gosh, what?"

"Uh, nothing... only thinking." I decided not to tell Donna I'd talked with Mel. Not yet.

Traffic filled the streets as No. 5 wove its way toward the West Fifties. I stepped over Donna's feet to reach the aisle. "Bye now. See you tomorrow."

"Right."

It was cooler than when we first arrived. The previous year, when I studied opera in New York, August was cold. I hoped this beautiful September would continue at least through our Long Island weekend.

After a brisk walk to my hotel, I unlocked the front door to hear the strains of "Happy Birthday." I stepped into the library to see small spirals of smoke wafting away from candles on a yummy-looking birthday cake. I was glad to see Vince there, obviously enjoying the entire affair.

Jenni glanced up from slicing the first piece. "Lisa, we wondered where you were. I blew out the candles already. Here, have some. It's..."

"I love Praline Crunch cake, especially with cashews!"

"But, Lisa, how did you know what kind of cake it is? Can you see through the frosting?"

"Why... I, I don't know... I just did."

With a questioning expression, Jenni handed me the plate.

I must have had the same expression, which I hoped a couple of blinks took care of. "Hey, your orchid is gorgeous."

"Isn't it, though? Vince gave it to me. I guess you knew about this surprise?"

"The girls told me earlier and I was afraid I'd be late. Vince, you never mentioned you were going to call Jenni, but I kinda hoped you would."

"My most brilliant ideas come without notice." He grinned at Jenni and she responded with a coy smile.

My roommate? Coy? "Here, let me finish serving the cake."

"Please. There's plenty, but if there are any leftovers, would you take them to our room? We might want a late snack."

"Be glad to." I reached for the knife. "Vince, are you having some?"

"I believe I'll pass on dessert, unless you think it's bad luck for the birthday girl. I made dinner reservations."

I continued serving and couldn't help notice the girls sneak extra peeks at Vince. We chatted a few minutes, while Jenni ate a last bite of cake before removing a red balloon from the party arrangement. "I appreciate it, everybody. You totally surprised me in case you wondered." When she and Vince reached the door, she turned back. "Lisa, would you please take my corsage box to the room, too?"

"Sure, I'll do that." I waved a good-bye. I thought they were so right for each other. After everyone finished, I helped clear the table. Holding what was left of the cake in one hand, I slung my tote over a shoulder, gripped the sticks of balloons in the crook of my arm, and considered balancing the corsage box on my head. I managed to make it to our room in one trip. Jenni's bed was the best temporary spot on which to unload the party remains. "Whew, what a day." No one was in the room to disagree with me.

I placed the corsage box on the table where the lamp cast a glow through the clear plastic. I couldn't miss the blue ribbon-trimmed florist card peeking out from a small envelope.

Chapter Eleven

Gregory Hardin almost pounced on me when I walked in the door, as if he waited in ambush. "Miss Warren?" The strident voice of our stage manager was unmistakable. "Do you check the callboard every day for rehearsal times?"

This might be the start of Twenty Questions. "Of course. Why do you ask?"

"Brad expected you an hour ago. You're late for your call."

My watch showed twelve minutes till eleven. "Actually, I'm early." Gregory reminded me of my mother, tapping a foot when I'd been a naughty child.

"You must have misread the notice." He stepped aside, with a wave toward the board.

I made a hasty move past him to see for myself. "When did the time change?"

"Yesterday afternoon. Did you check it before you left?"

I'd never run into a stage manager like this. "Donna and I had costume fittings at four o'clock."

I tried to control the pitch of my voice, which usually rose when I became irritated. And, if I grew irritated while singing, I found I could gain another octave. "We didn't finish until after five-thirty. No one expected us to come back to the studio."

Donna swept through the front door at that precise moment. "Wow, I made it. I should have walked. The cab got tangled in traffic."

My frustration level had not dropped a centimeter. "Your feet wouldn't have helped. The schedule changed after we left yesterday."

When Donna walked in, Gregory lost his motivation. Two against one. He inhaled and pressed his lips together. Pressing lips together and inhaling at the same time made eyes either squint or open wide. Gregory squinted.

"Gregory," I said, "I'll just take it up with Brad."

"All right. But in the future, check for changes." He added a guttural sigh and walked away.

"What's with Hardin?" Donna asked.

"As I've said before, he is really not fond of me. But you know what? I don't really give a—"

"Engh! Don't say it."

"I've never seen a stage manager like that one." I glared back at him and clenched my teeth. "If you inhale during this particular maneuver, your mood is evident."

After an explanation and a mini-apology to Brad, I jumped right into rehearsals. I didn't mind saying I was sorry if I had reason; otherwise, it made an apology difficult. Call it a character flaw. When we finished for the morning, I caught up with Brad at his office. I wanted to borrow his telephone book.

"Sure, use my phone if you like." He pulled the book from the lower drawer and laid it on top of his desk, a desk neater than Mel's. "Make yourself comfortable."

"Thanks, but I'd like to take it with me. I won't be long."

Brad held open the door for me. "Anything I can help you with?"

"No, I'm just searching for a florist." I wished I could snatch back the words. I wondered if his expression changed, or if I imagined it.

"You don't have to send me flowers for being late to rehearsal," he added.

"Okay, I won't. But I do have an errand to run." I smiled and proceeded down the hall to my dressing room. The envelope from Jenni's orchid had only the name of the shop, but the address should be easy to locate.

The Manhattan phone book was enormous compared to the Dallas directory. Uhm, what area... west side, east side? The right one could be any side. I tried west. "Royal Floral" on Broadway near Seventy-Second Street and another on Madison Avenue. The directory also listed Royalty Floral in the Village. No, the card definitely read *Royal*.

I could hear me now, "Pardon me, but do you use blue-trimmed floral cards?" They'd hang up. Nope, this was an in-person thing. I copied the addresses and phone numbers and folded the paper into my purse. I didn't have a lot of time, but I first returned Brad's phonebook.

If I could get to Seventy-Second and back on lunch break, I'd save Madison for after rehearsal. No matter what

Dulce's death certificate indicated, I believed thirteen roses meant something besides one more than a dozen. I took off and almost bumped into Orville on the way out. "Save me a sandwich, will you, Orville?"

"Yes, Miss Warren. One cheese with your name on it." He shook his head, perhaps mulling over the improbability of survival without meat. "These young people today don't know what's good for them," he muttered to his cart. I hoped he didn't hear me giggle.

I made it to Broadway as the bus pulled away. Lucky for me, a taxi was waiting for the light to change. I jumped in and gave directions to the cabby. The closer I came to the florist, the more I felt my trip would be a wasted effort. *What a strange feeling.* On the ride out there, I thought for all the world it was a good idea. Still, I couldn't shake the negative feeling.

I exited the cab in front of the small shop. It featured a window decorated with flowers, including a white glass container of carnations interspersed with two-inch long plastic baby dolls swinging from white pipe cleaners. Each baby held a miniature bottle and wore teensy diapers pinned with a single blue or pink safety pin. Of course, I thought, that's where pink leotards got their start.

As a customer exited, I entered. The shop was half-filled with floral arrangements and half with gift items. The woman behind the counter smiled in anticipation. I knew the look. I pulled the card from my purse. "Can you tell me if this card came from your shop?"

The woman squinted at the card. "No. No, it's not ours. We don't use engraved." As if a new idea danced into her mind, she said, "But let me show you these Gerber daisies." She started to open a refrigerated display cabinet.

"Thank you," I said, "but I need to know where this card came from. Is the Royal Floral on Madison Avenue part of a chain? I mean, are you connected with that store?"

"No, there's no connection." She quickly turned to another display. "But aren't these sumptuous roses, the most beautiful of our fall shipment."

"Yes, they're lovely. Not today, thanks. But I'll think of you the next time I order." The door opened and I saw my chance to escape, although not before the shopkeeper redirected her smile to a man who just entered. She had already dismissed me as a customer. *Whatever happened to "Thank you and ya'll come back now?"*

That visit lasted less than ten minutes. When I returned to rehearsal, Orville had scribbled a note on the callboard. He'd left my lunch with Steven.

I glanced up as Steven rounded the corner from the hallway. "There you are," he said, "I have sustenance for the runaway soprano."

"Orville is a thoughtful man. Thanks a lot, Steven. Now, if only there's time to eat. I don't want Gregory after me again."

"Giving you a hard time, is he?"

"Somewhat. But he's never been friendly." I unwrapped the sandwich. "Pimiento this time. A lot of pimiento cheese." I walked over to the coffee urn and poured a cup, adding a smidgen of cream.

Steven had some for himself. "I've missed you. You vanished after break. Brad said you were out picking flowers. Find what you wanted?"

"No, not yet, but I'm working on it." I began work on my sandwich, too. It's funny how hungry a girl can get when chasing a possible suspect. A suspect for what, I wasn't certain at this point. I turned to hear some hammer-like noises. A couple of prop men were building a rehearsal runway with three-quarter-inch plywood and two-by-twos for legs.

"Are you sure that's going to be strong enough?" I asked one of the men. "Raymond and I will come down pretty hard on it."

"Absolutely," he replied. "Count the legs, plus the angle irons. It's all finished."

"Don't worry about it," Steven said, "they know what they're doing."

"Then I guess it's time to check it out." I gulped the rest of my coffee. "Here we go. See you later, Steven."

We climbed on the mock stage that extended between chairs and simulated a theater. As Raymond and I danced out on the runway, Mel used the peashooter. I clicked my castanets as fast as I tapped. When Mel aimed the shooter at Raymond's feet, Raymond reacted much like a Mexican jumping bean, only he jumped higher and faster and in different directions.

After three run-throughs, Jerry said, "Okay, that's great. Take ten."

I had almost danced too close to the edge. If I'd fallen off the runway, I might have seen Saturday's show from a hospital bed. This hectic day had not dispelled my annoyance at Gregory. I noticed him reading his ever-present clipboard and decided to venture over.

"Gregory, may I speak with you a moment?"

He seemed surprised at the suggestion. "Yes, certainly."

I determined not to mince words. "I know you adored Dulce, but why did you dislike me from the first day I walked into the studio?"

"Nonsense!" he scoffed.

"No, not nonsense. I've noticed from the beginning that you don't mind whose feelings you trample over, except Cassie's, of course."

Cassie? You think I'm partial to Cassie?"

I didn't particularly care for anyone to overhear our conversation, so I kept my voice low. I hoped he would do the same. "It's apparent, Gregory, and that's fine. It's your business. She's your friend. But you clearly vent your frustrations, if that's what they are, on me."

"All right, since you're so set on knowing," he said. "Dulce knew theater, but she never understood comedy the way Cassie does. Somehow, she succeeded at it." He turned away. "But me, adore Dulce? Hardly. She was a bitch of the first order."

That would be bitchier than the second order. Still, his remark stunned me. "I thought you were in love with her. You were jealous of Vince's dating her."

"Me? In love with Dulce?" His questioning smile stopped short of a laugh. "I was jealous of her, not Vince. Think about it, Lisa."

I thought about it, but not for long. Naïve me for not having perceived the obvious. My comments changed only a little. "I know Cassie thought she should have taken Dulce's place on the show. That's what understudies are for. They offered the contract to an outsider, and you felt the same way she did, maybe even more."

"You win the prize. But I admit, so far, you've interpreted every skit better than Dulce would have."

"Not better than Cassie?"

"Cassie and I are friends. With her flair for comedy, she could have done it."

"Thanks for being honest with me, Gregory. I'm sorry things didn't work out the way you wanted. Since it is the way it is, do you think we can be friends, too?"

Although he nodded, I detected subtle reluctance in his expression. After we rehearsed the Magic Flute scene, I called Royal Floral on Madison to ask what time they closed. After a run-through of one scene, with a couple of notes, I checked the callboard twice within five minutes. Any changes would have to be made after my official going-home time. I darted out the door, too fast, it turned out. I could have broken my nose on the glass.

Brad spotted me. "It's best to open the door first." He grinned. "Did you find the flowers you wanted?"

Glancing back at him, I said, "Thanks, I have everything taken care of."

"Wait, I'll walk with you. I'm on my way to my apartment for a bit, but I'll be back to the grindstone till who knows when."

We small-talked our way to the corner and said good-bye. Brad crossed the street and I turned right.

I strolled by a couple of stores and stopped in a doorway until Brad was out of sight. Retracing some of my steps, I hurried on toward Madison and noticed a fashionable woman's leather and tweed shop. When my bank account allowed, I would buy that coat on display. While I fantasized over a leather coat with a gold-striped lining, I almost went into shock. A reflection stared back, drawing me in like a magnet. Dulce Carter!

"Oh, my Lord," I said too loud and hoped no one heard me gasp. But Dulce's image vanished as soon as it had appeared.

I brought myself back to reality and, still shaken, approached Royal Floral, its double windows displaying masses of flowers. Less than ten feet from the door, the most unnatural sensation flooded through me—like a transparent scrim washed down, taking my breath. I gasped for air, but little came into my lungs. I thought perhaps steam was curling through a manhole cover, but it was more than that—and cold. The mist circled me like a small whirly and then dissipated, drifting upward.

In a moment, my normal self returned. I drew in a deep breath and opened the door to the bustling shop. The name, "Royal Floral," suited the décor. I noticed many arrangements labeled, "Silk imports from France." Sure beat plastic.

Customers cleared out one by one until only three remained, me included. An attractive woman, whose dark hair hung to her shoulders, welcomed me with a smile. "May I help you?"

"Yes, please. Can you tell me if this is your shop's card?"

The salesperson took one glance. "Oh, yes, it's ours. We use only engraved cards and this is one of our original designs. Is there a special reason you wish to know?"

"I'd like to know how far back you keep your records. That is, can you tell me who ordered flowers about two weeks ago for a specific person?" Noticing her hesitation, I hoped that meant she would come up with an answer.

She turned toward a man in a dark pinstriped suit, assisting two customers. One, a well-dressed woman, I presumed to be the mother of the girl with her. The latter, maybe twenty, wore a pear-shaped diamond large enough to illuminate a subway, except she'd probably never been in a subway.

"Ah," the saleswoman said, "I guess Mr. Holton, the manager, will need to help you."

Mr. Holton was discussing a large wedding breakfast. With a floral order so huge, I'd sure like to see the wedding. When he finished and the couple left, he turned his attention to me. "Now, what may I do for you, Miss?"

"Warren, Lisa Warren." If my name rang a bell, it was less than a jingle. I decided Mr. Holton wasn't a TV fan, or maybe I expected celebrity status too soon. "Can you tell me who sent red roses to Dulce Carter, the television actress, about a week-and-a-half ago?"

"You understand, Miss Warren. Our records are confidential."

"Yes, sir, I do understand. But Miss Carter died soon after she received thirteen roses. I replaced her on the Mel London Show and, since that time, I've received thirteen red roses, possibly from your shop. Frankly, it's a little scary. I'd really like to know who sent them."

"But there's no way I... thirteen roses?" He paused, as if giving serious thought to my question. "Let me check a moment." He departed for the shop's back room.

I leaned over to sniff some double-red hibiscus in a blue and white Oriental container. "I keep forgetting these don't have a scent. And they should, they're so beautiful."

"I agree, but it's the plumeria that is so divine," the young woman commented.

"Miss Warren?" Mr. Holton said, returning from his office. "I don't have a name for you, because I remember now the gentleman paid cash. I recall because of the odd number, thirteen American Beauties. He returned later and placed a duplicate order, deliverable to... yes... Lisa Warren."

I felt I was getting somewhere. Where, I wasn't sure. "Thank you very much," I said. "Do you know who ordered them?"

"No. As I said, he paid cash."

"Can you at least give me some kind of description? Please, it's important. Was he tall, blond, brunette?"

"That was two weeks ago and we have so many customers." He paused. "I'd have to say maybe six feet tall, average weight.... I'm sorry, Miss Warren. Beyond that, I can't help you."

Chapter Twelve

I thought I'd never go to sleep last night. In my entire life, I never had trouble sleeping. I often retired early, rose early, and dressed for school to the radio's tune, "Griffin Time is the Time to Shine." The Light Crust Doughboys didn't broadcast until noon, and I suspected they'd still be singing long after I gave birth to my first child.

Last night I must have heard every ambulance siren in Manhattan. My thoughts wove in and out like basket weaving. The card read: "I'm sorry, but I loved..." *Sorry for what and who loved whom? It would have to be Dulce.*

Sleep finally came, interrupted too soon by morning. Careful not to awaken Jenni, I slipped out of the room and stopped at the bulletin board. Mrs. Jordan sometimes posted sign-up sheets for free tickets to Broadway plays and musicals. It wasn't so much for filling the houses as for giving tickets to young theatrical aspirants who couldn't afford to buy them. It's tough—constant auditioning and little money until you land that first job. I signed up for tickets to *Fiddler on the Roof*. The good thing about our room location, besides the proximity of the atrium, was we had first chance to peruse the bulletin board notices.

The dining room closed for breakfast at nine o'clock. I went down the short flight of stairs and conversed with other late diners. Most of the hotel's residents fell into that category. After breakfast I returned to my room and found Jenni still asleep. I tiptoed into the bathroom while a mental checklist clicked through my mind. Uppermost was whether to tell Steven about the Royal Floral Shop. That could wait. It was time for rehearsal.

"Hold it!" Jerry interrupted the flamenco scene in the middle of Raymond's and my dance on the runway. "Lisa, you missed your first turn. Right foot first on the runway, not left. That throws Raymond off and there isn't much room to correct it out there. Remember, the space is narrow."

"I know, Jerry. Sorry. Can we try it again?"

"Okay. From the top."

The second time the scene played through, with chickpeas, machinegun, and all. Part of my energy remained somewhere between the hotel and the studio. "Raymond, don't worry. I'll have it."

"Who's worrying? I found it enormously fascinating you erred," he said, patting me on the back. "See you later."

"Break, everyone," Jerry announced. "Back in two hours with orchestra. Flamenco first, followed by the bird scene."

I headed for my dressing room to decide what to do with the two hours. I knew the choreography but needed to review the lyrics. My mind was over-crowded.

Steven stopped me before I reached the hallway. "Hey there, how about a break date? We can go to the park or down to Rock Center and sit with the flowers."

"Actually, I was planning to meditate." But my thoughts turned toward the begonias.

When I returned, Steven waited with a cold drink. "Thought you might like this."

"A good idea, thanks. Is it chic to stroll down Fifth Avenue with bottle in hand?"

"Not chic if it was a whiskey bottle."

We left the building and arrived at Rockefeller Center in time for the man in a white uniform to accept our empties in his clean-up cart. Steven and I strolled down the sidewalk to the ice rink. Or at least it would be an ice rink when winter came. Big-city air always smelled fresher there.

"I'm not much on the ice," I said, "but I was a whiz on roller skates. Didn't you love going over hollow sidewalks and hearing the echo your skates made?"

I have no idea what you're talking about. Rode a bike myself. But yes, I probably would have enjoyed the echo. Let's sit."

"How about here?" Inasmuch as the other benches were taken, we had no choice. "It's a nice day to watch people."

Puzzled, Steven asked, "Watch people do what?"

"You mean you never simply sat and people-watched? If so, you've not enjoyed some of the freer things in life. It's educational. We used to guess who they were and what they did."

He laughed. "All right, I can play that game. See the couple over there on the bench? The woman has on a red jacket. They have three kids. Two are behaving, but not the little guy. The Mrs. is having a small argument with the Mr. and neither of them is watching Junior."

"You're right. They're not. Oh m'gosh, he's running off, and they don't even see." I jumped up, with Steven close behind. The boy reached the third bench and stumbled on the flowerbed's curb. You could hear his screams in Times Square. While onlookers looked, I reached for the child to pick him up. Blood dripped from a split in his lower lip. "Now, now, you'll be all right. Bless your heart...."

"Stop her! Kidnapper! Somebody stop that woman." The Mrs. ran toward me and began to pummel me with her handbag.

Steven reached out for her arm. "Madam, wait a minute there. This young lady merely tried to help. You weren't watching your son, and he ran away."

Her husband stood, opened his mouth as if to say something and stopped, with a slight shrug of his shoulders.

The woman, obviously flustered, snatched her crying child and then shifted her attention to me. Still frowning, she offered, "I guess I might have been distrac... Say! Aren't you the actress who took that poor Dulce Carter's place on TV?" Animosity in her eyes fell like a snake sheds skin.

"Uh, yes, I am," I said.

"I thought so!" The woman proceeded to dig around in her purse, squeezing her child close to her ample bazoom. "May I have your autograph?" she asked, digging pen and paper from her handbag. "I thought you were wonderful."

I hoped my enthusiasm at being recognized didn't show too much. "Why yes, certainly. I'm glad you enjoyed the show."

The excited woman thanked me and blotted the boy's lip with a handkerchief as she walked back to her family. "There, honey. We'll get you an ice cream."

Steven let out a sigh. "So, I guess I'll consider myself educated." With that comment, we walked up the sidewalk to a Chock Full o' Nuts. "You need to eat," he said. "What'll it be?"

I ordered nutty cream cheese on raisin bread, with orange juice. After quick service, we stood at the counter. Steven was a difficult man to figure—friendly, but distant. I had begun to like him and wanted to know more, so I put on my interview hat. "How did you break into this business? Did you do summer stock first?"

"As a matter of fact, I did a season in the Catskills, two in St. Louis and one more in the Catskills before I landed this job."

"Someone got you the job? You mean another contractor, like you recruited me?"

"No, I mean my agent arranged it."

A couple barged in toward the tiny counter.

"Pardon me," Steven said, "maybe we'd better stand aside here."

We moved, but I wasn't through listening. "Please go on. I'm really interested."

"Everyone thought Mel's show would be a hit, but not until after the first reviews did we feel it would have a long run. The cast stayed up to wait for the papers. Critics said Mel gave a fresh quality to comedy. The fact he's so spontaneous makes a big difference. There's nothing he can't do."

"That's my impression, too. Let me ask you, which came first, your being assistant director or talent contractor?"

"I worked as assistant director for the outdoor theater in St. Louis, and that position's what they hired me for here. They added the contractor part soon after, so actually, I do both."

Steven's explanation had a touch of nostalgia, but more than that, I noticed a slight underlying thread of resentment. I couldn't blame him, though.

"Would you like something else?" he asked.

"No, thanks. This is fine."

He took a sip of orange juice and continued, "To answer your question, I want to direct. Believe me, an assistant doesn't direct, not enough, other than continue what's already been set by the real director."

I hadn't considered his being unhappy with his work. An assistant-anything could generate a person's desire for more recognition. "Did you ever think about leaving?"

"Would have last year but didn't have another offer. Besides, I felt loyalty to Mel. But I guess Brad's here to stay. He's the one with the dream job." Steven finished his lunch. "If I didn't get a monthly check from a few inherited Oklahoma gas leases, I might be worried."

He seemed caught up in his thoughts, as if I weren't there. Then his tension lessened. "But I'll think positive. You have to in this business to get a break," he said, almost to himself. "Sorry, Tex. Are you ready?"

"Yes, I am. Thanks." I reached in my bag for my sunglasses and realized I must have left them at the studio. Glasses reminded me of Dulce. "You know, Steven, it's bizarre that Dulce didn't want anyone to know she wore contacts."

"Are you still on that?" He hesitated a moment. "I may not be the only one who knew."

Again, the basket weave. I didn't comment. "Thanks for lunch. I guess we'd better hurry. We're in for a big afternoon."

I couldn't tell how much of my feelings for him resulted from his giving me a big chance in show business, or if it was Steven himself. Clearly, his present status hadn't kept up with his ambition. I thought he deserved more. One day, perhaps, it would happen.

"Bravo," Jerry said, after the Flamenco routine. "Lisa, you needed a long-stemmed red rose between your teeth."

"Or maybe not." I laughed at the thought.

After the bird scene, Mel collapsed into a metal chair. Not only did he sweat, he breathed hard. "Whose idea was this, anyway?" He swiped a handkerchief across his face. "Didn't you say Mozart began composing at the age of five? If the kid had started later, maybe he would never have written this opera. It's for the birds."

Faux-shocked, I said, "Don't you know it's a sacrilege to insult an old master?"

"Hey, the only old master I ever came close to insulting was my father when he wanted me to be a dentist. Can't you just hear me tell a patient to say 'ah'? I'd probably start singing a duet with him."

"Actually, Mel, little Wolfgang began composing at the age of four, and he once told Marie Antoinette he would marry her when he grew up."

"See there? He was the first to lose his head."

I threw up my hands. "Are we through here, director?"

"The orchestra is, but Jerry, do you want to go over the scene with piano?"

"No, I think not," the choreographer answered. "I have only a few notes to give." He turned to Donna. "A little more body English for the Queen of the Nightie, all right? Everything else is working great."

"Okay, coach," she said, shimmying her hips.

Brad was speaking to the orchestra leader when Donna came up beside him. "Excuse me, Brad. May I see you when you have time?"

"The time is now. What can I do for you?"

"How's the guest list coming for my party? I figure I need to know, although my parents will be prepared anyway."

"It's filling up," he said, as he pulled a copy of the list from his shirt pocket.

Donna read the names. "Gregory's coming, but so far Cassie hasn't signed. That's almost everybody. I'll check with Mr. Scofeld to be sure he knows to bring his wife."

I peered over her shoulder to see the list. "Uhm, there's twenty-two."

"This is a great response," Donna said. "Many thanks, Brad. Would you mind making an announcement in the morning before rehearsals? Anyone's welcome to stay the night. We can have a gigantic slumber party. Otherwise, bring bathing suits and appetites."

"Be glad to," Brad said, "I'm looking forward to it."

"Fine, see you tomorrow. Lisa, let's get out of here."

"That's good with me." We turned to leave. "Oh, wait, I need my tote bag. You go ahead."

"I'll wait up front for you."

I returned to the rehearsal hall for my tote, but it wasn't there. Thinking it would be in my room, I headed for the stairs and pushed open the door to the stairwell. I took one step inside to switch on the light.

I froze. A scream spiraled through the stairwell. Mine.

The illusion of a skit emerged before me. But this was no illusion and no skit. It was real. A body lay motionless on the stair landing. Cold eyes stared upward, seeing nothing; an arrow embedded in the man's chest—dead center.

Chapter Thirteen

"Lisa! What is it? Are you all right?"

Donna's voice sounded like an echo. "Yes, I think so—mostly all right." I'm not the screaming type, but I must have let out a pretty good shriek. I leaned against the wall, hoping it knew to hold me up.

Donna pushed open the door. "Lisa, what's happened? Oh, my Lord! I... I'll get help. You stay here."

I wondered why I should stay, but, at that point, I didn't care. I was shaking too much to move, anyway.

In less than two minutes, Donna returned with Jerry. He knelt beside the body, but don't ask why he felt for a pulse. No mistake. The man was dead.

"Some way to die—an arrow!" Jerry said, as he stood. "He's still warm, but he'll get a lot colder. Lisa, did you open the door and find him like this?"

Yes. I almost tripped over his body." A shiver went all the way to my toes. "I didn't touch him."

"Did you see anything? Hear anything?"

"No, no. Only him. I heard nothing."

Jerry stood, rubbing his hands together, as if drying sweaty palms. "You two call the police. I'll check out things upstairs. Gregory Hardin won't be going anywhere."

The closest telephone hung in the front hall. It took only a minute to get to it. I reached into my pocket for a dime and dialed the operator. After a short exchange with the police, I cradled the phone.

Donna, anxious, asked, "What'd they say?"

"They told us to remain right where we are and not to touch a thing." I had already touched the telephone, but I felt certain the killer wouldn't have stopped to make a call.

In a short while, we heard wailing in the distance. That didn't mean it was headed to our building, but the wailing did come to a sudden halt while I was staring through the window. Two uniformed officers climbed out of the patrol car. The driver needed a little more space between his stomach and the steering wheel to allow an easy exit. The other one, blond and tall, reminded me of my high school beau.

The policemen came inside, and after brief introductions, the heavyset one asked to see the victim. "Who found him?"

"I found Mr. Hardin, officer. I'll show you." As long as I stood in one place my legs cooperated, but they trembled when I asked them to transport me. We made it to the stairs where Jerry held open the door.

The blond policeman took one glimpse at Gregory and then turned to his partner. "Geez, Tony. Can you believe it? Guy's got an arrow in his chest."

The red-feathered shaft could have been the prop I used in my *Annie* skit, but this one had a real point—a chilling thought.

Officer Tony examined the body before directing his gaze to Jerry. "And you are?"

Jerry introduced himself and identified Gregory.

"Is anyone else on the premises?" the officer asked.

"Everybody left for the day, at least as far as I know," Jerry said.

The burly officer scrutinized Gregory once more and quickened his gaze at the three of us. "I'll have to ask you not to discuss this among yourselves just yet." He turned to his partner. "Al, after you call for the ambulance, have Mr. Mindel give you the lay of this place. You better see if anybody else is around."

"Officer," I asked, "is it all right if Miss Springston and I go now?"

"No ma'am, not yet, but I'll tell you what you can do. That room off the lobby? You can wait there. And do not use the telephone."

We did what he said. "This can't be happening. Gregory's dead! Who would have done it? And with an arrow."

"Not any arrow," I replied. "My arrow. Wait until homicide gets here. If it's who I think it is, he'll love this."

"Well, well, Miss Warren, our paths cross again."

No mistaking the voice of Detective Douglas Sander. "I see they have, Detective. And no, I didn't kill him. I merely found him."

"Why, Miss Warren, that was the furthest thing from my mind." He tilted his head and pulled out the familiar notepad. "But since you did find Mr. Hardin, I'd like to ask you some questions."

Detective Sander gave orders to his assistants to take prints from the arrow and doors. "Check the banisters and don't forget the downstairs exit," he ordered. "Oh, and one more thing, check the elevator button. If our killer wore gloves to shoot an arrow, he may have taken them off, if he was stupid enough to use the elevator."

Sander also arranged for someone to call company personnel, including Mr. Sherman. No one could dispute who held authority here. Sander's tone was more abrupt than when we first met after Dulce's death. Maybe he viewed this murder as the real thing.

"Miss Warren, what can you tell me about the weapon? Is that an item from the studio, or I think you would call it a prop room?"

"Yes, props provided it. As a matter of fact, I used a bow and arrow in a skit on the show."

His eyebrow arched. The left one, I believe. "Was the arrow that killed Mr. Hardin the one you used?"

"It's possible. There are only two or three in props."

"But was it the arrow you used?" he emphasized.

"I did use an arrow with red feathers and a walnut-stained spine. It looks the same, except mine had a soft-pointed end. The tips can be interchanged."

"Pretty good shot, are you?" Without waiting for an answer, he said, "We'll need you to come down to the station and make a statement."

And I knew why. I found the body. That much I learned from Uncle Hamp, but still, I'd rather not.

"And in the meantime," he said, "we need to find your bow. Pardon me, Miss Warren, *the* bow."

We left the stair landing, and the detective proceeded to question Jerry and Donna. By then, Mr. Sherman arrived, along with Brad. I don't know who else they called. Detective

Sander ordered one of his officers to take me down to the station.

It didn't take long at the police station, once I answered their questions. By the time the officer returned me to the hotel, everyone had finished dinner. Hunger hit me. I hadn't become used to the fact easterners ate later than Texans. Sounds came from the kitchen, and I hoped some dinner remained. Sure enough, cook found some food, heated it and sent me on my way.

Before I opened my door, the hall phone rang. I held my plate in one hand and answered. It was Brad. I assured him everything was fine and thanked him for his concern. I cradled the phone and went back to my room.

Jenni turned from her desk and took note of my food. "Hi, Roomie. What are you having for dinner?"

"For one thing, London broil, which I had never heard of before coming to New York. The same for kale."

"Don't knock it until you've... but you may as well skip the kale.

Suddenly, my hunger evaporated. I set my plate on the nightstand.

"Hey, what gives?" Jenni said. "I'm thinking you're not batting a hundred percent. Are you sick?"

"No. My mind is going in too many directions to allow sick."

The phone rang again. "I'll get it," I said. As soon as I hung up, another ring. After promising both Steven and Donna that everything was under control, I decided not to answer the phone again. If it rang long enough, one of the other girls would get it.

"I heard that one-sided conversation," Jenni said. "Did you have a hard day at rehearsal?"

"You can ask that again, but please don't. You won't believe the answer."

"Try me." she said, folding her cardigan and placing it in her bureau.

Jenni couldn't be a better listener. I decided to sit down for the next explanation. "Someone murdered Gregory Hardin."

My roommate reacted much as I thought she would. With an audible gasp, she asked, "Murdered? You're sure?" Her eyes widened as she sank on the bed opposite me.

As if reciting dialogue, I told her I found him and the how, when, and where.

"Killed with an arrow? That's awful. And you found him. What about Cassie? As good a friends as they are, she must be devastated."

"I didn't see Cassie. Donna, Jerry, and I were the only ones there. And Gregory was near the top of my suspect list. I'd fallen asleep when you came home and left before you got up, so I couldn't tell you." I observed her sifting facts and suppositions.

"Tell me what?"

"Well, when I put the corsage box on your night table after you left with Vince, I noticed the card. It had the same blue spiral trim as the card on Dulce's roses. I traced it to a florist on Madison Avenue."

"So, who sent the flowers?"

"That's the point. The manager said he didn't know."

Several seconds passed. "Okay, now, hold on. That still doesn't mean whoever sent the roses killed Dulce or planned to harm you."

"Jenni, the police had to be suspicious, or they wouldn't have questioned all of us about Dulce in the first place. If they didn't find anything in the autopsy, maybe they didn't try hard enough."

"All right. What about the options? If not a heart attack, what? No guns, no wounds, the woman just died. What does that leave? It leaves poison."

"So what if someone put poison in the water and the roses' stems absorbed it," Jenni offered. "And... Dulce pricked her finger with a thorn.... Nah... that's too far-fetched. Sounds like something out of *Grimm's Fairy Tales*."

"True. But like I said before, why would she commit suicide with the future she had? I'm going to the library and read up on the subject tomorrow. My call isn't until eleven-thirty."

First murders first. One at a time is all I can handle.

Chapter Fourteen

New York businesses didn't open until ten o'clock, something else for me to get used to. I climbed into the Fifth Avenue bus and joined the standing-room crowd. Forty-Second Street was about a dozen blocks from the hotel.

When I arrived at my stop, I felt like a student with a notebook under my arm, as I walked toward the concrete steps of the largest public library in America. It differed quite a lot from the one in my hometown, which was a stately structure centered on green grass with an expanse of pecan trees.

I hurried past the huge lion statues and reached the last of many steps. Inside the heavy doors, the spacious interior affected me like my first view of the Grand Canyon. I drank it all in for a moment before inquiring at the information desk, where the attendant directed me to the card catalogues. I planned to research the same way I used to for a term paper, except speedier. Surely, poisons would be in an alphabetical listing with specific definitions. It wasn't that easy.

Offhand, the only poisons I could think of were strychnine, rattlesnake, or anti-freeze, if you drank it.

Starting at the top of the list, I copied call numbers and trotted off to the stacks. After perusing six books and finding nothing helpful, I placed them on the return cart and selected four more. These next books dealt with toxins in general and their various antidotes. At this rate, I could sit here until my thirtieth birthday, and still not come up with anything.

The search was difficult because I didn't know what specifics to search for. In my memory bank, I recalled a poison that wouldn't show in the victim's system. I read about it somewhere, saw it in a movie, or perhaps made it up. I brought three more books to the reading table and opened the first one. It mentioned muscle relaxing drugs and new synthetic curarizing agents under "Anaesthesius:

Myanesin" and another, "Galamine Triethiodide." I wouldn't remember those, let alone know how to pronounce them.

I think I had made headway, but time was fleeing. Before returning for more books, I heard a loud bang, as if something had been thrown against a wall. Then an eerie whooshing noise emitted from the stacks where my original choice of books was. No one else had come into this particular area.

Stepping back to the shelves near where the sound came, I glanced down at the floor. An open book lay there with its pages turning as fast as fire moved. Whoosh! Whoosh! Short jagged strips of flame reached out from within the pages.

I sensed a presence, and for that reason alone, wouldn't turn away. As I moved closer, the flames dissipated. The pages slowed their turning and stopped.

Surprisingly, the book wasn't hot nor had it burned. I picked it up and read the title on the spine: *Curare*. Unlike other books, this one concerned only that one poison. Flipping through the pages, I noticed a photograph of a South American native using a blowgun. I had seen such pictures in *National Geographic* and couldn't help visualizing Mel and the peashooter. I quickly scanned the book, skimming over specific information. A physician in South America injected a substance, which natives used on darts, into a small cut on a donkey's shoulder. The animal went into a paralytic state, seemingly dead. *Seemingly?*

I had to be at rehearsal in thirty-five minutes. At least I hoped we would rehearse. Detective Sander may have his own ideas. I walked over to the librarian's desk. "I don't have a library card, but I'd like to check out this book. Is there an application?"

The librarian smiled one of those condescending smiles when someone is interrupting. "I'm sorry, Miss, I'll be with you in a moment. I need to help this other patron." A scholarly young student followed her toward a reference section. The fact he wore black horn-rimmed glasses didn't make him scholarly, but something about the pencil over his ear gave me the tip-off.

Since my own rudeness of interrupting the librarian embarrassed me, I returned to the table and began taking notes as fast as my pen would write. *A kingdom for a typewriter.* If only I could read my shorthand. What I didn't have time to note, I would try to remember.

In a few minutes, the librarian passed by on the way to her station. "Miss, I can help you now."

I accompanied her to the large oak counter. She handed me a questionnaire. "Fill out the information. Your permanent card will be available as soon as possible."

After writing my name, I stopped. "I don't have enough time to do this now. Can you hold the book for me, please?"

"We can hold it for one day. After that, it goes back on the shelf."

I thanked her and dashed down the steps toward the bus stop. By the time I reached the studio, a swirl of investigations would probably be in progress. Maybe Detective Sander had dismissed me as a suspect. I figured he had considered me one.

It was weird not to see poor Gregory inside with a stopwatch. Calling him "poor Gregory" all of a sudden sounded right, now that he was dead. A ten-minute countdown remained until rehearsal, and he would never know I had arrived early.

Officers had been around all morning and questioned everyone who set foot into our building. After each person's interview, Brad continued with the discussion of sketches for Saturday's show. This lasted a little more than an hour, including changes in camera angles, particularly for the flamenco scene.

"That does it for now, folks," Brad announced. "Break and be ready to run musical numbers from the top. Again, the show must go on. We have to hold together."

The familiar voice of Detective Sander rang out. "Miss Warren, do you have a moment?"

I stopped short of making a dash out the exit. "Why yes, of course, Detective."

"I promise not to keep you. You have work to do. I merely want to verify you don't remember seeing or hearing anything unusual prior to Mr. Hardin's death. You had no idea something like this was about to happen?"

"No, nothing. Gregory's murder surprised me as much as anyone. We know he didn't commit suicide, or it would've had to have been a very short arrow."

"That's true, he didn't." He almost smiled. "You may be interested to know we found the bow in question, with no fingerprints, of course. But if you do think of anything later on, you will contact me?"

"Certainly. You'll be the second to know."

He finished the conversation with, "Thank you, Miss Warren. I know where to find you, if necessary."

I wondered what else he figured I could offer. No matter what the top brass thought of my talent, the number one rated television show did not need the diversion of a scandal. And Gregory killed with an arrow—I could see the *Variety* headlines now: "Well-known TV Stage Manager Gets the Shaft."

The cast sat in a semi-circle for orchestra rehearsal, beginning with the *Chocolate Soldier*. If anyone tried to follow along in the original score, they'd be lost. After a dance routine with Jerry and Cassie as leads, followed by the *Magic Flute* skit, we spied the week's guest performer, Herculano Piñero, a famous baritone from Mexico City.

He directed his gaze to Donna as he turned the corner to the music room.

"He's gorgeous! I'm sure he's in love with me."

"*Pero si!*" I encouraged.

Brad got the signal from the stage manager. "Break, everybody. Take ten."

"I'll take ten of Herculano." Donna pretended to swoon.

"When you pull yourself together," I said, "will you come with me to my dressing room? I have something to tell you and we haven't much time."

"Sure, my crushes don't last long." She rose from her chair. "Let's go."

I owed her an explanation and had already put it off. My intermittent attempts at solving a murder, not yet officially called one, could lead to a problem with my contract. I didn't like the word, fired. My obsession with Dulce's death was stubbornness on my part. Once we were inside my room, I closed the door.

Donna plopped down on the chaise and pulled a throw over her. "It's still like a refrigerator in here, Lisa. You're going to catch a cold and then where will the show be?

"Maybe so. I haven't taken time to inquire about it. Listen, Donna, I want you to know why I was sort of out of it yesterday and not only because of Gregory. I traced the source of the roses Dulce received before she died, as well as my own thirteen American Beauties."

She listened with interest to my story of the Madison Avenue florist. I knew she was interested because she didn't utter a word throughout the entire explanation.

"The store manager didn't know who sent the flowers, but he said the same man placed both orders."

"You're kidding," she said. "I don't know how to answer that one. But the roses may have no connection with Dulce's death, in which case there would be no danger to you."

She had said virtually the same thing as Jenni.

"But if whoever meant to send me flowers as a welcome to the show, he would have signed a card. And Mr. Holton, manager of the Royal Florist, said the man made it clear he didn't want a card enclosed." I checked the time. "We'd best get back. I don't want to bother you with my theorizing."

"It's no bother. I'm not saying you're wrong, but I still think you shouldn't put yourself in jeopardy, if any jeopardy exists."

The remainder of the rehearsal presented no problems, and the cast departed. Brad reserved the evening to review technical aspects of the show. Donna and I gathered up our things and walked to the front of the theater.

"What did you do with your morning?" she asked. "I had to talk to Detective Sander again, as if I knew anything. I was second on his list, since I found you with Gregory's body."

"My morning contrasted from yours." I didn't want to keep throwing my theories at my friend, but she did ask. "I spent two hours in the library."

"The library?"

"Trying to find exotic poisons."

"Now that, I'm interested in," she said, "but I've never thought of poisons as exotic."

"Even if Dulce's autopsy didn't show anything suspicious, they could have missed something. According to what I read, it—"

"Aha!" a voice interrupted. Steven stepped up behind us, placing his arms on our shoulders.

"Is our company detective still at work?"

I hadn't planned to discuss my findings with anyone but Donna and Jenni, and I sure didn't want to seem as if I knew more than the police and medical examiner combined. "No, I'm not moonlighting, really. And speaking of moonlight, it's time to go home. See you guys in the morning, okay?"

"I'll be here," Steven said. He dropped his arm from Donna's shoulder, but kept the other one on mine. "Get some rest, Tex. You've had a strenuous couple of days. But I'm still telling Sander you're after his job."

Steven's smile proved hard to resist.

Rain clouds rolled across the sky, so Donna and I decided to share the only available cab in sight. I was anxious to get home to tell my roommate about my discovery. She would call it an espial, but I'll stick with simple discovery. The cabby dropped me off first.

I hurried to our room. Luckily, Jenni was there. "Good, you're home," I said. "Listen to what I found in this book."

"What book?"

"I don't have it yet. That's why I took notes. Sit down. I want your opinion."

Jenni got comfortable on her bed, and I curled up in the armchair, tucking my legs beneath me. "This isn't a direct quote. I wrote down the highlights and I can remember the rest. I want you to hear this. Back in the 1800s, a physician injected a donkey's cut shoulder with the poison, curare." So far, the explanation apparently captivated my roommate. "The doctor attached bellows to a tube and inserted the tube in the donkey's windpipe. He pumped air into its lungs for an hour."

I shifted in my chair, even more enthused telling my story aloud. "When the physician withdrew the bellows, the donkey raised its head, peered around and then plopped over and stopped breathing. So the doctor resumed the respiration for two hours this time, and the animal started breathing again. Can you believe it?"

Jenni nodded, eager to hear more.

"Now get this. The animal recovered and lived a fat and sassy life for twenty-five more years. Well, they called it a she-ass. I call it a donkey."

"But would you tell me exactly what you're trying to tell me?"

"The point is, the heart continues to beat even after breathing stops. A person can have small amounts of this poison injected, swallowed, whatever. You don't have to inject it into the blood stream. If you give artificial respiration long enough for the effects of the poison to wear off, the patient might survive, providing the person hasn't had an overload of the stuff. Stop respiration too soon and the patient dies, like what almost happened with the donkey. But as long as the person's heart is beating, you think she'll live."

"Utterly amazing. So you're saying if Dulce was poisoned, but her heart still beat, they thought it was some kind of seizure that they could treat?"

"It's possible. From what Steven told me, they gave Dulce oxygen and she came out of it alert. They thought she was going to make it, and the next thing they knew, she turned blue and died. If she was poisoned, I have no idea how she ingested it. It's almost as if she died twice. According to this information, curare doesn't show in an autopsy." I coupled a shrug with a sigh. "Even if what I found means nothing, I feel better for having tried, but still..."

"Now what are you thinking?"

I uncoiled from the chair and brought out my nightgown from the bureau. "That's a good question. I'd like to speak with the doctor who attended her at the hospital. Can't you see me now? 'Excuse me, doctor, but I think there's something you should know.'"

"Why not? You said yourself, it doesn't show up in an autopsy."

"I'll have to think hard about it. I plan to call Uncle Hamp. But for now, I'll see if there's any hot water." I started for the bathroom and stopped in my tracks. Proverbial tracks, I believe they're called. "Jenni! I forgot to ask. How was your evening with Vince?"

A flush touched her face, and I couldn't help an inner smile.

"It was good," she said, "I mean, really. Professorial comes to mind, but just enough. He's a sweet guy."

"I had drifted to sleep by the time you came home. Either you enjoyed a ten-course dinner or you had a lot to talk about."

"The dinner was great. Italian, of course. As for talk, we covered a lot, but he was hung up on your murder theory."

"Why would he bring up my theory? What did he say?"

"He wanted to know what you'd discovered about Dulce's death and if you were still working on it. 'Course, you hadn't told me about the library yet, but—"

"What did you tell him?" I sat back down on my bed, expecting a dissertation.

"I didn't know that much to tell, nor would I have told him if I did. Anyway, I changed the subject to Lucrezia Borgia—one poison for another." Jenni turned over on her pink-flowered sheets and fluffed her pillow.

"You're brainy, roommate. Okay, you can go to sleep now. I'll see about that hot water."

I wondered why Vince chose my sleuthing as a topic of conversation when they had all those other subjects to discuss.

Chapter Fifteen

Jenni volunteered to check out the library book on her card. I had the necessary information about how the poison works, but the book could verify my theory to Detective Sander.

For the time being, a TV show waited for me. I arrived at the theater with fifteen minutes to spare. Promptness was one of my attributes. If my seven o'clock date rang the doorbell at seven, he was on the brink of being late. Being on time meant early. I learned that long before I met Gregory Hardin.

The cast entered through the building's side door. By coincidence, Cassie arrived at the theater the same time I did.

"Hi, Cassie. I haven't told you how super yours and Jerry's dance sequence is. You're a perfect dance couple." I couldn't see them as a couple anywhere else.

She halfway smiled while I held the door open. "Thanks. Coming from you, that's a compliment." She wasted no time entering ahead of me.

"Are you going to Donna's cast party tomorrow?" I sprinted to catch up with her. "We noticed you hadn't signed the list."

She responded with an insulting glare. "How could you go out for a good time when Gregory's been murdered?"

"I know he's dead, but... everyone thought since the Springstons already planned the weekend, we'd have nothing to gain by canceling the party."

"By 'we,' you mean it's your party, too?"

"No, of course not. Donna and I read the list and didn't see your name."

With a big sigh, she said, "Oh, all right, I guess I'll go, as long as everybody else is."

I thought she might pout, but I decided she wasn't the type.

The theater was cool and still. A dramatic production once aired on Wednesdays from the same theater. After a long run, it sank. But now, the aroma of fresh coffee and sweet rolls covered any leftover dusty smell from the building's being closed a week.

We walked to the front lobby where the cart of Danish waited. I mulled over the selection of goodies and chose my usual. Cassie went for something equally squishy.

During the week, Vivian, the entrepreneur of the portable bakery, purchased a small microwave, which occupied half the cart's lower rack. She plugged it into the nearest wall socket. I opened the door and slipped a maple roll inside for several seconds. After one bite of the sugary topping, I melted along with it, knowing full well its complete lack of nutrition.

We stood, waiting for the coffee to finish brewing. My immediate plan to open a sociable conversation hadn't worked so far. I counted in silence, giving Cassie time to open her mouth for some reason other than eating a fried twist.

She broke my silence. "Lisa, tell me, how did you really get on this show? Did you talk Steven into it, or who did you sleep with?"

I never walked away from accusations, except when I spilled my sister's favorite perfume when I was ten. I consider myself a nice person but could change that with the blink of an eye. "Why, you henna-dyed phony! How dare you make such an accusation. You know very well Steven is a talent contractor. It's part of his job to find talent."

"That may be, but I've been Dulce's understudy for three years. Her role should have been mine. Gregory spent hours with me, rehearsing numbers after everyone else left for the day."

"But he was the stage manager."

"And also a damn good choreographer. That's the job he wanted when they gave it to Jerry. And now Gregory's dead."

I wondered if she planned to cry and almost felt sympathy for her. Almost. "I'm truly sorry about Gregory. I know you were close friends. They'll find out who killed him, you'll see."

"If only they do," she said. "Believe me, he knew the business. He told me... " She stopped.

"What did he tell you?" I didn't want this conniving redhead to stop now.

"If anything ever happened to Dulce, like being offered a movie role or something she'd quit the show for, I would replace her." Cassie swung back, facing me. "But no, you came in as if you owned the place. You should have seen yourself that first day. 'I'm to take over for Dulce Carter,' like no one else mattered but dear little Lisa."

"I didn't mean to give that impression. Besides, I didn't know Dulce was dead. I regret your plan didn't work out, but you can't blame me. I'd been in New York for two weeks, with a contract for a network spectacular."

"Please. Spare me the speech."

Striving to keep the pitch low, I talked faster. "That's where I met Steven. The last day of the spectacular, he said they might call me. That was before Dulce died." I was about to run out of breath. "So if you have any questions about my being here, suppose you ask Brad or Mr. Sherman." I could feel my face flushing.

"I know all I need to know," she snapped.

Cassie turned on her heel, and off she wen—oh m'gosh. She fell! I instinctively ran toward her. "Are you all right?"

She picked herself up, screaming, "You pushed me!"

"No, I didn't. I was six feet away." I had been watching her leave, and she just fell forward... like someone pushed her.... But it wasn't me.

I tried once more. "Cassie, listen. You have talent, and you'll have another chance, perhaps even better. This is show business! Sometimes you get a break and sometimes you don't. So why don't you take it for what it was. You just didn't-get-the-break. I suggest we make an effort to get along because we may be here for some time to come." I'm not sure my speech phased her.

Cassie gave me one of those glares like I told Donna about—the one with spikes—and left.

I walked toward anybody with a friendly face, the first in line being the pastry lady. "How about a chocolate lattice, Vivian. Wait, I believe I'll have a dozen."

* * *

Since not everyone had checked in, Jeff, the assistant stage manager and now Gregory's replacement, called the role. "Meyer... ? Raymond, are you here?"

A voice echoed from the hallway leading from the men's room. "I'm here, Chief!" Raymond hastened to join the group. "Sorry. Just one of those crazy things."

"Mr. Meyer, we can't proceed without you."

"I don't have control over everything, Mr. Stage Manager, sir."

The cast snickered, as Raymond probably expected. When I thought about it, he took getting used to, love him or not.

Brad made his first announcement of the morning. "Everyone concentrate. This is a complicated show and we don't want to spend all day at it. I take that back. We're already scheduled for all day."

We made it through with frequent stops and starts, like a taxi in a rainstorm. After the initial break, Brad called for specific scenes rather than a full repeat. He let the next break go by without comment.

Before we resumed in early afternoon, he said, "We go on live TV at nine o'clock tonight. Not tomorrow or Monday, but tonight. I'm not pointing a finger at any one person. It's the lack of enthusiasm, plus a very difficult week. Now let's run over this once more. I don't want any slipups on cues and timing. So will you please set the pace and stop insulting the writers?"

Brad succeeded in making his point, and I knew he meant it. It was almost show time.

After the complete run-through, Jeff announced, "Be back in costumes and ready to go in an hour-and-a-half."

I left for my dressing room, which deserved its makeover. Work had already begun. I made my way around a few strips of two-by-fours and three cans of paint. A ceiling fan hummed overhead, gently swaying the costumes on a portable rack.

At least this production gave me no hair-styling problems. The flamenco sequence required a wig, and for the bird scene I wore plumage from the top of my head to my ankles. No wonder birds make it through the winter. I dressed and hurried to take my place on stage.

The dress rehearsal literally glided. Tempo picked up and the show fell into shape. Again, Mel watched from the control room, except for the *Magic Flute*. He wanted to rehearse it himself. I sighed with relief at his decision.

When we finished, he said, "Lisa, I'll have it right, but we move so fast, I may have to ask for cue cards."

"Never mind. It went really well. You'll be great." Like Steven said, Mel could do anything, so I felt strange giving him a pep talk. I wiggled around in my uncomfortable feathered costume and let out a sneeze I couldn't stifle. "S'cuse me."

The announcement from the stage manager sounded loud and precise. "All right folks, gather round. Brad has notes."

"My heartfelt thanks," Brad said. "A fine dress. I have only a few remarks, but I'll talk to you individually on that. Lisa, did Mrs. Bjornson alter your costume?"

"Yes, you should have seen it before. I still feel trapped, but through no fault of hers. Ah-choo! S'cuse me."

"Bless you," Brad said. "What is this? Are you catching a cold?"

"Oh, no. I, uh, think it's the feathers. I've always been allergic to feathers. I don't even eat fried chicken."

"Jeff, would you mind giving Mrs. Bjornson a call to see if she can work with Lisa's costume? She could hand-sew a few seams."

"She won't be here till later," Jeff said, "but her assistant can mark it."

I headed toward the back of the theater when Steven called out, "Slow down there, Tex. Are you going to the green room?"

"As soon as I have my costume fitted. It won't take long, and I need to talk to you."

"Good enough," Steven said.

I put the costume on wrong side out and the wardrobe assistant pinned the inner seams. I sneezed twice. Mrs. Bjornson would be embarrassed that the costume was still too big, but she'd have it adjusted by show time. I dressed and went to meet Steven.

"What a day this has been," I said, sitting next to him on the sofa. No one else was in the green room, at least for the moment. "Steven, I have something to tell you, and it can't wait."

"A mysterious secret you had to think over before telling me?"

"No, not that. I couldn't find the time. I traced the card that came with Dulce's roses. It was from Royal Floral on Madison Avenue."

"You mean there really was a card?" he asked.

"I found it the day you asked me to go to Schrafft's. I put it in my bag and forgot it. Later, I washed it by accident, and Jenni and I couldn't read the smeared signature."

"So if the writing smeared, how do you know who sent the flowers?"

"That's the trouble, I don't. The store manager remembered the order but not the customer. I still believe whoever sent the flowers had something to do with Dulce's death. I thought Mel had searched my room for the card, but he denied it."

"You mean you asked him?"

"He didn't mind," I said. "I had to know, didn't I? Mel was my first big clue."

Steven laid his hand on my arm. "Tex, your flowers could have been from a secret admirer."

"Why don't I believe that?"

His laughter didn't sound altogether forced. "Want my opinion?"

"Of course, I always appreciate someone else's opinion, as long as—"

"As long as you agree with it?" At least he smiled when he said it. "Why not go on being a new shining star on the television horizon? There's no question someone murdered Gregory. That's the important thing now." He got up and put coins into the vending machine. "Would you like something?"

"Oh, no, thanks. You know, Steven, it's difficult to mind my own business when I can mind somebody else's. Besides, I don't see the police doing anything about Dulce's death. And have they done anything to find Gregory's murderer?"

"Miss Marple, there's no getting through to you. And yes, they're working on Gregory's murder."

I debated with myself. "While I'm into true confessions, I may as well tell you something else." *What man wouldn't want to hear a girl's true confessions?*

"All right, let's hear it."

"We already know the unusual way Dulce died. Think about all the famous 'poison' writers: Hawthorne, Sayers, Kipling. Their murderers used poison because it was simple, and best of all, many times undetectable." I wasn't sure what affect my soliloquy had on Steven. Perhaps my lifetime powers of persuasion had vanished.

He gave a reproving shake of his head. "But think of your position if Brad or anyone else on the show thought you made accusations against them."

In retrospect, I didn't believe I could put anyone at risk, including myself. "Okay, you win, but I'd better tell you the rest. I found a remarkable book in the library. It's all about a poison that leaves no trace."

Steven's eyes locked with mine. "I guess that could make a little sense, but perhaps because you want it to fit your murder theory."

"Why do I have the feeling you're humoring me?" I wanted to have the last word. I just didn't know which word. Cast members entering the green room stopped our conversation.

"You better get ready to go on," Steven said, and winked.

"I'm going." I knew what he meant. He didn't really think I was onto something. In all honesty, I couldn't assure him I would give it up.

Before airtime, Mel had one thing to say to me. "Keep the sneezes in the bird scene."

"Are you kidding? I can't keep them out."

As the show progressed, it was obvious this live audience needed no overhead sign telling them to applaud. It was a smash. Afterward, fans detained a few of us at the stage door. I didn't notice any Johnnies of "Stage Door Johnny" fame. I thought that might all be a bit of folklore. If fans waited as long as it took for us to get out of costumes and ready to leave, they had to want an autograph pretty bad. I couldn't imagine they would want mine, but I'd practiced my whorls and flourishes and was flattered they asked.

Believe it or don't, Mel joined the cast next door at the Grill for our regular after-the-show meeting. Mel and Raymond seldom joined the group, and I heard Dulce never did. I hadn't considered myself a star, but they apparently considered me one, and I felt a sense of belonging.

We found our tables, and Donna stood, getting everyone's attention by striking a fork on her water glass. "Okay, now about my party. Does everybody know the way to our house?"

I counted two yeas. The rest, nays.

"I'll be taking my car from the city. If anyone wants to leave as early as I do, you're welcome to ride along. It's a rental car, but you know how it is when... uh, your own gets wrecked. She grinned at that comment, reminding everyone of our accident. "If you're not familiar with King's Point, I've made maps leading you right to our drive. If you have problems, call at the first phone you come to, and we'll send someone to meet you."

After everyone had consumed much food and drink, Vince went for papers. He returned, a smile across his face. "Okay, you guys. We did it! It's still a hit, and they love Lisa." He read a review aloud and passed the papers around.

Gregory's murder had a column of its own. "No suspects as yet." Of course, I could have told them that. So much for my headlines about the shaft thing. I tried not to think about reviews.

Who was I kidding? I thought about them all the time.

We made a toast to ourselves, and the waiter carried out his own congratulations by singing "O Sole Mio."

After we left the Grill, Vince said, "I'll have a car tomorrow. Do you need a ride? I don't know the way, but you can navigate."

"Thanks, Vince. Mr. and Mrs. Sherman are picking me up. But getting to the Springstons is simple if you have a map."

"In that case, you can give directions while I walk you home. It's on my way, remember?"

"Good, I was going to hail a cab, but I'd rather walk." Perfect timing, now that my roommate already told me about their date. "Jenni enjoyed dinner with you the other evening, Vince. How'd it go?"

"If you mean is there something going on, I don't know. Not that she said in so many words, but I think she has a journalistic interest."

"You may be right. She's had a couple of dates with an editor. Still, you must have found a lot to talk about. Why not call her again?"

"I might. Jenni and I discussed everything from the meaning of the universe to Rodin's love life. The conversation made thinkers of us both."

"I'll pretend I didn't hear that. But you two have so much in common, you'd have to get along. Now about the directions to King's Point. Everyone's excited about going. But you know something, Vince? I'm not really fond of the water. A pool is okay, but big water is dark."

I gave him clear instructions for the turn-off to the Springstons, plus one sharp curve to watch out for—the one that could send you into the water with one wrong twist of the wheel. "It's going to be a weekend to remember."

Chapter Sixteen

I awoke early. Of course I did. I found it difficult to sleep for thinking of the cast party. After breakfast, I stood in the entry hall, checking the time every two minutes. To keep the producer and his wife waiting would not be smart. I peeked through the window as a black limousine pulled up.

A tall slender man dressed in a chauffeur's uniform, his billed cap covering all but a ruffle of light brown hair, climbed the hotel steps. I moved around the corner past the entry so he couldn't see me through the glass door. An appropriate thirty seconds would do before I answered the bell. Not that I was anxious, but that might be too long.

I wore a nifty little outfit with an Italian cotton pullover. How maritime could a girl be? My lightweight blue jacket would come in handy if we sailed into the evening.

The driver rang the bell and I stepped outside. "Miss Warren. My name's Paul, ma'am." He took my travel case and we walked down the concrete steps. He opened the door and I climbed into the back seat of the limo. "Mr. and Mrs. Sherman... Hello. Thank you so much for picking me up."

Nate Sherman smiled cordially. "Our pleasure, Lisa."

This man exuded self-confidence. He should, I thought. He had been a successful producer of several Off-Broadway shows and at least two TV Spectaculars. His first try at a television series resulted in a winner for three seasons. Even now, he was in the planning stages of another TV project, a variety show starring a well-known comedienne, her name still unannounced.

"It's good to see you again, Mrs. Sherman." I thought that was the best line to begin with. Maybe she would buy it.

She half-glanced back at me. "I'm glad to see you too, Lisa. And I'd like to say last night's show surpassed your first."

Uhm. Did she say it, or just say she'd like to? "Thank you. It was even more fun than the first, although it required more effort."

"Are you saying you're not up to the challenge?"

"No, not at all. Challenges make a better performance as well as a better person." That sounded pretty good, profound, yet intellectual.

The "duchess" wore a celadon raw-silk pantsuit and a strand of large white pearls and matching earrings. I couldn't help notice her ring. Two large baroque pearls separated by a swirl of diamonds. It reminded me of one Jeannette MacDonald once wore in a production of the State Fair Musicals in Dallas.

With her pearl-burdened finger, Audrey lifted a lock of auburn hair from a mascaraed eye. "Goodness knows, I've been to King's Point on numerous occasions, but never to the Springstons. I'm sure I didn't know they lived there."

I did not feel free of insecurity in Audrey's presence. Her attitude didn't make it easy.

"This is going to be a beautiful clear day, at least, so far," I said. "Do you go to all the cast parties?"

"As a matter of fact, not often," Mr. Sherman said. "However, since Dr. Springston is my ophthalmologist, I thought it would be appropriate to attend. And as you mentioned, it's a beautiful day."

Audrey cast a questioning glance toward her husband. "But darling, isn't that a conflict of interests, being associated in such a way with the father of one of your performers?"

Mr. Sherman laughed. "It's no conflict of any kind. You think someone's going to take me to court for going to a party? I thought I told you, sweetheart. Several months ago, I was referred to Dr. Springston." His voice dropped to a confidential near-whisper. "It had nothing to do with his daughter."

I knew they were joking, or so I thought. As we drove out of the city, a cloud cover glazed the sky. "Oh no, tell me the weather isn't going to mucky up."

With a slight toss of her head, Audrey said, "'Mucky up'? That must be one of your quaint Texas terms."

I hoped I wouldn't throw up in the limousine.

Nate Sherman gazed out the window. "Oh, I think the weather will pass."

During the remainder of the drive, I asked him about the production process behind the scenes that were behind the scenes. He hastened to tell me how ideas came about and how he found enough people with money to back TV shows, as well as Broadway plays.

A slice of light blue peeked from behind breaking clouds. That was a relief. "Mr. Sherman, that curve ahead must be the one Donna mentioned. We're getting close."

"I think you're right," he replied. "Watch for the curve up there," he said to the driver.

"Yes, sir."

Without warning, the motor revved and the car raced forward.

Mr. Sherman called out, "For God's sake, Paul. What are you doing—"

Audrey stopped him mid-sentence with a scream, while I landed on the other side of the car, courtesy of the sudden excessive speed.

We were headed for huge boulders at the tip of the curve. Paul anchored himself to the wheel, his hands twisting so fast they lapped over each other. He was obviously braking, but the car pitched in one direction, then another, and back again, as it kept speeding.

The boulders loomed closer. I held my purse in front of my face, just in case. In case what? We hit boulders?

Paul made one last swerve to the road. And... the car died. No jolt. No grinding to a halt. It just stopped. The silence was deafening.

"Paul, what on earth happened?" Mr. Sherman asked.

"I don't know, sir. I slowed to maneuver the curve, and the car took off. My foot was on the brake, to the floorboard, and it wouldn't stop. The emergency brake was frozen."

"Nevertheless, that was some driving. You kept us from crashing into those rocks, if not into the water."

"I'd better check under the hood," Paul said, as he got out of the car.

Mr. Sherman leaned over to his wife. "Are you all right, sweetheart? Lisa, are you?"

"Of course I'm not all right," Audrey exclaimed. "We could have been killed!"

I could see Audrey wasn't bleeding. "Thanks, Mr. Sherman. I'm shook up is all, not injured."

In a moment, Paul climbed back inside. "I don't see anything wrong. But I'll take it easy up to the house, in the event the brakes are goners."

After we regained our composure, if that's what we could call it, we sat back and let Paul take over. I didn't trust myself to speak when we drove toward the Springstons. Their house was so large, it looked like two. We pulled up to the entrance where Paul applied the brakes and pressed the intercom button.

"That's good news," Mr. Sherman said. "Brakes worked fine."

Paul announced our arrival and the scrolled iron gates swung open.

We approached the house from a rosebush-lined entryway. The red brick drive circled at the right spot to allow a glimpse of flowers in every bed. Fall was beginning to show, but it took nothing away from the beauty before us.

You could tell Audrey was absorbing it all. "Nate, darling, Dr. Springston must have a lucrative practice. I didn't realize ophthalmologists were... well, you know."

"As a matter of fact, William Springston made a break-through in cataract surgery a few years ago. Success generates money. You should know that." He reached over and patted his wife's knee.

Mr. Sherman gave directions and the driver parked near where our host waited at the front of the house. Again, there was no problem with the brakes. "Paul," he said, "maybe you'd better stop somewhere and have the car checked, to be safe.

We thanked Paul again, and Mr. Sherman told him when to return.

Donna's father was just as I had pictured him—tall, slightly graying, a mustache, and very distinguished. "Come in, come in. We've been expecting you."

Two taxis pulled up behind us, followed by a limo transporting Mel, his wife Marty, and Raymond. Donna stepped outside the house, accompanied by a boy in his late teens, blond and tan.

"Is this Lisa?" He nearly tripped in his hurry to reach for my overnight case.

Donna rolled her eyes. "Yes, little brother. Lisa, this is Billy. He graduates from high school this year."

His dejection showed at his sister's public announcement that indicated his age.

"Billy, I'm sure Lisa is already spoken for. By the way, he likes to be called Bill, now that he's a senior."

I noticed her brother winced at her last remark.

"Hello, Bill. Thanks for taking my case. Donna, this is beautiful," I said, taking a quick scan at the expansive grounds.

"I thought you'd like it. I kinda love it myself."

We entered the house, and I could see Donna's mother coming from the hallway to meet us.

She wore winter white slacks with a snazzy black and white sweater. Her blonde hair, perfectly coiffed, had to be natural color. Donna surely inherited her good looks from both parents.

After introductions and how-do-you-do's, she escorted the guests into a living room, with its multiple conversation areas.

In this homelike atmosphere, my friends presented different personalities, except for Raymond, whose personality never changed. Such an impressive house, somewhat pretentious. The Springstons were impressive, but not at all pretentious.

Dr. Springston invited the guests to play croquet, tennis, or relax on the lanai or on any of the three covered porches. "Make yourselves comfortable. We promised our daughter we would go sailing, which I think will be more pleasant a little later in the day."

Donna's mother took over as a welcoming committee. With a charming smile, she said, "If the idea of a swim is appealing, slip into your suits whenever you wish. Our housekeeper, Sarah, will show you to your rooms." She started to turn but reversed her steps. "A light lunch and other refreshments will be served by the pool. Now, if you need or want anything, I'm sure we can find it for you." She made another turn to go, and then stopped. "Oh, there is an assortment of bathing suits in the cabana."

While the housekeeper escorted the guests upstairs, I took Donna aside. "Your mother is lovely. I can tell she has energy. She hasn't met Audrey yet, right? I mean close up?"

"No, I'm seeing to that personally."

"Well, forewarned is, well... forewarn her."

"I think Mother can handle the duchess."

No time for fore-anything. Audrey had already approached Donna's mother. "Mrs. Springton, such a treat it is to visit your beautiful home. You have my favorite colors, paintings, favorite everything. I must have your decorator's name."

"You're standing next to my decorator," she replied, "and please call me Anna. When I met William, I was studying interior design but never entered the profession. I'm sure it's for the best because I'd always wait for something new or better, or a more fabulous antique. I'd never get anything done."

"I would adore seeing the rest of your house." Audrey reached for Anna's arm and led her to the first available hallway.

Rather presumptuous, I thought, not to give her any choice in the matter.

"We'll see how that turns out," Donna said. "Now, let's go upstairs." We climbed the circular staircase with its smooth walnut banisters, perfect for sliding down. Forget it, I told myself.

Donna opened the first door on the left. "This is your room."

I entered with an audible gasp. "I'll take it. It's beautiful."

She laughed. "Come on down when you're ready."

"Thanks. If I can pull myself away." I could scarcely pull myself out of the thick carpet. A classic Greek wallpaper, designed with faux columns on either side of the bed, almost had me fooled. Feeling proud of myself for discovering the closet door covered in matching wallpaper, I hung up my clothes. Columns with carved caps flanked the entry to the area, leading to the bathroom. The gold and white basin was a porcelain shell. Of all things to covet—someone's bathroom.

I walked to the bedroom window and viewed the most breath-taking peaceful openness. I don't know why, but my thoughts drifted to Donna's and my near-accident. *Was it only a coincidence? Who would've tried to hurt us? Hurt me, would be more like it. And why did I see Dulce's vision in the leather shop?*

I was thinking too long. I slipped into my bathing suit and scurried to meet Donna, whom I found in the kitchen. We strolled outside before anyone else came down. The expansive lawn turned into a gentle slope toward the water.

"Our grounds aren't quite as pretty as in summer, but the grass is still good for croquet."

"The view is spectacular. Oh my, is that your boat? I mean, of course it is." The yacht rocked in the gentle ripples. "I've sailed a few times at Lake Texhoma and once along the coast, but not on something as imposing as this."

"She's a 48-footer. Sleeps six, or eight, if we squeeze."

I stepped aboard the sleek vessel and followed Donna to the cabin area. "This is really special." I ran my hand over the teakwood paneling. The galley was fully equipped with food, coffee, and bottled water. "You could take a vacation right now. Wait a minute. This is a boat. Am I walking on an Oriental rug?"

"That's right. Mother thought it added a nifty touch."

"And it does. Donna, I wonder. Maybe you can help me with something. I've had more thoughts about Dulce and can't find the right answers—only threads of ideas that unravel before they start. I hate it that Gregory's dead, but if we knew who killed Dulce, Gregory might have his justice as well. Do you know if Detective Sander has been back since Tuesday?"

"Yes, Thursday afternoon. He and Brad stayed a long time in Mr. Sherman's office. I know because I needed to see Brad. Mel wasn't around, or he might've met with them, too."

"I think the police should have something to go on by now. If it weren't for Nate's being at the hospital with Dulce, someone could have suffocated her with a pillow." I grimaced at the thought. "But that would be easy to determine."

"Sander may have given information to Brad or Nate, but I don't know anything other than what I've been told."

"By the time they decided on an autopsy, all kinds of clues might have been lost. Detective Sander didn't find anything in Dulce's dressing room." I paused a moment to ponder my next statement. "If I planned to commit suicide, I'd make darn sure I looked my best. Dulce wouldn't have poisoned herself in the middle of taking off her make-up."

We decided we'd better head back to the house before anyone missed us. Once in the kitchen, we perched on barstools. Mrs. Springston checked the refreshments. Another nifty touch she possessed was that of a culinary artist.

"So, Mom, how did it go with Mrs. Sherman?"

"Mrs. Sherman? Well, dear, she's charming enough. She especially liked my baroque mirrors. I know, because she stopped in front of each one."

"Do I detect a note of sarcasm?" Donna asked.

Mrs. Springston didn't respond, but removed a dish of parsley sprigs from the stainless steel refrigerator and placed them among the finger sandwiches. She retrieved another bowl. "Lisa, will you try this, dear? I don't want too much brown sugar, but enough." She pushed the bowl of off-white mixture toward me. "Now dip one of these strawberries and tell me what you think."

I let my mind absorb the visual and dipped a plump strawberry into the mixture and popped it into my mouth. "I don't know what you put in this, but it's scrumptious."

"Thank you, dear. It's only sour cream and brown sugar. I'll chill it a while longer. Cook will take everything to the cabana."

"Mother, why do I think you've omitted something about Audrey Sherman?"

Mrs. Springston put a manicured hand to her forehead for no apparent reason. "Nothing, really. It's that she was so preoccupied with her husband. When she didn't see him anywhere, she abandoned our tour and went in search of him."

Donna crossed her eyes in my direction and then rolled them toward the ceiling. It's amazing what you can do with your eyes.

"Okay," she said, "shall we adjourn to the great outdoors? Everyone should be out by now. You find a good spot, Lisa. I'll check with Dad about sailing."

Billy... or rather, Bill, Springston had already formed two teams for croquet. One of the dancers must have impressed him, either with her athletic prowess or her legs. As I passed by, he lowered his voice.

"Say, Lisa, what can you tell me about that little dancer, Merle? I could see myself goin' out with her."

"She's a good girl, Bill, so don't lead her astray. I haven't seen anybody waiting for her at the stage door. Keep in mind she's at least a couple years older than you." I patted him on the shoulder. "Have fun."

On my way to the pool, I spied the large round target set up for archery. I noticed three arrows in the bull's eye. A few of the guys had just applauded when Brad pulled off his glove. He walked toward me, almost as if he had been waiting.

"Hey," I said, "are you the sharpshooter?"

"Me? Hardly. That was Nate."

Chapter Seventeen

White wicker chairs, set up on the veranda, spilled over to the smooth tree-shaded lawn. The landscape architect had created luxury surrounded by impressive gardens, although William Springston's green thumb was evident.

Brad and I strolled back toward the cabana, the most popular gathering place. Tall urns of flowering plants stood by the corners nearest the house. At one end of the pool, water cascaded over several levels of stones, from which delicate ferns grew. Closer inspection showed them in their own containers tucked into crevices.

"This is a beautiful place," Brad said. "It must be great to close the door on the city and drive to another world."

"That's a nice picture. Come on, let's try the buffet." Food was artfully arranged on a rectangular table with an island-patterned cloth of plumeria, hibiscus, and antherium. I chose dipped strawberries, some cheese things, and a few colorful items I couldn't identify.

Brad selected more than a little bit of food. "I may eat some of these great tidbits and then put on my sailing clothes. Say, is our network detective still detecting?"

"Don't jest, and yes, I'm thinking about it."

He dropped the subject and we chatted a few more minutes. 'Which trip are you taking?"

"Flight Two, I believe, to see the sunset."

"Then that's the one I'll take. If you've seen one sunset, you haven't seen them all."

I picked up a cup of mango punch and we found poolside chaises. The atmosphere of the afternoon provided a relaxed mood, until someone mentioned Gregory's murder, causing solemnity to set in, but only until dessert arrived.

Nate Sherman arranged a few morsels on a snack plate, with Audrey draped on his arm. *Ye gads, lady, don't cling.* Her all-white swimsuit sported a large rhinestone buckle at the base of a low-cut back. Well, of course they were rhinestones, but how could I be sure?

She needed nothing else to call attention to her svelte figure. For someone who lived in New York City, she had a great tan. They probably spent summers on a beach somewhere in France. I had used sunlamps myself, until the one time I stayed under too long.

Steven and Raymond stood talking by the side of the pool. Steven was trim in his striped trunks and white terrycloth pullover, topped with a nautical scarf that I wished were mine. I wondered when he had time to work out, or if he came by his physique naturally.

Jovial Raymond drank iced coffee. I hadn't detected an area devoted to anything stronger. That would, undoubtedly, come later. With a long afternoon and evening, I figured the Springstons paced the serving of alcohol.

Cassie strolled down the walkway with a couple of dancers. She wore a teensy polka-dotted something or other. I calculated it was seventeen dots short of a swimsuit. She pranced out on the diving board and executed a perfect swan dive.

Raymond chose not to be outdone. He removed his shoes and ran fully clothed to the end of the board. He leaped off in a grab-your-knees cannon ball.

"Somehow, I knew he would do that," Brad said.

Donna tossed a terry robe over to the side of the pool. "I was supposed to laugh, right? Okay, extra swimwear in the cabana."

"Why get perfectly good swim trunks wet?" Raymond replied, glancing over his shoulder. He swam the length of the pool, picked up the robe and ambled to the dressing room.

Donna shook her head and scooted a chair over near Brad and me. "The afternoon is turning out great. Even Cassie is civil to everyone. I forgot to tell you the Scofelds had a previous engagement. Kurt's nephew is getting married."

"We're also minus someone else," I said. "Vince isn't here."

"He arrived a little while ago. Something to do with a flat tire and no spare—his Aunt Sophia's car. He's over there with Billy, learning to play the great American pastime."

I'm pretty sure not everyone accepted croquet with such fervor. At one o'clock, Dr. Springston called for our attention. "Hear ye, all you landlubbers. It's almost time to sail the ocean blue. Of course, the Sound isn't blue, or an ocean, but we're fortunate to have a good day. This morning I thought we might be out of luck."

"Dr. Springston," I said, "I'd like to take the last cruise. I've seen a sunset on Lake Erie and would love to see one here if we're out that long." As soon as I heard myself say the words, I wondered if that was the real reason, or did I want more time to gather courage?

"Of course, Lisa. Second cruise it is. We'll have a beauty."

The first group set out on the vessel of Captain William Springston at 1400 hours. The entire family had sailing experience, but they sometimes hired a crewman when entertaining guests. Those of us who waited for the second trip had fun anticipating more fun.

After an hour, Donna suggested we go inside. "If we stay in the sun till they come back, we may be sorry."

"Good idea. The last time my skin peeled, my make-up resembled a smeared numbers painting."

"Oh, one thing, everybody," Donna said. "Change clothes if you like. At least you can start out dry."

I ran upstairs to change into my sailing outfit. I had hung it in the closet, and now it was gone. My closed luggage sat on the rack. I raised the lid, and there lay my sailor outfit, neatly folded, as if ready for me to go home. But why? What unnerved me was I didn't do the folding! I couldn't take time to think about it now, so I dressed and walked down the curving stairs.

Vince was eyeing the Steinway and proceeded to slide onto the bench. He noticed me enter the room as his fingers rippled across the keys. "How about singing that duet we've never sung?"

I had planned to relax in a plush velvet chair until the boat docked. But I cleared my throat and ventured over to the piano. We decided on a song we both knew, and judging from the response, we made the right choice.

Afterward, Mel said, "Lisa, you took the starch right out of my shirt with those high notes. If you two have the remotest idea of signing with the Met before your contract expires, forget the possibility."

"Thanks, Mel, that's real encouragement," Vince said.

We devoted time to conversation and laughter until Donna cupped her hand to her ear. "Okay, I think they're coming." She walked over to the window. "I see the boat docking, so it's our turn on the water. But if anyone's prone to sea-sickness, sail at your own risk."

"I fit into that category," Marty London chimed. "I get seasick in the tub."

Mel kissed her on the cheek. "Remember, love, once if by land, twice if by sea."

"I haven't the vaguest idea what that means," she said, "but good sailing."

We heard a distant chorus of "Ninety-nine Bottles of Beer on the Wall." Mrs. Springston sang as loud as anyone on the way to the house. "Who's next?" she called to us would-be voyagers. "The breezes are shifting a little, but your sail should be yare. Now, everyone else, enjoy the library or whatever you like. Relax until dinner. If you need me, I'll be somewhere near the kitchen."

"Donna, give me a hint," I said. "What does 'yare' mean?"

"It refers to a good boat. Something to do with Katherine Hepburn."

In one fell sloop, the seafarers ascended the steps into the house. Jerry Mindel brushed against me as he entered the side door. "Go to it, Lisa. Did you bring your metaphors?"

"By all means, Jerry. You never know when an SOS may be necessary." I took off down the path, camera swinging from my shoulder.

Brad caught up with me. "I wish I had a rakish sailor's cap like yours."

"It's the only one I have, but you can borrow it sometime."

As we strolled toward the dock, Nate and Audrey walked in front of us. "What a divine afternoon," Audrey said. "Anna

Springston is charming, but she does tend to talk, don't you think? And Dr. Springston is such an attractive man."

Somehow I expected Nate's answer. "Yes, she's charming, but you'll have to be the judge of William."

I gazed heavenward, wondering how a brilliant man like Nate Sherman could take it day after day. Maybe night after night made it worthwhile.

Dr. Springston met us at the dock, ready to help us board.

Brad took a step back and perused the side of the white and blue yacht. "Optical Illusion," he said. "Now that's some name for a boat, Captain."

"You like it? I wanted something unique and personal, so my wife named her in honor of my profession."

I thought it was a great name but hoped we boarded the real thing.

Nate paused for Audrey and me to go first. "Everybody listen up," he said, "I'm a pretty good swimmer. What about you, Lisa?"

"No problem, but I've never been put to a test."

"There's little chance you'll be tested today," Dr. Springston said. "I haven't lost a passenger yet."

Once on the yacht, Donna led a brief tour. "First of all, here are the life vests. You can buckle up now, if you like. Otherwise, don't forget where they are, just in case."

"In case what?" Mel asked. "Are you saying we might spring a leak?"

"It isn't probable," Dr. Springston said, "but if we didn't have vests and needed them, we would be in deep trouble."

"He means deep as in six." Raymond started for the galley and stopped. "I'm not waiting for trouble. I've done some sailing in my time. Doc, if I can help, let me know." He put on his vest and fastened it.

"Thanks, Raymond. I think we have it covered. Anna supplied the galley with refreshments. Help yourselves to what's in the fridge." Dr. Springston went about his duties and in a few minutes, the sleek sailboat skimmed over glassy waters.

For the present, I disregarded my fear of the water and enjoyed the scenery, preferring for the most part, to see where we were going rather than where we had been.

After a few moments, Brad joined me. "Lisa, may I get you something to eat or drink?"

"Thanks, I'd like a cold drink, but take your time and check out this vessel."

"Fine, I will, but I won't be long."

Raymond and the Shermans found the fridge. I could hear the duchess pleading. "Darling, please get me something. I do believe a glass of wine would make this outing about perfect. Then let's go up on deck and take in the view."

I recognized Raymond's voice in the background and suspected he was investigating the stronger liquid stock. He would probably mix his drink with the expertise of a pharmacist compounding a prescription. I walked up to the bow to share the calm beauty with Donna and her father. "I'm wondering, Dr. Springston, were you in the navy?"

"No, I wasn't. I wanted the navy more than anything, but my eyes wouldn't let me. The Coast Guard didn't need me either, for the same reason."

"Let me guess. Is that why you became an ophthalmologist?"

"How astute of you." He smiled and gazed into the distance a moment. "As a matter of fact, that's exactly why, and I've never regretted it."

"Anything you want to know about sailing, my father can tell you," Donna said. "I'd better go below and see what's happening."

"Okay, I'll take a stroll to the other end, or is it aft?" Instead, I stopped at a blue and white-striped deck chair, adjusted it and leaned back. I closed my eyes and listened to the water trying to catch the boat. This fun day didn't require cerebral meandering, and I could take time to think about arrows and poison. I felt like a psychic failing to contact a bereaved's dearly departed. Something refused to show itself.

"A penny for 'em, Tex."

I almost jumped out of my chair, even though I knew no one but Steven called me Tex. "So far, my thoughts aren't very productive."

He put his hand on my shoulder. "Sorry. I didn't mean to startle you. This is special, don't you think? Everybody needs a yacht."

"'Need,' I'm not sure. But want, is something else," I said.

"Did you ever see a sky like this in Texas?"

"Since we don't live near an ocean, we have to settle for the sun's reflection on the prairie. You remember that song, 'Sunset on the Prairie'?"

"Yes, but I was under the impression you were reared in the city. That is what they say in Texas, *reared*?"

"You're right—reared, brought up, raised. And we do have a little bit of prairie in North Texas. Anyway, this view is gorgeous. I'd like a picture of it right now." I reached for my camera and took two shots.

Donna and the rest of the guests returned topside. "Hey, Donna, would you get your dad and come over here so I can get a picture with all our shipmates?"

"I heard that!" Dr. Springston called. He and Donna gathered everybody into a group.

"All right, y'all," I said, "Everybody be beautiful." Audrey struck a glamour pose. Brad still held my drink, the doctor had Donna's hand in his, and Raymond made a face. Oh well. "Vince, get in there. Okay now." I clicked the shutter. "Don't move! One more."

"Wait a minute," Brad said. "Lisa, I want one with you in it."

I exchanged the camera for the drink and Brad took a picture.

"Thanks, everyone. I'll see you each get a copy."

"Now," Brad said, "shall we go speak to the captain about his next holiday cruise to the Caribbean?"

After viewing the shimmering waves, two or three guests retreated to the galley for more samples of Anna Springstons' scrumptious hors d'oeuvres. The rest joined our host to discuss sailing and, in general, to enjoy our atypical Sunday afternoon.

Cassie stated her thoughts in a memorable way. "Don't look at the view. Look at the panorama."

"That's what it is, Cassie." Dr. Springston said.

"But I've never been on any kind of boat before. I should think once a person's sailed, he could never stop."

"My sentiments precisely," the doctor replied, removing his cap to brush a stray hair into place. "I believe the wind is picking up a little, though."

Yes, it had, I thought. Quite a bit. While Brad and the others chatted, I returned to my chair. The afternoon that began so bright had turned dreary. Shadowy clouds covered the sun, growing more ominous as they traveled across the sky. Little by little, the boat took on the feel of riding a bicycle down a gravel road. The quick change in the weather was eerie.

I could hear Donna ask, "Dad, what do you think?"

"It's one those freakish things we've run into a couple of times. Makes me think of the Bermuda Triangle. Now you see it, now you don't, or in this case, vice-versa. Better make sure everyone gets a vest."

Donna delivered vests to those who earlier had returned below. Her voice carried upward. "Folks, Dad says for you to put these on. Raymond, I think we have it under control, but would you come topside?"

Soon, everyone else came on deck before Dr. Springston suggested they might be safer below, for the time being.

The trip began on calm waters but had changed into choppy waves. I found a vest for myself, and no sooner had I slipped it on, than a gale struck. I reached for a chair, but whirling winds swooped it from my grasp.

By this time, rain shot from all directions, like piercing needles. The boat rocked while I fought to keep my balance. Trying to see through the blinding rain for something to hold onto, I glimpsed a slash of white, maybe a torn sail, coming at me. As I turned to duck, I felt a terrific pain in the back of my head.

Dreamlike, and floating in air, I grasped at raindrops. Slamming into the water did not render me unconscious, but for a split second, I thought it had. The next thing I knew, I struggled in the rolling waves, swallowing too much water. My head hurt, but my fear hurt worse. I tried to focus on something, anything. The icy water brought me to reality as I flailed to the surface.

With a semblance of consciousness, I could see the Optical Illusion. Or was it an optical illusion? The thought of the boat moving away panicked me. "Wait! Come back!" I screamed in my highest soprano, hoping it would pierce the wind. How could anyone have heard me?

It was impossible to swim against the waves. I tried to tread water but kept going under. I didn't have the strength. I fought my way back up every time but felt it was a battle lost. A flash of lightning soared the sky. In its brief light, I scanned the surface and could see dark images in the boat's wake. Then one of those images began moving toward me.

I tried harder to swim to the shadow and prayed it wasn't a shark. I know I didn't imagine it. There was something—I couldn't tell what it was until... "Vince!" Saying anything more would've been difficult. He must have pushed me overboard and now came to finish me off. He didn't need to finish me off. I would've drowned anyway.

"I've got you now," he yelled. "Stop fighting, or you'll sink us both!"

Vince was my only choice. I threw my arms around his neck and didn't let go.

"Take it easy. My Lord, your vest isn't fastened." He managed to hold me while he buckled it. "Listen! I think they're coming back for us."

I believe I heard what he said. My head throbbed. "Do they know where we are?" I clung to him, fearful of slipping away.

"I certainly hope so," he said. "It won't be long. Stay calm."

The awesome waves dissipated, but white foam floated on the water's crests. After what seemed hours, the boat reached us. I could make out a ladder on the side and a floating life ring. We made it to the ring and paddled to the side of the boat. A flashlight shone down on us.

Vince grabbed my wrist. "Lisa, you have something in your hand. Let it go," Vince yelled.

I hadn't realized I held anything, but I loosened my fingers and it floated away.

Keeping a firm grip on me with one arm, Vince placed my hand on the ladder. "Get your foot up on the rung. I'm right behind you. Now climb!"

Chapter Eighteen

After I clamored onto the deck, Steven was right there to help. "Let's get you below and find some blankets!"

Brad came running from the steps and threw a rain slicker around my trembling shoulders. It was dry and warm on the inside. He gave Vince another. "A fine time for a swim," Brad said.

Dr. Springston called out, "Lisa? Are you hurt?"

I wanted to answer, but I could only smile through chattering teeth.

"Aside from the shock," Vince said, "I think she's all right if she doesn't catch pneumonia."

Dr. Springston sent Raymond back to help Gordon, the crewman. Then he stepped down to join us. "Lisa, I can't believe this." He put his arms around me. "I am so sorry. I feel responsible."

I thought he would cry, but perhaps not before I did. "No. Of course you're not. I'm okay." I lied. My head felt like an anchor.

Steven said, "My God, Lisa, I was so worried. Are you sure you're all right? No broken bones?"

"My head hurts, and I'm half-frozen. Other than that, I'll probably make it."

Dr. Springston had turned his attention to Vince. "And what about yourself, young man?"

"No problem with me." Breathing hard, he shivered and slapped his legs to bring back circulation.

"Well done," the captain said, "but I think you're turning blue. Go with Brad and he'll find you something hot to drink. And Vince, in the remote case something like this comes up again, it isn't smart to jump overboard."

"Yes, sir, that's true. But it depends on the circumstances."

A cold rain still peppered down, but the needles had dulled. We managed to get below and found Donna heating water for tea. Everyone hovered around. We huddled on a bench, grateful for blankets Brad took from the closet. I stopped trembling long enough to hug Vince. Thanks, friend. You'll make a snazzy lifeguard, should you ever lose your voice."

"Yeah. I've done that and I'd rather not." He planted a kiss on my cheek.

"I am so sorry," Donna said, "but I have no dry clothes to offer you. I just never thought of it."

"Don't worry. The blanket's fine."

She reached for mugs and poured tea for each of us. "You guys scared us. Please don't ever do an encore."

"Not if I can help it." I grasped the mug, not waiting for the tea to cool.

Vince drank his, almost all in one gulp. "I'm going topside to see if I can help."

"Wait. You have to tell me how you knew I went overboard."

With a grin, he said, "As my Irish-Italian grandmother would say, that was a little bit o' luck. Donna tried to calm the passengers, or rather calm Audrey. I thought I heard something and asked Dr. Springston if he heard it too. His precise words were, 'That's known as thunder, young man.' He must not have heard what I heard."

"But, how did you know it was me?"

"I didn't, but whatever I saw had arms. I asked the doctor if he could turn this thing around. Before he had a chance, I went swimming. Simple as that." Vince headed up the steps.

"Hold on, I'm coming, too." I wrapped myself in the blanket, half dragging it, and followed him. During the last few minutes, the wind had finally lost its intensity. The sky, still ominous, rumbled with the sound of distant thunder.

Vince quickly scanned the yacht. "Any damage, Dr. Springston?"

The doctor shook his head. "Not as far as I know. She's a strong one. Normally, the family can handle our little outings, but I'm glad I had help this time." He paused a moment and then looked over at me. "Lisa, how did you fall overboard?"

"I don't know, and my vest wasn't fastened, either."

"It's the only accident we've ever had, but this surprise storm was a first, too. There have been small ones, but nothing like this." He gazed at the sky. "I think the worst has moved on. We'd better get this baby home."

Soon we pulled into the dock and saw Bill running down the path. "Hey, Mom's worried sick, and I was, too. Is everybody okay?" He caught the rope his dad tossed to him.

"I'd like to think so," his dad answered.

I grabbed my jacket. When we touched solid ground, Dr. Springston all but counted noses to be sure we were all there. "Raymond, thanks for your help. And of course, yours, Vince. I couldn't have done it without you both."

Audrey Sherman was calmer than I expected, but maybe she suffered from shock. She didn't even cling to Nate.

Bill asked, "What about the boat, Dad? Any problems?"

"We'll check the sails later. Can't do anything about it now anyway." He explained about my accident, leaving his son much in awe.

"Gee, I knew the storm had to be bad out there. Here, too. Lightning struck the greenhouse. But Lisa? Overboard? You're darn lucky Vince heard you."

"More than lucky," his father replied. He shook the crewman's hand and asked him to take care of the boat's temporary needs. "Thanks, Gordon. I'll call your wife. She's sure to be worried."

I had already reclaimed my slicker, and we trekked in the light rain toward the house, Bill taking the lead.

Anna Springston greeted us at the door. "Oh please!" she said. "If you hadn't planned to stay until tomorrow, reconsider and get a good night's rest. I'm changing dinner to informal buffet. You deserve to be comfortable after all you've been through. Sarah has everything ready for you, and William will charcoal the steaks out on the lanai."

Her words made me hungry. The aroma of hot apple cider permeated the kitchen. Sarah offered me a cup, which I accepted without hesitation. Even my toenails were cold.

"Lisa," Dr. Springston said, "wait a moment. I want to check you out." He relayed the details of our boat trip to his wife.

"Oh, my dear," she said, "I worried about everyone, but never dreamed of such a thing. Are you positive you're not injured?"

"Well, I do have a headache from this bump." I flinched when I touched the back of my head.

"Here, sit down," the doctor said. With deft fingers, he examined the back of my head. "Now I'd say that's a lump-and-a-half. If I had to guess, I'd say one of the deck chairs hit you and knocked you overboard."

"I remember I started to grab the chair and the wind came up...."

"What lump?" Brad asked.

I started to say the wind sucked the chair out of my hand, and I saw it go over, but Dr. Springston answered for me.

"Lisa fell overboard."

Steven asked, "Any chance of a concussion, Doctor?"

"No, I don't believe so."

"How can you be sure?"

"Well, I guess I can't be absolutely sure for right now, but... just a moment." Dr. Springston pulled his chair around and examined my eyes for any dilation. "Everything is fine, as far as I can tell. You're still chilled from the cold, which is expected, but not clammy, which is good." He placed his hands on mine. "And now, young lady, if you start seeing double, you'd better tell me pronto."

"Thank you, but I'll be fine. It would do me good to move around. I might go to sleep and not have sweet dreams. I'm only a little shaky, but I'd like to go to my room for a while."

"Fine, but if you feel like sleeping, don't. Not just yet."

"I'll go upstairs with you," Brad said.

"Thanks, but that isn't necessary. I'll be okay. Say, maybe Mel can come up with a skit, like 'How Deep is the Ocean'." I joked, but I felt more angered than injured.

I stepped into the spacious bathroom and gazed at the marble tub. Urns of dainty maidenhair fern sat on the window's ledge. The lacy fronds moved when nothing else in the room did. A tray of salts, bubble bath, lotions and a small book of poetry lay on a gold leaf stand by the tub. Without another thought, I turned on the water and poured in soon-to-be bubbles. I could've showered and washed my hair, but I really wanted to soak.

I removed my still-damp clothes, thinking I must be crazy to get in more water on purpose. This wasn't quite the same as getting back on the horse that throwed ya, but it was a start. I eased my body into the mountain of froth and cautiously washed my hair.

As I relaxed, something kept niggling at my subconscious—something about my going overboard. How easy it would have been to take a nap, but I reached for the poetry book instead.

".... Like leaflets in the pauses of the wind." Lovely.

Time rolled by too quickly, and I made myself replace the book and exit the tub. I slipped into a tan short-sleeved dress with matching cardigan. I brought nothing else, since I had planned to return with the Shermans after dinner.

A man's voice accompanied a knock on the bedroom door. "Tex?"

I opened the door to receive Steven's immediate hug. "Thank God you're safe. You sure you want to go downstairs?"

"Yes, quite sure. I'm almost ready." I hadn't taken time to use the hair dryer, so I fluffed with a brush, avoiding my injury as if cordoned off.

The aroma of charcoal-broiled steaks led us downstairs. Dr. Springston, an accomplished chef, accepted assistance from Sarah and anyone else who offered. He deserved some help after our stressful afternoon.

The main buffet table held a bouquet of fresh flowers in an epergne of silver and cut glass. Or, pressed glass. I couldn't tell the difference but knew you better learn before you bought it.

Donna's mother had subtracted flowers from a large arrangement in the entry and placed them on the small round tables. Apparently, her version of informal.

Mel made an announcement. "Ladies and Gentlemen— and you are—please know I feel as close to you right now as family."

"This isn't going to be maudlin, is it, Mel?" Raymond asked.

"On the contrary, we've had a great time, thanks to the Springstons' hospitality."

"Hear, hear," someone called.

"And for my next number," Mel added, "I propose a toast to Vince Varcasia, that sad-eyed Italian who saved Lisa from the depths."

Applause erupted. Mel quieted the group. "Third, I have a great new idea, and while it's still fresh on our minds, we should get to it soon. Why not write a sketch based on our experience of the day? We can call it 'How Deep is the Ocean!'"

Great minds, I thought. Everyone whooped at the idea. Knowing Mel, we would have the skit soon.

Our hostess stepped into the room and invited us to the buffet. I realized I had no appetite and even less energy. After dinner, we adjourned to the veranda for a last glimpse of the moonlight on the water. The sky had cleared and I watched gentle waves shimmer. They seemed to stay in the same place, but I knew they had to be on their way to somewhere. Waves did that.

When the evening turned chilly, we meandered inside, and everyone said goodnight. I adjourned to my room and slipped on the nightgown Donna left for me. With no effort, I sank into sleep in the luxurious silken comfort of the bed.

Morning came as if night never happened. The previous day's events played over and over in my mind—the boat caught up in waves, the scramble for life vests, the thing with the chair and the pain in my head, in that order. My thoughts went back to finding my sailor outfit neatly folded in my luggage. I know I didn't put those clothes there. Was it a warning for me not to go sailing? And from whom?

A light tap sounded on the door. I shoved aside the thought of the paranormal warning I had earlier ignored and managed to get myself into an upright position. It was difficult to move my aching body.

"Lisa? It's Donna. Are you there?"

"Yes, come in." I was trying to think of something to wear, as if I had a choice.

Donna provided the answer. She entered the room with a pair of clean white slacks and my pullover. "Mom took care of these, but your sweater may never be the same."

"Oh, they're great." I held up my clothes and sniffed. "The only thing I smell is fresh."

"Hey, fresh tuna can't be all bad."

"I was about to put on my I-wore-it-last night dress. I must thank your mom."

Donna sat on the corner of the bed. "Lisa, I'm sorry. First, the car accident, and now, the yacht."

"Hey, none of it was your fault." I couldn't help smiling, even though I knew she was serious.

"Still, I'm sorry. How do you feel this morning? I can't imagine what it must've been like."

"It was strange. Every time I went under, it was as if something pushed me back to the surface. There for a moment, I wondered if the dead-man's float would take me to shore. But by then, I probably would've been a dead woman floating, or at least a frozen one."

"Listen to you, joking at a time like this. I hope you didn't have nightmares. I would have."

"As a matter of fact, I had a good night until about four this morning. I was half-asleep and relived the storm and all its shadows. Donna, this is serious. Someone pushed me overboard. I know it." How seriously she regarded it, I couldn't tell. But right now, I couldn't keep my hands from trembling.

You mean you think someone tried to kill you?... For what reason? Lisa, I'm not saying I doubt you, but it doesn't make sense. Couldn't you have lost your balance?"

"The reason is, when I put on my vest, the wind snatched the chair—like a paper cup. It couldn't have hit me because I saw it go overboard. I remember a flash of bright white and thought for a moment I saw Audrey's white bathing suit, but maybe it was the furling sails. And immediately, I felt the blow on my head."

"Who would have done such a thing?" Donna asked. "And why?"

"I can't answer that." I finished dressing and sat down to slip on my sandals. "I wouldn't say it was no accident unless I was sure. I can't accuse anyone on Mel's show, or Cassie might get my job after all."

"Ha! Like that would ever happen."

"What do you mean?"

No sense of secrecy showed on Donna's face. "This is what happened. Nate hired me in the original company, right along with Raymond. He signed Mel as the star of the show. It was Nate's baby. He was responsible for the orchestra leader, stage manager, choreographer... everybody concerned with the production. I mean he's a hands-on producer."

The telephone's jingle interrupted her. "That's Mom." She picked up the handset.

"Hello.... Okay, we'll be right down." She put the phone back on its cradle. "Breakfast is about ready, but I'll finish this first. Anyway, Cassie's agent called Nate, urging him to hire her for the role. But he gave Dulce the contract and offered Cassie a secondary part, which she reluctantly accepted."

I didn't miss a word. "What does that have to do with their choosing me over Cassie? Sounds as if she came in second in the first place."

"Un-uh." Donna shook her head. "Mel didn't like her from the start. She was too much a single and it takes more than one to make a good duet. This time he told Steven to find someone not all out for herself. So, now you have it."

"How did you know this?"

"I sensed it when Cassie first auditioned with Mel. And I overheard Mel asking Nate and Steven to find somebody else. They had to be quick. Believe me, I waited for sparks to fly."

"Thanks, Donna. That helps make more sense of it." On the way downstairs, I said, "It's best no one knows what I told you of my so-called accident. Either time will tell, or I will."

"My lips are sealed," she assured me.

Continuing through the spacious kitchen and into the morning room, I recalled what the word *famished* meant. Although a vegetarian, I didn't even mind the smell of bacon frying.

"There you two are," Mrs. Springston said. "I was about to come up and get you. And Lisa, how did you sleep?"

"Like I didn't want to wake up. And I do thank you for resuscitating my clothes."

"You're welcome, dear," she replied, patting my shoulder. "William is outside with Vince and Raymond, checking any damage to the boat. The greenhouse is a shambles, and debris is everywhere." She picked up a delicate glass and handed it to me. "Here, dear, have some nectar. I'll watch out the door for them."

Donna poured us juice from a pitcher. I had a sip from the offered glass, painted with tiny orange blossoms.

"Donna, I don't even know who stayed the night. I went to bed before anyone left."

"Vince, Raymond, and two of the dancers, and you can guess that includes Merle. Everybody told me to give you their best."

"Ahoy, the house," called Dr. Springston. A minute later, he and the others came inside. "Nothing to worry about. The sails are fine."

"Thank goodness for that," his wife said. "Now, shall we have breakfast?"

I sat next to Donna's father at the large round table, again centered with flowers. Mrs. Springston later told me she kept them fresh in their over-sized refrigerator for the night.

"Doctor, may I talk to you in private before we leave?" I asked.

"Of course, Lisa. Do you still have a headache?"

"Oh, no. It isn't that. I need to ask your medical opinion about something."

"I will certainly be glad to give it if I can."

Vince and Raymond sat to the other side of me. "By the way, Lisa," Vince said, "last night I told the Shermans not to worry about you. I'd drive you back to the city, unless of course you'd rather take the train."

"Sure, Vince, I'd rather take the train."

"Look at me," he said. "See me smile? I know when someone's serious. The bad news is Raymond will be going with us," he joked.

"Too late," Raymond said, "you're committed."

We continued with coffee, listening to our hostess' happy talk.

"I'm sorry, I've monopolized the entire conversation," Mrs. Springston said. She reached for my hand. "I can't tell you how much I regret this dreadful accident."

"Please think no more about it. We appreciate your hospitality so much. You've been grand to let us barge into your home."

"Any time, my dear. Come back any time at all."

"I think we should let this family get back to their lives,"
I said.

"Yesterday's excitement is worth remembering. A lot of
fun," Raymond added. "No offense, Lisa. Your experience is
the obvious exception."

"No offense taken. And there's every chance I'll
remember it."

We arose from the table, and Dr. Springston turned to
me. "Now, you wanted an answer to a question?" He
escorted me across the marble foyer, and we entered
through the ornately carved doors to the library.

Chapter Nineteen

The next morning's humidity-sodden air gave the impression clouds might rip any minute, releasing another downpour. How could more rain be in the sky? I wanted to return to the city before Mother Nature presented us with an encore.

Donna's father carried my overnight case to the car. "Lisa, I insist on giving you the name of a physician in the city, in case you have any problems. I'll also be in my office this week."

"I appreciate that, but I'm sure I'll be fine. My hotel has a doctor on call."

"All right, but get in touch with me if you have any questions."

"I will. I promise."

Mrs. Springston came bounding out of the house, as much as a graceful lady can. "William, you didn't give Lisa her camera. Here, dear." She handed it over.

"Oh, thank you so much. I never gave it a thought."

"I found it on the boat," the doctor said. "It's a little damp, but you're fortunate to have a good camera case."

"If the film isn't ruined, I'll have it developed and send you copies. I took shots of the garden and pool before. I'm sorry, Mrs. Springston, no afters."

She sighed. "I'm afraid I wouldn't enjoy afters, dear. The damage is a mournful sight."

"Hard to argue with that." I turned toward Donna and gave her a quick hug.

"I'm so grateful you're okay," she said, "I'll see you soon."

Our car pulled away from this lovely family.

I didn't realize how glad I would be to get home until the car stopped in front of the hotel. "Lisa, I hope you're all right and not merely saying so," Raymond said.

"I'll be fine, really. I'll see you tomorrow."

Vince accompanied me to the hotel entrance. "Thanks more than you know, Vince. Isn't there a culture that believes the person whose life is saved owes the rescuer a lifetime of servitude?"

"I didn't know about that," he replied, "but it sounds good to me."

"If you didn't know, I'll not do the research; however, I could buy you lunch. Fair trade?"

"I'll remind you." Laughing, Vince waved and drove off.

I felt tired, although anxious to tell Jenni of my weekend's experience. Jenni attended class until two o'clock on Mondays and always returned soon after, unless a modeling assignment delayed her. This was one of those Mondays. Our quiet room was waiting for me when I entered. Only on sunny days did light flow through the windows. I flipped on the switch.

As I dropped my overnight case on the bed, a small scratching sound came from across the room. I turned toward the windowsill and there sat Fossil, wet and rejected. "Oh m'gosh." I raised the window and opened the screen. She scrambled inside and began rubbing against my leg. "Hey, wait a minute." I grabbed a towel and dried her wet fur. "There, there, poor kitty. I know how you feel."

Jenni popped into the room. "I'm home. Anybody here? Oops, who's our visitor?"

Fossil snuggled in my arms. "She was in the atrium getting drowned."

"Mrs. Jordan's in her office. Here, I'll take Miss Fossil home."

"Good. I'd let her stay all night, but we couldn't get away with it." Jenni left with the tortoiseshell bundle. I sneezed. Oh well, feathers and cat dander.

I changed into a robe and prepared to get cozy before reviewing my script. The door squeaked open and Jenni entered empty-handed. "I'd say Mrs. Jordan will give you future cat-sitting privileges for rescuing her baby. Now, tell me about King's Point." She plopped down in our chair.

I ooched back on my bed and raised the pillow against the headboard. "My adventures yesterday would make a fine movie. Three-fourths of the day was spectacular."

"Who went? Did Steven go? Tell me." Jenni eagerly awaited each detail.

"Yes, Steven was there. The other fourth of the time... " I could feel my voice begin to shake. *Get control of yourself, Lisa.* I buried my hands in my face and refused to cry.

Jenni jumped up and ran over to me. "Lisa, what is it? What happened?"

Reaching for a tissue in case I changed my mind and blubbered, I relayed yesterday's events. "Now that it's safe, I realize the danger. And the worst part is, everyone is calling it an accident."

Jenni remained silent for a moment. I could tell she was sifting conjectures again.

"Lisa, I suggest keeping your suspicions quiet, unless of course, you tell the detective. And that might not be a bad idea. Tell him about being pushed overboard and let him take it from there."

I could sense the frown on my forehead. "Think about it, Jenni. I go to him and say, 'Detective Sander, somebody on Mel London's Comedy Show tried to kill me this weekend. What are you going to do about it?'"

"But you can start with your poison theory."

"We've already been through that. According to the police, Dulce was a statistic who had an unexpected heart attack."

"Okay, Roomie. Keep a low profile and be careful not to pull anybody's chain."

"You left one out. Don't leave rehearsal or the theater alone, particularly after dark."

"Yes, that too." Jenni gathered up her books and sat at her desk. After a moment, she turned around. "I'm not kidding, Lisa. Be careful."

"I know. I will." I reminded myself somebody killed Gregory in broad daylight and I'd best find out who it was, and soon. After my Long Island experience, I might not be so lucky next time.

Mel scanned the scripts Brad handed him. He shifted in his chair. "I could say what is *this*, but what I really mean is, what *is* this?"

"It's a winner, that's what. I'll explain it to you."

I giggled. "Mel, this is Smetana's comic opera, *The Bartered Bride*."

"That's not quite right," Brad said. "We're calling it *The Borrowed Bride*."

Raymond stared into space. "One of my lifetime desires."

"He who borrows must also lend," Mel announced.

"But I've never found a bride of my own!"

"Let's get serious, shall we?" Brad asked. "This scene is the one with the circus bear. And you, Lisa, are Esmeralda, except it's Esmereldi in our version."

"Who plays the bear?" Mel asked.

"Not to worry." Raymond stood up, in the stance of Hamlet. "I bear the weight of the brawny bear, I say bearily unto thee."

"Good Lord, Raymond, put it in a sack." Mel headed for the water fountain.

Donna nudged me. "I hate to think we're experiencing the birth of inner-circle dissention."

Raymond, sitting next to me, leaned over. "Hey, Lisa, I was trying to be humorous, but did it come across as obnoxious?"

"Not at all, Raymond. I believe you're having one of your better days." At least I smiled.

"Thank you, I think," he said, ducking back to his chair.

Later, Mel was in a better mood, and after a rough run-through, he and I went to meet Kurt. Our likeable music director was sorting stacks of music that decorated the top of his piano. An ashtray containing several cigarette butts sat at the end of the keyboard. Bass keys showed scallops of eaten ivory, outlined in tan, where a pianist had rested cigarettes. That would be a left-handed pianist, in the event the point ever needed clarifying.

Kurt grinned when he saw us standing before him. "Ah, you are early. But never mind. I am ready. Now, shall ve begin?"

The completed rehearsal lived up to Brad's prediction. I meant it when I told Mel he should have seriously studied voice. "You sing well, but this is the first time you've gotten to show off. As my grade school teacher would have said, 'You have resonance.'"

"Is that so? And what does that mean?"

"What it means is, the intensification of vocal tones during articulation, but you can call it tonal quality."

"Then I must work on that." Mel walked out, clearing his throat. "Me-me-me. La-la-la."

After rehearsal, I planned a quick stop to have my film developed. Donna had a friend who would put a rush on it. As for friends, many of the cast inquired how I fared after my dunk in the depths.

"Lisa," Brad said, "I'm sorry about your unplanned swim. I hope there are no repercussions from your accident."

Accident? I exchanged my preferred answer to say, "The lump on my head is down to a hardly-can-tell-it's-there. And thanks for checking."

Donna approached us in an obvious hurry. "Hi, Lisa. Are you ready?"

"Ready? Oh, yes, of course. I'm ready." *For what?*

"But wait," Brad said, "I was about to invite this young lady to lunch, although I extend the invitation to you both."

"That's a top invite and we hate to pass it up, but Lisa and I planned to eat at my apartment. She's never seen it, and I have everything a chef would need. We better rush so we can get back in time."

"Thanks, Brad," I said. "Another day?"

"Okay. I'll hold you to it."

At the elevator, Donna pressed the down button and the door opened. Once on the street, she said, "So, we're going to the Springston apartment."

She raised a thumb and finger to her lips and whistled as loud as a Texas cowboy calling his horse. A cab screeched to a halt in front of us and Donna grabbed my hand. "Let's go."

We jumped into the mud-spattered vehicle and made one stop for Donna to leave the film at the camera shop. Back in the cab, she said, "I thought you were going to be a loner for a while. I mean, doesn't that include Brad?"

"I guess it does, but I don't want to be obvious."

In a few minutes, we arrived in front of an imposing East Sixties apartment building, where a spiffy doorman with smiling eyes stood under the protective fringed awning.

After greeting us, he opened the door and Donna and I headed for the elevator. We exited on the ninth floor into a foyer with taupe and white striped wallpaper. The apartment was small compared to the Shermans' penthouse, but no less impressive.

I surveyed around the large, and mostly white, living, dining and kitchen combination. "Now tell me again why you have this apartment when you have a remarkable house in King's Point?"

"It's invaluable for Dad in his practice. He performs surgery in New York and sometimes, after a long day, it's nice to stay in the city. He and Mom occasionally see a show and then spend the night here. I think their real reason for leasing it is for me to have a place to live."

Donna turned to the fridge.

That eerie feeling again, the one that made me lightheaded. I knew she wouldn't find food in that fridge. Weird, but all of a sudden I had a craving for Italian.

Donna opened the door and stared at limp lettuce. "So I don't really have everything a chef would need. Nothing in the freezer except bread. Let's see what the pantry offers. Aha! Spaghetti. Okay?"

"Sure," I said, blinking to clear my head. "Just what I wanted."

She reached into a cabinet for a pan and filled it with water. "Stroll around if you like. You can't get lost."

I took her up on it. A color scheme in shades of taupe, with occasional teal accents, and a touch of peachy coral, decorated the larger of the two bedrooms. In the living area, a round glass-topped cocktail table stood between two white leather sofas.

"This is a marvelous apartment." I ran my fingers over the base of an antique table lamp.

"Mother enjoyed decorating it. She always had her favorite colors, no matter what was in vogue. You won't see ashtrays. She doesn't allow smoking in the apartment. At home, it's different, a courtesy to their guests, but this is harder to air out." Soon, Donna brought a pitcher of iced tea and set plates of spaghetti on the marble-topped bar. She returned for hot garlic bread.

"Smells divine," I said. "This is what I miss at the hotel, not being able to prepare meals. But I find a way to get the three C's: vitamin C, chips, and chocolate."

"Maybe you could write a hotplate cookbook."

"An amusing idea. But, maybe I won't."

"Now I know how Mother Hubbard felt. I didn't realize I left the cupboard so depleted. It's my job to keep it stocked, and I forgot this week."

I twirled spaghetti around my fork, a skill perfected years ago. "Now back to my secondary preoccupation. What do you know about Dulce's ex-husband? I caught a glimpse of him at the memorial service. I thought he was rather shook up."

"Oh, I almost forgot." Donna scooted off the barstool and reached for tea. "Sorry, I don't have lemon. Want some sugar?"

"No thanks. I try to skip it."

"Now for Dulce's ex-husband. I met him at the show's opening night cast party. If you can believe it, I felt the flu coming on. Trooper that I am, I made a token showing and left soon after." Donna scrutinized her food and stood to fetch something else. "During other cast parties, B.J. impressed me as an all-right kind of person. As far as I know, everyone liked him." She handed me a small green container. "Here, have some Parmesan."

I decorated my spaghetti with cheese sprinkles. "This is great, Donna. Anyway, I wondered about the ex. Do you know if they ever saw each other after their divorce?"

"Maybe. He came around a few times, as I recall. They might have been ironing things out about the settlement. How about more tea?"

I accepted it and decided on sugar, after all. "What was his name again?"

"Who?"

"Donna! Dulce's ex-husband."

"Oh, I thought you knew. His last name is Carter. Dulce's career hadn't progressed too much at that time so she kept his name. She liked it better than her own, which had six or eight syllables."

"First name?"

"I have no idea. All she ever called him was B.J."

Chapter Twenty

I still had B.J. Carter on my mind when Donna and I returned to rehearsal. I almost expected Gregory to surface, but of course, it was Jeff who greeted us with a pleasant smile.

We walked toward the music room where Vince stood listening outside the door. From the intense expression on his face, someone could have yelled, "fire," and he wouldn't have budged.

This room was reserved Tuesday afternoons for the guest performer of the next show. I took a step closer. "Vince? You working undercover for the FBI?"

"Oh, hi," he said, perhaps a little embarrassed at the obvious eavesdropping. "Not quite, I'm listening to Saturday's guest."

I moved as close to the door as possible, without being in the room. "Who is it? I haven't heard."

"Sylvia Delgado, the movie star."

"Delgado? I remember seeing that gorgeous woman in movies when I was a kid."

"She's supposed to sing 'Zigeuner' from *Bittersweet*," Vince answered. "I just heard her go over it with Kurt. Not... very good."

I wanted to hear for myself, but only silence came from the music room. Then sobs filled the silence.

Kurt yanked open the door like he expected us to be listening. "Vell, come in, don't stand in der hall. This is vot ve are going to do." He went over to Sylvia and put his arm around her shoulder.

Tears streamed on her cheeks. "Do you think they will do it, Señor Scofeld?"

"Do what?" I asked.

Kurt cracked a big smile. "Ve are changing Frauline Delgado's solo to an operatic trio, but no satire. Her voice is not as bad as she thinks," he added.

"Please," Sylvia said, "it is much worse than I think. My agent, he wished me to have a go back in America. It has been so long. He wished me to appear on national television so people in your country would remember me." She brought a handkerchief to her eyes. "Would you do it?"

Oh dear, she means comeback. And Kurt, such a sweet man, is probably dying.

Of course, Vince and I agreed to the trio idea. Besides, this would give Vince the opportunity for recognition, a definite plus for him. As for me, singing something classical and unspoofed on Mel's show could showcase my operatic talent.

Sylvia bubbled with enthusiasm. "Thank you. Thank you," she said, her tears subsiding.

Kurt's relief was evident. "Go along now. I vill make arrangements."

Vince and I left a smiling Sylvia Delgado. "This is a most interesting development," I said.

"But right now, I need to locate Nate."

"A development I hope develops in a big way," Vince replied. "I think Nate's in his office."

"I'll try to find him. See you later." I thought how we all called him Nate behind his back. He didn't make my suspect list for now, but I'd bet money his wife dreamed of Dulce's early departure, one way or the other. I needed to think of a good reason for asking him about B.J. Carter.

Nate stepped from his office. Turning, he saw me. "Ah, Lisa, I'd like to speak with you. Do you have a moment?"

There are those who would have called this a coincidence. "Of course I do, Mr. Sherman."

"I talked with Kurt about Sylvia Delgado. I hope you agreed with the plan. I'm not sure what her agent had in mind."

"We're glad to do it," I said. Glad didn't sound like a strong enough adjective. I hoped something might come of this operatic performance and felt certain Vince did, too.

Nate led the way to the coffee bar. "I telephoned you yesterday evening but didn't get an answer."

"I'm sorry I missed you. The phone's in the hall and we don't always hear it."

"I called to see how you were. You made a valiant effort at dinner Sunday night. Let's face it, you had a traumatic incident."

"Thank you, Mr. Sherman. I don't think I'll be suffering any lingering physical effects from the experience." I didn't mention mental.

"Wonderful. But what else would I expect from you?" He picked up a cup and filled it from the coffee urn. "Sure you won't have some?"

"No thanks, I've reached my quota." I studied his face, thinking he had something else to tell me.

He considered his coffee a moment, stirring it more than I thought necessary. "Lisa, your replacing Dulce was a choice of great importance. You may think it unusual for us to sign an unknown. To a certain extent, that's true."

"I guess I was an unknown by New York standards. But still, I got the role on the Franks Spectacular without an agent."

"That proves you have talent. But Brad thought we needed a more experienced personality and he had a particular actress in mind. Since it was Steven's responsibility to help replace Dulce, we planned to do the one show with you while we found a permanent replacement."

I memorized every word he said.

"So," Nate continued, "after the first show, you became our choice, and we looked no further. I preferred to answer any questions you might have harbored. That's all I wanted to say."

At last, a clear explanation to go along with what Donna told me earlier. Now I knew what Brad and Steven argued about the first day I arrived. Brad wanted someone else for the role, and Steven wanted me. Maybe one day I would have the chance to ask Brad about that someone.

"I appreciate your concern, Mr. Sherman. I do have another question. Have the police learned anything about Gregory's murder?

"They're still investigating. The killer undoubtedly would have worn gloves, but if not, he wiped the bow clean of prints. They'll check it out anyway." I decided not to ask Mr. Sherman about B.J. Carter. I trusted Steven. He could at least hang an opinion on the man. Even though there wasn't much left of the afternoon, I planned fifteen minutes on the barre. Afterward, I'd locate him.

Donna had almost finished working out, along with the other dancers. Even when damp, her hair turned to curls. When mine got damp, it turned to straight. Oh well, it beat the early Romans. They put mud on their hair and rolled it on sticks.

Donna picked up a towel and blotted her face. "So, Lisa, how did the thing with Sylvia turn out?"

"Great. She does pretty well and is beautiful, besides. The woman can act."

"But can she sing?"

"Actually, she doesn't sing alone much, so it works. If Vince and I pull it off, it could be super for us. I love television, but I still want to do opera and Broadway before I die."

We continued with practice for another ten minutes. Afterward, I gathered my things up off the floor and headed for the dressing room. I changed clothes and guided a brush through my hair, still being cautious with my tender head.

I left, hoping to see Steven without making a point of it. Luck responded and I almost bumped into him when I left the rehearsal hall.

"Hello there," he said. "How is our Olympic swimmer today?"

"That's funny, Steven. Say, are you busy?"

"Never too busy for you. On your way out?"

"You're saying that because I'm carrying my tote bag and have my jacket on?"

"That gave me a pair of clues. You're free this afternoon, and I have an errand. If you're going home, I'll walk with you, if you don't mind."

"Please do."

I do think everyone in New York decided to walk down Fifth Avenue at the same time. Soon after rounding the next corner, I asked him, "What was B.J. Carter like?"

My question caught him off-guard. "That was out of the blue. Why do you want to know?"

"I'm wondering what kind of man Dulce would have chosen for a husband."

"Tex, I have a feeling you're coming up with a new angle." We stopped for a traffic light.

"Maybe you could trade your AFTRA union card for a gold badge."

The light changed to green but we didn't cross. We moved over to keep from being stepped on by the crowd. "Steven, can you tell me who asked for the divorce?"

He paused a second. "I don't know. There's a fifty-fifty chance Dulce did."

Fifty-fifty didn't offer much help.

"Hey, Tex, there's a flower stand. Let me buy you flowers." He pulled me by the hand. "What's your pleasure?"

The floral scent didn't quite cover the exhaust fumes of 5th Avenue. "They're beautiful," I said to the vendor. "I haven't seen you here before."

The man greeted me with a cheery smile. There were more smiles in New York than I'd thought, if one noticed them. He said, "I changed my plan of attack and switched corners. How can I help you?"

"What'll it be?" Steven asked. "How about yellow roses, or do you prefer red?"

I had only one answer. "Yellow, please."

The vendor wrapped the roses in tissue and Steven paid him. "I have to get these papers to the network offices, so better hurry on." He moved closer and put his hand on my arm. "And Tex, I'm glad you're okay."

"Thanks, Steven. The flowers are lovely. You better hurry or you'll be late."

He hurried down the sidewalk and I walked the two blocks to my hotel. I located a vase on the closet shelf, and even though it wasn't much of a vase, it worked. I was no flower-arranger, but Mother always arranged them the way they grew. I could do that. The stems go down.

After finding a spot for the roses, I brought the telephone book in from the hall. How many Carters could there be in New York City? Uhm, plenty of B-something Carters, but not a B.J. among them. A thought hit me. I guessed he and Dulce attended the same church. If so, the secretary might give me the information.

I called the church first thing the next morning. My idea paid off. The secretary gave me his telephone number. Of course, with the story I told her about being on the London show, the request presented no problem. That, and the promise to hold two tickets for Saturday night.

My first calls resulted in busy signals. Finally, a ring.

"Carter here."

His secretary must have been late to work. "Mr. Carter, you don't know me, but my name is Lisa Warren."

"I may know who you are. I watch television. What can I do for you, Miss Warren?"

So far, so good, I thought. I found it interesting he still watched the show. He had a pleasant enough voice, but now that he was on the line, I felt ridiculous. "Mr. Carter, I wonder if I could speak to you, I mean, in person?"

"Regarding what, Miss Warren?"

"It's a little difficult to discuss over the phone." Now what do I say, I wondered. Did you murder your ex-wife? "Are you located anywhere near the West Fifties?"

"Not far. I won't be free until about twelve-thirty and then only until one o'clock or so. I'm going to Boston." He paused. "If it's important, I could see you today, or perhaps you'd rather wait until I return on Monday..."

Quick to answer, I said, "Yes, today would be fine."

He gave me directions and I figured fifteen minutes would get me there. "Thank you, Mr. Carter."

The man sounded businesslike, shy of being abrupt. But now, I needed to sprint to rehearsal and pray we wouldn't work through lunch again.

Our schedules indicated more piano rehearsals scheduled for the morning, and Mrs. Bjornson would come in later to make notes on the *Fledermaus* costumes.

The only glitch concerned Frank, the lead male dancer. Dashing onto the subway train, he broke his little toe. Furious, Cassie gave him no sympathy whatsoever, calling him a clumsy oaf. They had a dance routine for Saturday and now she would have to work with someone else. If a fiery temper and red hair did go together, Cassie proved a good example. And the peculiar thing was, I think I would have liked her if I could have gotten past not liking her.

Sylvia Delgado dropped by to meet with Mrs. Bjornson. We didn't have to rehearse our trio again until final dress at the theater. No sooner had I registered the thought than

Sylvia asked to run through the music during our lunch break.

Vince agreed, but what reason could I give for saying no? It turned out Jerry skipped our flamenco practice to work with Cassie and her new partner. They broke early, so Kurt took us through the trio. We finished before noon.

Afterward, I ran to my dressing room to change clothes. In anticipation of meeting with B.J. Carter, I had brought a suit. Somewhere I had heard that a woman wearing a tailored suit indicated seriousness, whatever that implied. As an afterthought, usually my first thought, I sprayed on cologne.

On the way to Mr. Carter's office, I tried to remain focused on what to say. When I arrived, I noticed the building was one of the upscale varieties, so business must have been good. Until I read the notice on the door, "Attorney-at-Law," I didn't even know his business.

His secretary reminded me of Perry Mason's Della Street—cordial, but rather formal. She picked up the phone and announced me.

Carter's office door opened, and Mr. Carter stepped out. "Good afternoon, Miss Warren. Please come in."

My present impression of B.J. Carter didn't match my recollection of him. An athletic build enhanced his six-foot-two-inch frame. While I thought he wasn't all that handsome, he wouldn't go unnoticed. I understood how Dulce was attracted to him.

"Please, sit down," he offered.

I sat in a high-back upholstered chair and felt I needed to sit close to the edge or I'd never get up. Carter had either excellent taste or a talented designer.

"Mr. Carter, I don't know where to start."

"Had you considered the beginning?" he asked, an unexpected twinkle in his eyes.

I told him the circumstances of Dulce's death and how the doctors thought she would pull through. Then, she suddenly died. He knew nothing of that detail. And why should he? They had been apart for quite some time.

"And how does this concern me, Miss Warren?"

"Oh, I didn't mean it did. My question is, do you have any idea who your ex-wife might have been seeing after your divorce? I mean, someone with whom she may have had problems?"

"Problems?"

"I'm sorry, I know I'm intruding."

He leaned back, made a steeple of his hands and tapped his forefingers together. "If you're trying to ask me about our marriage, cut to the question." He put his arms down, resting them on the desk. "Never mind, I'll tell you."

I sighed with relief.

"I loved Dulce and grieved when she died, but it was also a grief for our past. We had two years of marriage, less than one of them happy. And now, you want the reason for our divorce?"

So far, he was right on cue. I nodded.

"Only if you tell me why you're so interested."

I nodded again and didn't move another muscle.

"Fine. I'll tell you. When we married, I knew Dulce loved show business. That wasn't an issue. But, her interest in other men was. You see, I put her on a pedestal." He stopped for a moment, fingering a memo pad. "When I finally had enough, I asked for a divorce, but she didn't want one. Marriage was too much fun for her. It provided a safety net."

"So when did you get divorced?"

"Over a year and a half after the London show premiered. By then, she agreed without hesitating. She had a long line waiting."

"Line?" I asked.

"Of men, Miss Warren. Men." He angled his leather swivel chair toward the window and paused. Turning back, he said, "I gave you this information because I'm curious. Now it's your turn."

"I have to tell you, Mr. Carter, my uncle is the Dallas police chief. Anything I consider suspicious gets my undivided attention. It's hereditary." I smiled and received a smile in return. "I couldn't see Dulce taking her own life. From the time I learned about her death, I thought maybe someone... helped her along. Does that make sense to you?"

"It might, depending on why you believe somebody wanted her dead. But don't you think the police would have figured it out by now?"

I let his question go for the moment. "First, one more thing, if you will. Did Dulce have a heart condition?"

"A heart condition?" He sounded surprised at the suggestion. "None whatsoever. She was in perfect health."

I stood, ready to leave. "The police don't share my suspicious nature, Mr. Carter. I guess that's why they never talked to you. They saw no reason." I glanced at my watch. "I must be getting back. I hope I haven't—"

"Of course you haven't." He moved from behind his desk. "You will let me know if something comes of your, ah, investigation? I would appreciate it." He escorted me to the door.

"I will, and thank you for your time."

"You're more than welcome." He extended his hand. "And incidentally, Miss Warren. I'm not the someone you're looking for."

Chapter Twenty-One

I reviewed my meeting with B.J. Carter while riding the bus back to the studio. I found him disarming and courteous, and I couldn't think of a chance in a trillion he had anything to do with his ex-wife's death. If guilty, he sure carried a grudge a long time before doing anything about it. Besides, he wasn't on the boat, and I'd sure have to be wrong about my so-called accident.

I figured I might prove how Dulce was killed easier than who killed her. I mentally analyzed those I knew to be her close acquaintances. Knowing what I did about Dulce, she wasn't Brad's type. I had my own opinion of Brad Hunter, but a person doesn't always see a picture the way an artist paints it.

Raymond? He made his stand the night of the Shermans' party. Cassie probably hated Dulce more than anyone. Enough to murder her? I hadn't uncovered any more reason for Steven to kill her than B.J. Carter. Kurt and Jerry are married to lovely women. What reason would they have?

Audrey Sherman often came to the studio to see Nate, or to check on him. I wondered how far her jealousy could lead her. Maybe not far enough for murder, but who knew? She wouldn't win a popularity contest, that's for sure. And Marty's out of the question. She and Mel seem devoted, unless Mel had strayed and no one realized it.

Here I was, a long way from my first list of suspects, with Gregory the leading man. He was obsessed with Cassie's career and jealous of Vince, or rather Dulce. I sure missed the obvious there.

And speaking of Vince. He had loved Dulce, or was at least infatuated with her. I didn't like her for not treating him right. Besides, it wasn't credible for anyone who saved my life to have taken someone else's. Not everything fit. Still, I had conjured up an overpowering array of possibilities.

My thoughts came to a halt along with the bus. It squealed to a stop at the corner—nothing a shot of brake

fluid couldn't help. I exited the back door with ten minutes
to spare.

When I stepped off the curb two blocks from rehearsal,
the signal light turned red, and a couple of police cars
zoomed by, careening around the corner. Turning the same
corner, I noticed they had stopped alongside an ambulance
parked near the studio. People gathered on the sidewalk and
across the street. The police warned them to stay back. I
thought someone had robbed the women's boutique close
by. When I caught up, medics were loading a stretcher into
the ambulance and then slammed the door with a sickening
thud.

I suddenly realized it wasn't the boutique. "It's the
studio," I gasped. I ran to the entrance where a policeman
stopped me.

"But I have to go inside!"

"Sorry, Miss."

"What's happened? Who's in the ambulance?"

The policeman raised his arm, blocking my entry. "I can't
tell you, ma'am. You'll have to wait."

At that moment, I could see Brad standing inside the
doorway. As he started to move away, I called to him. "Brad?
Tell him to let me in."

He whirled around and hurried over to me. "Officer,
Miss Warren's in the company. I'm sure it would be
permissible."

The man scrutinized Brad, then me, and asked for my
identification. "All right, Miss Warren, they'll probably want
to question you anyway." He stood aside and let me enter.

"Come with me to my office," Brad said, walking at a fast
clip.

I accompanied him, struggling to keep up. "Will you
please tell me what's happened?"

He pulled me into his office and closed the door. "Sit
down and I will."

I remained standing.

"You really should sit down," he said, sucking in a deep
breath. "It's Steven. Somebody stabbed him. It's serious."

Brad was right. My entire body trembled and I dropped
into the Milano chair. "Stabbed Steven? But why? Who

would do such a thing?" I think I said that aloud. I didn't know until Brad answered me.

"I found him in the lounge. He'd lost a lot of blood."

Thoughts raced through my mind, jumping from one gray cell to the next. Dulce, Gregory, and now Steven, and not to forget myself. I was in a daze.

Brad leaned down a bit. "Lisa, are you there?"

I blinked a couple of times. "Yes, I'm here. Brad, do you think Steven discovered who poisoned Dulce?"

"No one has proved she was poisoned. Are you forgetting about Gregory? For whatever reason, whoever killed him might have attacked Steven."

A knock sounded on the door and Nate Sherman stepped inside. "I thought I saw you come in here, Lisa. Detective Sander wants to talk to you."

We walked down the hall to the rehearsal room where the detective was questioning the dancers. Cassie hadn't rehearsed with them this morning because she worked with her new partner and finished early.

After a few minutes, Sander completed his questioning and then zeroed in on me. "Ah, Miss Warren. Tell me you know who killed Hardin and attacked Mr. Drake so I can get out of here."

"I have no idea, Detective." I wasn't ready for sarcasm and for sure not from him.

He proceeded to ask my whereabouts for the last two hours.

That wouldn't be difficult to validate. "I had an appointment. I took the bus before noon and the driver recognized me. He even asked why I hadn't taken a cab." My explanation evidently satisfied Sander. Besides, I wouldn't have time to stab someone and get to B.J. Carter's office, although I'd prefer no one knew I had been to see him.

"All right, Miss Warren. I may ask you for more information concerning your appointment."

Mel, Raymond, and the rest of the staff took turns answering Sander's questions. When he finished, Bert called to him. "Detective? Telephone for you."

Sander walked over to the wall phone and answered it. "Is that right? You're sure?" He hung up the phone and rested his hand on it a moment. He didn't make an announcement about the call, but asked everyone to remain in the room until his officers could search the premises.

Mrs. Bjornson marched up to him in her military manner and, with her strong Norwegian accent, said, "I have measurements to take of three people in this room, young man. If you don't like it, perhaps you would be good enough to alter these costumes yourself."

Something about the sergeant's speaking nose-to-nose with Sander lowered him a rung or two. "Yes, well, I think that will be acceptable if you can accomplish it quickly."

"Thank you, Detecktif."

I moved to go with her when Sander said, "Miss Warren, another question, if you will." He directed me away from the others. "As you have never before hesitated to show me your suspicions, do you have any thoughts on who disliked Mr. Drake enough to do away with him?"

"Not a soul," I said. "Everybody likes Steven. This makes no sense." Until I heard from my uncle concerning the package I mailed him, I had nothing further to say.

"Well, I dunno. The way I see it, a thief wandered in and Mr. Drake caught him. That's one theory, mind you. The other is we have some kind of cuckoo-head running around here, flailing knives and shooting arrows."

"I haven't another suggestion," I said.

"I figure a thief wouldn't want to be caught with the weapon, so he left it in the room where Hunter found it. And Miss Warren, that call I just received? The knife had no fingerprints—only the victim's blood."

"So you couldn't prove who did it."

Sander's expression brightened. "See there, I knew you paid attention to details."

"Don't make fun of me." *Ooh, this man has a hold on sarcastic.* "I know what it means. If it wasn't a thief, then maybe one of us is guilty; otherwise, the attacker wouldn't have left a knife. Where would he put it? He had to leave it."

"No offense, Miss Warren. If you had done it, you would probably have a little blood on that pretty suit of yours. You will call me if anything comes to mind?"

"Yes, of course." I went back to Brad's office and found the door ajar. I peered inside. "Brad, do you have a minute?"

"Lisa, come in. Yes, certainly. I have for you."

"I'm wondering if you've heard news about Steven?"

"The emergency room won't release any information, but Nate's at the hospital and he'll call us. Audrey was here, but I don't think she went with him." He walked toward me and placed both hands on my shoulders. "You've heard this before. We have a show to do. We'll have to focus on that and on Steven's getting well."

"I must see Mrs. Bjornson, but I won't be late for rehearsal. Thanks, Brad."

As it turned out, Mrs. Bjornson didn't wait for me. She took Sylvia Delgado's measurements, made adjustments for Vince, and left a message for me not to worry about my costumes. They would be ready. This wardrobe mistress was a perfectionist on her own terms.

Jeff arranged chairs in a circle for our dialogue rehearsal. The writers changed lines in each sketch, to rev them up, they said. It's scary to discard learned dialogue for new on short notice, and we were already on edge about Steven. The head writer said if they thought of something else, they could always change it by airtime, but no major changes. I hoped he meant it.

About that time, Bert came in with another note for me. Miss Warren, you have a message from a Miss Morris. She said she worked at the Royal Floral." He handed me a memo.

"Thanks, Bert." According to the note, Miss Morris wanted me to call and ask specifically for her. I tucked the memo into my pocket, thinking I must have left my sunglasses at the shop after all but wondered why that would be so secretive. Calling her right now wasn't a priority.

After our line reading, we tried conversation. Nobody wanted to leave until we heard from the hospital. We didn't wait long before Mr. Sherman telephoned and talked with Brad.

When Brad finished with the call, he said, "Steven is going to be all right. The knife missed everything vital, although I'm sure everything is vital to Steven. Even though he lost a lot of blood, knowing him, he'll be back to work soon."

Sighs and smiles filled the room.

"Listen, people," Brad continued, "I know this is a relief, but the fact remains, it may not be over. We've had two deaths and Steven's attack. I'm sure Nate would agree that you should have a buddy. Don't leave the studio, theater, or go anywhere alone."

Everyone exchanged glances as if never contemplating danger. Donna was an exception. "I'm not about to go anywhere alone. There's a lunatic running around this place."

"That's what I mean. Be cautious," Brad said. "Okay, check the callboard. With any luck, this show goes on the air tomorrow."

I hadn't talked to Donna since Steven's attack, so I asked her to wait for me.

"Sure," she said. "I have to change for a dinner date. Give me fifteen minutes."

"I'll be here."

After Brad answered a few questions from the cast, I sauntered on over to him. "Brad, would you show me where you found Steven? I think the police are finished with the room, aren't they?"

"Yes, they're through. Why would you want to see it?... Never mind, I'll show you."

We rode the elevator to the next floor and entered the lounge. "Where exactly was he?"

Brad stopped a moment and walked over to a spot about eight feet from the entrance. "He was lying about here, with the knife over by the door. As a matter of fact, when I came in, I heard something scrape on the tile. It must have been the knife."

I tried to envision the moment when Steven fell and then turned my attention to the door. "I don't know why I wanted to see, Brad, or what it served, but thanks for showing me."

We left the scene. I didn't plan to return.

"You are something else, Lisa Warren," Brad said, "I suppose you're going to solve this, too. Now you've got a poisoner and a knife-thrower to track down, to say nothing of a master bowman."

I had no idea why he had to be so stubborn. "I don't see why you won't listen to my theory about Dulce.

He took a deep breath. "Lisa... "

"I know. I'll be careful. Whether the police act on it is up to them. Frankly, I don't think they're attending to business."

"Okay, okay." He put up his hands in surrender. "Now, back to safety first. Are you and Donna leaving together?"

"Yes, we are. Donna has a date, but we'll leave the building at the same time. Don't worry."

"I'll worry if I want to." His expression sobered. "Be careful, Lisa. When Nate gets back in the morning, he can tell us more about Steven's condition. He sounded optimistic when he called."

I walked on toward the entrance, since Donna had asked me to wait for her. She soon caught up with me, ready to leave in an obvious going-to-dinner dress. "Well, here I am. What do you think?"

"Positively great is all," I said.

"Thanks. It's a joy to hear an unsolicited compliment," she said, winking. "My date will be out front. We'll drive you to the Fine Arts."

"No, I wouldn't dream of it."

"I didn't ask you to dream about it," she said. "We'll just drive you home."

"Has Bjornson been giving you lessons?"

Chapter Twenty-Two

I dropped on my bed and would have fallen asleep at once had Jenni not been rummaging in her books. The abnormal quiet on my side of the room must have gotten her attention.

"Lisa? You okay?"

I stared at the ceiling.

"Want to tell me about it?"

"Yes. I do." I unfolded the news about Steven. "Jenni, I can't make the pieces fit."

"I'm so sorry, Roomie, but from what you say, I'm sure Steven will be all right. You're a little whey-faced, though. Did you even have lunch?"

"I don't remember lunch. Maybe I did," I groaned.

"Here, take this root beer. It's still cold, and here's some pretzels."

"Thanks, I believe I will." I opened the bag of pretzels and popped the cap on the root beer.

Jenni said, "Oh, your uncle called from Texas." She reached for the notepad we left on the table for messages. "He wants you to call him."

"He did?" I sat up straight. "Did he say anything else?"

Jenni read the note. "He says for you to call him as soon as possible." She laid down the pad, shaking her head. "Sounds salient to me."

"If you mean important, you bet it is." I almost forgot my concerns about Steven and dumped my purse for phone money. Bert's memo fell out along with everything else. *Ask for Elizabeth Morris. Royal Floral. After four-thirty.* I would call her, but first things first.

I grabbed a handful of change and headed for the phone in the hall, where I shoved a coin in the slot. "Operator? I'd.... Oh, no. Can you hold?" I was so nervous, I dropped half my change. "I'm sorry, Operator. I need to place a person-to-person call to Police Chief Hamilton Warren in Dallas, Texas." I gave her the number and plunked in the coins. Three, four, five rings. *Come on, Uncle Hamp. Be there.*

The operator finally put me through. *Good. He answered.* "Hi, Uncle Hamp, how are you? ... Yes, I'm fine. Uncle Hamp, I got your message. What did you find out? ... You did? ... They did? Will there be any trouble because I sent it to you? ... No, Detective Sander wasn't interested in what I thought. Not then, anyway... I know. I'll be careful. Send the box and the toxicology report to the hotel. Send it airmail special delivery, insured. I'll leave a note at the desk... I love you, too. Thanks so much. And oh, tell Mom and Dad I'll call them soon."

I hung up with a sigh of satisfaction. That's a sigh with a smug smile. For the time being, I planned to keep the information secret from anyone at the studio, including Donna, but only because Uncle Hamp warned me. He kept a few cc's of the lens wash. If the package became lost in the mail, insurance couldn't replace hard evidence.

After my call, Jenni's relieved expression indicated my attitude had changed. It had indeed, by many percentage points.

"I always feel better after talking with Uncle Hamp. When this package arrives from him, you'll be the second to know the results." I checked the time and figured the florist would be open. I reached for another coin, returned to the phone and dialed the number.

"Royal Floral," a woman answered. She must have been holding the phone when it rang.

"Miss Morris?"

"This is Elizabeth Morris."

"I'm Lisa Warren. You asked me to call you?"

"Yes, Miss Warren. I saw the London Show so I thought I might reach you through the studio. I wanted you to call me at this time because Mr. Holton wouldn't be here."

"What does he have to do with my sunglasses? I did leave them there, right?"

"No, I haven't seen any glasses. It's the card. You know, the one you asked about that came with the thirteen roses?"

My adrenaline surged. "What about it?"

"Well, as you know, and as Mr. Holton said, we didn't have a record of who sent the roses. After hearing you tell him why you were interested, I'd be scared to death if I were in your place. I thought it over and decided to call you."

I'll scream if she doesn't tell me soon. "What about the card, Miss Morris?"

"I remember that card all right. I took it from the man, myself. You see, it's my brother's name. That's why I couldn't forget."

Please, get on with it, lady.

"He signed the card, 'Brad'."

I felt myself go hollow.

"Miss Warren?"

Her voice sounded a hundred miles away. *Could I even speak?* "You're not mistaken?" I asked. "You're sure?"

"I am not mistaken. If I noticed what else he wrote at the time, I didn't have reason to remember it. But 'Brad,' I'm certain of."

The next day's schedule involved going through every scene with scripts. Although the actors had the dialogue memorized, we could still have changes. Two or three words, or even only one, might make a difference in the timing, and every laugh counted. I was pretty sure I'd never laugh again. I exited the elevator on the fourth floor and Brad was the first person I ran into.

"Lisa, good morning. Are you all right? I worried about you last night."

I had little control over my anxiety. Casual wasn't simple. "Yes, thank you, I'm fine. But how is Steven? Have you heard anything more?"

Brad paused an instant. "He slept well. Nate spoke with his doctor and his recovery now is no more difficult than after an appendectomy."

Thank the thespian gods for that. "It would be awful if someone in the company stabbed him. The guilty are seldom easy to spot, especially among friends."

"I have trouble thinking anyone with the show attacked Steven," Brad said. "From now on, we'll have a security man on duty. If anyone's name is not on the list, he'll call and check with us."

Right now, I wanted to join the others in the rehearsal room. "I'll see you later." My heart pounded. Security man or no, it didn't make me less nervous. I sat in one of the folding chairs, studying my script. I couldn't concentrate and reread it almost sentence by sentence, urging my mind to join me.

Mel and Donna came in, and Raymond followed. After the four of us discussed the day before, Brad launched into the first scene.

The writers made only a couple of changes. They revised the traffic cop skit by inserting rain. Mel rolls up the car window and he can't hear Raymond, the patrolman. Then a chimpanzee in the car bangs on the window, scaring the patrolman. They added rain so he can slip on the wet pavement. He breaks his leg, but Mel keeps talking while the patrolman is writhing in pain on the ground. Comical, yes, and I always wondered how that rain thing worked.

Between skits, a noticeable quiet carried through the studio. Even though we knew Steven would be okay, the absence of laughter was foreboding. At break, Donna and I talked. "You want coffee?" she asked.

"No, not now, thanks." I was tempted to tell her about Uncle Hamp, but I wanted to see what he sent first. I had called him, Texas time, before the post office closed. I should receive the package by noon tomorrow.

"Lisa, do you remember where everybody was before Brad discovered Steven? They said he'd been attacked less than an hour before."

"I think we were doing a sketch with Raymond, Mel, Vince, and the three guy singers. We broke for a few minutes but returned and finished the trio before noon. I had this appointment with B.J. Carter at twelve-thirty."

"You didn't tell me about an appointment."

"I know, but I'm about to. After rehearsal, I went to my dressing room and changed. I caught the bus to Carter's office and when I returned, the ambulance was out in front. I don't know anyone's whereabouts before then."

"Neither do I," Donna said. "I mean we're all actors. A guilty actor can look innocent right after he commits murder, for heaven's sake."

"Good point. I do remember seeing Audrey go down in the elevator. And Brad mentioned seeing her, too."

"You saw Audrey?" Donna asked. "I didn't know she stopped by yesterday, although she's been rather visible ever since Dulce died. I kinda thought she was checking on you—you know, to make sure you weren't stalking her husband."

Hardly. I took a few minutes to tell Donna about my visit with B.J. His schedule evidently occupied his time before ever meeting with me and I believed him. We decided he couldn't have been at the studio so I dismissed him from my list. Besides, what motive would he have?

The stage manager's voice sounded through the megaphone. "Places, everyone, for *Annie, Get Your Gun.*

A brilliant scene. It still amazed me how bullets appeared to shoot a message into a board—all an illusion, with a metal attachment on the back of the wood. And I always thought Matt Dillon was that good a shot.

Brad put off someone trying to ask a question and walked toward me. "Lisa, I need to talk to you."

Need or *want?* Fumbling for words, I settled on, "I have a couple of minutes."

"What's wrong?" He reached for my arm, then pulled back. "You've been avoiding me."

"I... I'm not avoiding you. It's that we've been so busy."

"Then have dinner with me. I promise I won't keep you out late."

If I ate with Brad, what would he do, stab me with a fork? I couldn't think of a rational refusal. "All right, but do you mind if we go from here? I really am tired."

"Of course not. We can do that."

The rehearsal day came to an end at six, later than anyone expected. Brad and I took a cab to a small out-of-the-way place known for good southern food. No matter how out-of-the-way in New York you were, you're still in the City. On the drive over, I sat so close to the door, I was almost out the window.

Once inside the restaurant, we followed the waiter to a booth with red-checked placemats and napkins. I sat first and realized Brad started to sit by me, paused and then decided on the opposite side of the table. Gratefully, this widened the distance between us.

Brad ordered fried chicken, and I chose a vegetable plate with cornbread. Our conversation was forced, but we small-talked until our food came.

"The chicken is first rate," he said. "How is your vegetarian dinner?"

"It isn't Texas southern, but it's good."

Brad took a sip of water, put the glass down and said, "Lisa, if you didn't want to have dinner with me, you shouldn't have come." His comment caught me by surprise, although I knew so far I had been as charming as a black widow spider. *I expected him not to notice?* "No, no, it's nothing," I lied. "I wanted to come to dinner."

He leaned across the table, putting his hand over mine. "You can't tell me it's nothing."

I started to draw away, but he kept a firm grip.

"Lisa, what is it? I know something's the matter."

At least the restaurant wasn't crowded, so no one could hear. I decided I'd best grasp hold of my nerves. "I'm sorry, Brad. This week has been stressful, and I want to do my best for the show. Go ahead and finish your meal. I've had all I want."

"No, that's it. I'll take you home." We left, and, as if we had called it, a cab pulled up at the entrance and transported us to my hotel.

Walking up the steps, Brad said, "Lisa, I'm sorry if I did or said anything to upset you."

"Don't worry about it. See you in the morning."

"You don't come in until eleven?"

"Yes, but I may come in earlier to work out. Thank you for dinner, Brad."

What an evening this was. I looked at my reflection in the mirror and smeared vanishing cream on my face. It didn't work. I was still there, tired and unnerved. Even my lashes had lost their curl. At least my room provided a safe haven.

Mrs. Jordan had screens installed on the ground floor so her kitty wouldn't make herself at home on our beds. I opened a window for fresh air, thinking I'd be secure until Spider-Man turned evil and slithered down the inner walls of the atrium. I fell asleep before Jenni came home, scarcely stirring as she puttered around getting ready for bed. I'd wanted to tell her what Uncle Hamp reported, but it could wait until I had the written proof in my hands.

It must have been around four o'clock when I awoke. I shivered as if the temperature had dropped to zero. Before I could move from my bed to close the window, the eeriest feeling came over me. What was it?

An apparition floated across the room toward my bed. The figure of a woman, not clearly outlined, drifted less than five feet away. Struggling to make out her face, I knew I wasn't mistaken. The image of Dulce Carter stood before me. She carried one red rose and remained for mere seconds. She smiled through tears and then vanished, leaving nothing but a ruffled mist until, it too, faded.

No one would believe this. I'm not sure I did. In the past, the incidents were frightening, as if she were seeking revenge for my taking her role on Mel's show. And now, she seemed to believe I was on her side.

I ignored the window and lay back in bed. Pulling up the covers, I waged an internal debate about my sanity. When early morning light touched the sill, I climbed out of bed, dressed, and went down to breakfast. None of the girls ate this early. I could think of nothing but Dulce's ghost. Any visions I'd seen before paled compared to this. Why did she come, I wondered.

Jenni had awakened by the time I returned to our room. "You up, roommate?" I asked.

"I will be, in about two minutes." She followed a yawn with a stretch.

I couldn't bring myself to mention my "visitor." Besides, a sensible girl like Jenni might not believe me anyway. "Will you do me a favor?" I asked. "You don't have a class this morning, right?"

"Sure, and right."

"If a package from Uncle Hamp arrives after I leave, will you sign for it, bring it to our room and call the studio? I would appreciate it."

"I will. And since you reminded me I don't have a class, I shall set my alarm for another hour. Bye now." She reached for her clock.

I soft-walked from the room, locking the door as I left. Friday would be a long day. If the show ran overtime, it was easier to change a sketch than a dance number. I'm glad they vetoed Mel's idea of cutting a girl in half. It had great laugh potential, but unfortunately, it elicited a visual of an arrow in Gregory's chest.

The morning flew by, and as soon as lunch break came, I escaped. I exchanged places with a passenger exiting a cab. The driver obeyed my plea to hurry and we pulled in front of the hospital in a matter of minutes. I found my way to the information desk where the attendant gave me Steven's room number. When I reached his door, a pretty red-haired nurse walked by.

"May I help you?" she asked.

"Thank you, I'd like to see Steven Drake."

"Mr. Drake is having a walk. He should be... oh, here he comes now." She smiled and scurried on her way.

With a nurse like that, I bet Steven would be better already. I zeroed in on the figure headed in my direction. I thought he would be limping, but any limp was minimal. He carried a cane but scarcely used it.

When he drew closer, his smile brightened. "Hi, Tex. Thanks for coming to see me. Don't you have a better way to spend your lunch hour?"

"Not at all. How do you feel?" I could hear eagerness in my voice.

"Come into my parlor. I'm almost well now that you're here." Steven reached to open the door, but I took the courtesy from him. He motioned toward the room's only chair.

"How's the wounded patient? Are you in much pain?"

He sat on the edge of the bed. "Nothing an aspirin can't cure. But hey, I'm getting out of here. I'll show up at work tomorrow."

"That's great. I'm surprised it's so soon. I can't wait to tell you about my research at the library. You knew I wouldn't let it go."

Steven's face sobered. "Tex, can't you see you could be putting yourself in danger? The police are taking care of it all—Dulce, Gregory, and now me. I've already talked to the police."

"That's the point. Do you have any idea who attacked you?"

"As I told them, it happened pretty fast. He wore something over his head, like one of those ski masks."

"This may sound odd, but could your attacker have been a woman?"

"What? I don't think so. Whoever it was took me by surprise, but I'm sure I would've known if a woman used that knife. Still, he or she wasn't so large, but who... "

The door swung open, and a hurried, or maybe harried, doctor acknowledged me with a polite hello. "Mr. Drake, I expect you're ready to leave this place. I need to reexamine that wound. We'll probably keep you one more night.

"I'm ready to go now, Doctor." Steven stretched back in the bed. "Dr. Berin, I'd like you to meet Lisa Warren."

"It's a pleasure, Miss Warren. Now if you will excuse us."

"Yes, of course. I'm due at the studio anyway." I headed for the door. "Bye, Steven. Everyone's anxious for you to come back." Although ready to divulge what I knew about curare, I had to put it on hold.

As soon as I returned to rehearsal, Donna told me Jenni called. "She said what you were waiting for arrived. I'm thinking the 'what' is a thing and not a person?"

"Oh, yes. But I'll tell you about it later."

I had only a little time to get to the hotel. The brisk walk made me aware of the city's exhaust fumes. Like I breathe 'em in and hope I can breathe 'em all out.

Entering my room, I found the small parcel from Uncle Hamp. I pulled out the scissors from the desk and cut the twine. He had wrapped the bottle of eye drops in shreds of paper. I read the toxicology report and replaced it in the box in the lower drawer of my bureau. Now if I could just return to rehearsal as fast as I got to the hotel.

Chapter Twenty-Three

I finally got the hang of this route to the studio. On foot was best. Donna walked in at the same time I did, but not as out of breath.

"You sure left in a hurry, Lisa. I wanted you to go down to A. C.'s with me, and poof, you had gone." Donna carried a small shopping bag from Arnold Constable's. "Here, sniff." She put out her wrist.

"Oh, 'Wind Song.' Prince Matchabelli came up with a good one." I was particular when it came to scents. I liked them light or tweedy and as far away from "Tabu" as possible.

"So where did you go?" Donna asked. "Somewhere special?"

"To visit a friend in the hospital." I smiled a smile between coy and sheepish.

"You went to see Steven! How is he?"

"Believe it or don't, they plan to release him tomorrow."

"That's great. You've got to tell me all about it... Uh-oh, tell me later. The stage manager's calling."

"Jeff's smiles get more cooperation than Gregory's scowls, rest his soul."

Donna stashed her things while I joined the others in the circular arrangement of chairs. This marked the first time we rehearsed the show from start to finish. Brad set aside Mel's phenomenal soliloquy from Macbeth because of the dagger-before-me bit. He had scheduled it before Steven's attack.

The writers had scrambled to put together "How Deep is the Ocean," plus an earlier rejected and now doctored, "Sixteen Tons and a Bucket of Spuds." The former takes place on the ocean floor. Mel and I are in diving suits, searching for treasure from pirate Captain Jacquard Fabrique's three-masted schooner, the *Goelette Avec Trois Mats*. The writers couldn't resist this one after they heard about our Long Island weekend.

The rehearsal progressed and then broke until a late afternoon theater meeting with the orchestra. When I left, I noticed Detective Sander coming from Nate's office. I hurried to catch him before he exited the building. "Detective, could you wait a minute?"

He spun around. "Why, Miss Warren, what have you uncovered now?"

As I've noted, he was a sarcastic man, although I thought he'd mellowed since our first encounter. I sensed his air of steadfast skepticism, but still, he did ask me what I'd uncovered. I took a deep breath. "Detective, I want to tell you how I figured this. It won't take long."

"Please go on. You have my undivided interest." He crossed his arms over his chest. Had there been a light pole, I was sure he would have leaned against it.

"It's about Steven's attack."

Sander's expression indicated a not-again attitude. "We've spent time on this and concluded, as I suspected, that somebody from the outside came in to steal whatever he could find worth burgling. He saw someone coming and ducked into the lounge where he encountered Mr. Drake. A ruckus ensued and he stabbed Drake. It had nothing to do with Hardin's murder. That's the way I see it. The culprit's long gone and I doubt we'll find him. We'll keep working on it, of course."

I struggled to contain the urge to kick his shins. "What I'm saying is, someone was after Steven, period." I talked fast to keep his attention. "And besides, maybe the person who attacked Steven killed Gregory. Had you thought of that?"

Sander all but snapped his reply. "Are you saying you've come up with an angle the police aren't clever enough to figure? And I suppose you still claim Miss Carter was poisoned?"

"That's right. See here, Detective, I need to go now. I don't have proof with me, but if you'll meet me later, I'll have it for you." I reached into my purse for paper and scribbled my phone number. "Call me if you wish, or meet me at the theater in the morning. I'll be there by eight."

He actually smiled at me. "If you've got proof, lady, I'd love to see that. Yes, indeed. I can't promise eight o'clock, but I'll be there before noon."

Tallying his smile and his sarcasm as a sort of compliment, I came up with maybe he's not such a bad guy after all.

"One thing for sure," he added, "if you haven't told anyone about this, ah—proof, don't. Your own life might be in jeopardy. Understand?"

Caught by his serious tone, I nodded. But I didn't think he believed me for a second, or he wouldn't have waited until noon tomorrow.

A blue-clad security guard checked my identification when I arrived at rehearsal the next morning. "I'm glad you're here," I said.

"Thank you, Miss Warren. I'll keep a close watch."

The guard could keep people from wandering in from the streets, but if the attacker belonged in our company, he'd have a valid ID. Once inside, I prepared for the underwater scene.

A few minutes later, Donna nudged me. "Would you see who just came in? He's standing there up front, by the pillar."

I squinted. "It's Steven all right. I should have known he wouldn't wait until tomorrow." Before we could approach him, others had closed in. After responding to their good wishes, he spotted us and headed in our direction.

"Steven, you look good. A little pale, but good," Donna said. "I thought it would be at least another day before you returned."

"Couldn't help myself."

"I guess I shouldn't have been surprised," I said. "Are you sure you feel up to it?"

"Yes, mainly because my doctor relented and told me to go home and rest. I figured I could rest over here. I'm not officially working, you understand."

I had to agree he could do anything he felt well enough to do. "I guess you know how lucky you are."

"That I do. Do you mind if I wait and watch rehearsal?" With a bit of a grimace, he pulled up a chair and sat.

"Of course you can watch, but it may be a while yet. Do you need anything? Water? A cushion for your back?"

He shook his head and waved me off. "Thanks. Believe me, I'm fine."

The underwater ocean scene with Mel and me proved hysterical. Such tricky timing, but the orchestra managed to crochet bubble music around our dialogue. Afterward, I returned to where we left Steven.

"Clever sketch," he said. "You ready for something to eat? Brad's already at the Grill, and believe it or not, Nate's there, too."

"Sure, good with me." Safety in numbers, so why not?

As we entered the Grill, Brad motioned for us to join them. "Come on, you two. Here, Steven, would a table be better? We can move."

"No, thanks, the booth is fine."

Brad moved for me to sit next to him.

After we finished our meal, Mr. Sherman said, "Lisa, I almost forgot. Mrs. Bjornson called to say she sent for another wet suit. She ordered your size, but she didn't like it, so she's bringing the new one over tomorrow."

"Good, I was afraid I would have to be a mermaid." It made me a little nervous to wait until the last day for a final fitting, but I knew the sergeant would take care of it.

"A mermaid would be interesting," Brad said. "Now if you'll excuse us, I need to get back to technical."

As soon as Nate and Brad left, Steven turned toward me. "Now, let's hear it."

"All right.... I think I have proof the police will accept."

"How could you have proof, Tex?"

My own words hit me like a falling sandbag. I was too anxious to tell Steven what I'd discovered, and Detective Sander's warning deserted me. He meant for me not to tell anyone, and that included Steven. A mixture of thoughts bumped into each other. I chose one. "After I went to the library to research poisons, I called Uncle Hamp. He agreed the symptoms showed Dulce could have died from a heart attack even if she was poisoned with curare. He did say it was a far-fetched theory." *He said nothing of the kind.*

With half-amused eyes, Steven asked, "And that's what you consider proof?"

"It could have happened." In explaining, I never told him about the toxicology report. "But Steven, why were you attacked? Had you discovered something?"

I know he was sick of my playing detective. He seemed a little impatient with me. "Like I told you before, I didn't know my attacker. He, or she, darted into the lounge like someone was chasing him. Before I knew it, he lunged at me with a knife. We surprised each other. Tex, please promise me you'll be careful."

"Of course." I didn't tell him much. How serious would he take me if I told him more?

Chapter Twenty-Four

During the night, the radiator clanged like a trolley, but it kept our room cozy. Thank goodness we had a reliable super. He'd prepared for the cold weather that now arrived full force. I awoke early and dressed. Trying not to disturb Jenni, I retrieved Uncle Hamp's package from the bureau. I had already told her everything about the poison.

She must have heard my silence. "Roomie," she said, "I'm sleeping in this morning. You be careful today, okay?"

"You can be sure of that. I'll see you later."

I checked my watch again and slipped out the door. Hotel breakfast on Saturday didn't begin until nine; one reason the theater's Danish cart succeeded, at least for me. However, my dunking in Long Island Sound five days earlier, along with a strenuous rehearsal week, had finally caught up with me. I refused to catch a cold, but still, I felt a sniffle coming on. Just in case, I allowed enough time to buy a miracle cure at the Warwick.

I headed straight to the drugstore's tall display island of over-the-counter marvels. I considered Aspirin and Dymatap. I figured one or the other ought to work, so I bought both. When I left, the cold wind stung my face and I pulled my coat close around me, wishing I'd brought a muffler.

At the theater, I showed my ID to the security guard. We exchanged "good mornings" as I hurried inside to escape the weather. It turned out that Vivian was late and some thoughtful body had made coffee. Good. Vivian finally arrived and remembered to bring chocolate lattices. Better than good.

Rehearsal opened with the trio of Miss Delgado, Vince, and me. Vince and I thought we sounded super, but did anyone else, I wondered.

Afterward, I noticed Bert heading my way. "Miss Warren, somebody called this in for you." He waved a small piece of paper above his head. "I wrote it down to make sure I had it right," he added, handing the note to me.

Bert had his own version of shorthand. *Uhm, I think this means Mrs. Bjornson wants me to come by the Costume Company to try on my new wet suit.* "But Mr. Sherman told me she was going to bring it here," I said.

"I don't know about that," Bert replied. "All I know is she couldn't be here until four o'clock and wants you to come on your lunch break, 'cause if your wet suit doesn't fit, she needs more time.

How did my life get so complicated? One day I'm going to actually have lunch on my lunch hour.

Did I understand that right, Miss Warren? You going to wear a wet costume?"

I couldn't help laughing. "It's a wet suit, you know, like for underwater."

"Oh, yeah, I should have known," he said, sheepishly.

"That's okay. Thanks, Bert."

The schedule called for the "Sixteen Tons" run-through before noon. It didn't include me, so I could leave right after the ocean scene. Oh m'gosh, I'd forgotten my appointment with Detective Sander. There's no way I can put him off. Luck cooperated. The scene went smoothly, with only one brief stop. I left and hurried to find a cab. Not enough time for the bus.

"Hey, Lisa, where you going?" Donna called.

"Mrs. Bjornson wants to see me for a fitting." I pushed open the door then stopped. "I'm expecting Detective Sander. When he comes, will you ask him to wait? I'll be gone about an hour, tops."

"You must have a good reason to see him."

"I do. But don't tell anyone, okay?"

"Absolutely. I'll keep him here if I have to stand on his foot. Oh, hold on." She reached into her tote bag and handed me an envelope. "You'll want these. Vince picked them up at the camera shop."

"So soon? Well, you said the shop owner was a friend. Thanks, Donna. I'll look at them on the way... "

"Yes, yes. Now go."

I hailed a taxi and told the driver to hurry. I pulled the packet of snapshots from my purse. The first picture showed the Springston's beautiful pool. I continued reminiscing until I came to the group picture. Ha! Cassie and her almost bathing suit, Donna, then Steven in that neat outfit with a sailor scarf. I believed a man shouldn't wear a scarf unless he was Sir Cedric Hardwick, but Steven was a cosmopolitan man. I lay the picture next to me and went on to the next one.

A sudden whirling began inside my mind, expanding until I felt dizzy. Then, the picture flew into my hand, landing face up and began to flutter. *What is this?* I looked at it again... *Oh, my Lord.*

The cabby bluffed traffic as only New York cabbies can and pulled in front of the costumer's. I shoved the pictures into the envelope and dropped it in my bag.

"You want me to wait, Miss?"

"No, thank you. I don't know how long I'll be."

I paid my fare and tipped him. Still shaken, I entered the building and pressed the elevator button. Lights were on in the third floor entry, but when I opened the Costume Company's door, darkness greeted me. I flipped the light switch. Nothing happened. I tried again. Still nothing.

"Mrs. Bjornson? It's Lisa." No answer. The sergeant didn't expect me until after twelve and I was a little early. Still, the light should've turned on. Costume racks almost reached the ceiling. I thought the shades were drawn, or at least some light would surely have come through the front windows. I might as well have been in a cellar.

"Mrs. Bjornson?"

The air was heavy. Tall racks didn't allow any circulation. *This is weird. I'm leaving.* Then I heard a noise. I thought it might be the sergeant's floor fans, but they wouldn't be on if the power was out. "Mrs. Bjornson, are you here? What's happened to the lights?"

My eyes began adjusting to the dark and I could see the outline of her desk. One more step caught me totally off guard. My foot connected with something soft and heavy— too heavy for a fallen costume.

Instinctively, I reached down... "Mrs. Bjornson!" Who else could it have been? I felt for a pulse, which was there, thank God. But she was not responsive.

Frantic, I rose to my feet and searched for the phone on the desk. Then I stopped. Silence closed in... Footsteps?... No question about it, Mrs. Bjornson and I weren't the only ones there. Slipping out of my shoes, I tiptoed down one aisle and halfway up another, barely able to see.

No way did I anticipate the box of clothes over which I stumbled. I scraped my knee and shoved the words I wanted to say through cracks in the floor. When my heart calmed, I got to my feet and made my way to the next aisle. Not knowing where the stairs were, my only choice was to jump out the window. And that choice would end three floors down.

The footfalls grew closer, reinforcing my fear. Now used to the dim room, I turned left at the next aisle, hoping it would lead to an exit. A figure stepped from behind one of the multitude of racks. Shadows covered the face, but I already knew who it was.

A voice broke through the dimness. "I wouldn't try to get away, because you see, this scene is my version of *From Here to Eternity*—and I will direct."

I found it difficult to accept any voice but Brad's. Still, I couldn't deny who stood in the shadows. I gasped when I realized I was right. My chest went tight with anxiety.

"But what about Mrs. Bjornson? What did you do to her? She may be dying."

"I'll have to say Mrs. Bjornson did present a small drawback in my plan."

"She needs help!"

"That can wait." He came closer, blocking any escape, but I wasn't finished yet. A stepstool was in front of me. I threw it as hard as I could, toward the direction of the voice.

"Hold on there! Your aim should be better than that. Oh, that's right, you didn't shoot an arrow into poor Gregory, did you?"

What options do I have now?... Running through the clothes rack? Of Course! I wrestled through the costumes. It was difficult and eliminated no problem at all. There he stood, right in front of me.

"Don't try that again, darling."

I tried to run to his right, but he grabbed my wrist.

"You're hurting me," I screamed.

"Lisa... Tex!... This is your own fault. We were beginning to mean something to each other. You wouldn't leave it alone. Your curiosity brought you closer to the truth and people would begin asking questions. I'd be discovered. But you never had a clue it was me."

I could smell his tenseness, his clammy sweat. I managed to break free. "Yes. Yes, Steven, I knew—only not soon enough."

"You couldn't have known!"

"When Vince rescued me during the storm, he told me to let go of something as I was climbing the yacht's ladder. I never gave it another thought until I saw pictures of the cast party. It was your scarf! When you knocked me overboard, I must have caught hold of it."

"Tex, darling. You really are clever, more than I gave you credit for."

"But what about the roses? Brad sent them. I know that."

"Oh, yes, the American Beauties. Shrewd of me, don't you think, signing Brad's name? I thought if you checked with the florist, his name on the card would give you another lead. Since you smeared the ink on Dulce's card, you had no way of knowing I sent the thirteen roses to her. Sending you thirteen was a scare tactic. It should have worked, too. But no, you were so damn stubborn, you kept right on with your little suspicions."

"But why, Steven? Why did you poison her?" Fighting panic, I still had to know. Now that I knew how and who, I could at least go from here to eternity with the rest of the answer.

He moved closer. "All right, I owe you that much. I met Dulce during summer stock in the Catskills. We were lovers. She was so beautiful. I adored her. My agent landed me this job on Mel's show and they were searching for a co-star. I told Nate how great Dulce would be and they signed her."

"Lovers? But she had a happy marriage. Her husband told me."

"Happy? Maybe at one time. She hadn't cared about B.J. for months." He stopped, a catch in his voice, like a forlorn teenager breaking up with his first sweetheart. "She promised when they divorced, she would marry me. But she kept putting me off."

The tone of his voice changed and he spoke faster. "Dulce said she loved me. I got her that first big break. Don't you see? She used me. Then laughed in my face. She didn't care! After the divorce, I no longer existed for her."

I fought for words to calm him. "Steven, you don't have to kill me for what Dulce did."

"You may not deserve it, but I can't have you telling the police, now can I, my dear Tex?" He stepped closer, reaching to brush my cheek with his fingers.

"But, you were attacked yourself." It was becoming clear to me, but I wanted to hear it from Steven. The longer I kept him talking, the better chance for escape. Inching my way down the aisle, I found myself with no place to go. I willed away the fear pulsing through my body. I needed to think clearly now.

"Surely you can figure out that one. Think about it, Tex," he said, moving closer. It's an old trick, turning suspicion away from myself. I admit I made it a little too authentic. In the end, that worked to my advantage. Everyone believed I was a victim. Lucky Brad found me when he did."

I didn't have to see the madness in this stranger's eyes. I heard it in his voice. "So you did murder Gregory?"

"Of course, I did. He knew from the beginning I killed Dulce. I thought no one was in the building the first time I went to her dressing room. You see, Gregory hadn't left, and he saw me unlock her door. He watched me prepare my little potion and then he followed me the last time. So I'd made a stupid mistake and hadn't given the creep enough credit."

I listened in wonder to his explanation.

"He didn't realize what I was doing until he added it up after Dulce died. That's when he began blackmailing me. But enough now. We must go on with our scene."

I tried again to scramble between him and the clothes, but he blocked my way. In the dim light, I saw him pull a sash down from a costume.

"And as for killing you? Strangulation won't last long enough to hurt, I promise. And then you'll be free to dream for ever... and ever..."

Steven threw the sash around my neck. I swallowed a scream as he tightened it. I didn't want to die now. Tugging at the noose only made it worse. Terror fell over me like a diaphanous scrim and I felt myself growing limp. Did I dream a faint whir of the elevator? Perhaps I did, since Steven showed no reaction.

Suddenly, the clinking of chains sounded as the old elevator swooshed to a halt. I heard the metal door open. The entry light cast its glow on Brad as he charged into the room. Detective Sander was close behind.

Brad dashed to the main aisle and yelled. "Lisa!" Then he saw us. "Let her go, Drake."

Steven jerked me off my feet. "Stay back, both of you!"

The detective had a gun. "Don't be a fool," he said. "One shot will take you down."

"If you want to risk my breaking her neck. I have nothing to lose. Back off." Steven let go of the sash and hooked me around the waist with one arm, curling the other around my throat.

I felt as if my breath was spiraling out of me.

"Keep away from me, Hunter.... Now, Tex, just take it easy. We're going out the door to the elevator." He readjusted his hold on me.

In an instant, I saw my opportunity and twisted away from him. I whirled around and with a high kick, slammed my foot into his wounded side, sending him sprawling. He howled in agony and staggered to his feet, reaching for me, but Brad darted between us.

Steven landed a glancing blow to Brad's jaw.

He responded with a short jab to Steven's ribs. Steven clutched his side and fell against a costume rack, but Brad lunged for him again.

"That's enough, Hunter. It's over," Sander aimed his revolver at the distraught man sitting on the floor.

"I'm bleeding." Steven groaned, holding his side.

"Go ahead! Do us all a favor and bleed to death for real this time!" Brad headed to the windows and raised two large shades, letting light flood in and hurried back to me.

I'm all right. It's Mrs. Bjornson" I pointed to the desk. "She needs an ambulance!"

"Is there a phone in this place?" Sander called out.

"It's right there on the desk behind you."

While Brad examined Mrs. Bjornson, I quickly drenched some paper towels from the water fountain.

"She's coming around," he said.

As I started to wipe her face with the wet towels, she took them from me. "Thank you, but I can do that." Still dazed, she tried to get up.

Brad helped her to a chair.

"I will be fine. Thank God, my head is hard."

That's my Sergeant Bjornson. Independence in human form.

The detective, still holding his gun on Steven, reached for the phone. "Hunter, can you strap that sash thing around Drake's mid-section? That is, if he's really bleeding. I'll get an ambulance for the lady and have the station pick up Drake.

By that time, Brad was preoccupied holding me close. I didn't want to move.

"Hunter!"

Brad let me go, and I found I could stand by myself.

He pulled Steven forward and wrapped the sash around him.

"Take your hands off me," Steven snapped, pushing away. He slumped against the rack and slid to the floor.

Chapter Twenty-Five

Still a little foggy, I unblocked my mind. "Wait, where's my handbag? It's important." I tried to retrace my steps to the aisle where I fell over the box of clothes. "No, wait. It was the next one. There it is, in plain sight."

Brad reached down and picked up the shoes I had scarcely missed. "Lisa, do these little things belong to you?"

As soon as I slipped them on, we left the library of clothes, to the sound of sirens. Mrs. Bjornson walked without assistance and protested going to the hospital. She was outvoted.

The ambulance drove up as we exited and the squad car came soon after. Detective Sander sent Steven to the station and said he would drive us to the theater before he went to the precinct.

Brad sat with his arm around me in the back seat of the car. I gulped air, reassuring myself I could breathe.

I caught Sander's glance in his rearview mirror.

"Miss Warren, you know I'll have a few questions for you. You'll need to come to the station to make a statement."

Before responding, I cleared my throat, hoping I still had a voice. "I'll be happy to answer your questions. But how did you know where to find me?"

"Easy," Brad said. "Sander came by wanting to see you. Donna told him you had a message to meet Mrs. Bjornson at the costumers and wouldn't be long. We had waited over an hour and you were already late for rehearsal.

"I'm just glad I told her."

"You should've seen Hunter when I told him you had proof Dulce Carter was murdered. He couldn't get out of there fast enough."

"I was really worried about you," Brad said. "But Nate's at the studio and needs to be informed, if you don't mind taking us by there, Sander. The rehearsal doesn't need me for a while. They can work on the music."

"I'm ready," Sander said.

When we arrived at the studio, Brad opened the producer's door without knocking.

"Come in. Come in," Sherman said, rising from his chair. Something tells me this isn't a usual visit."

"It isn't a usual visit," Brad responded. He gave him a hasty briefing of the last hour's activities, to which Mr. Sherman registered astonishment.

Sander took out his notepad. "I would like to pin down some facts. I can attest that Mr. Drake was ready to kill you, Miss Warren, but his being attacked still puzzles me."

It was all clear to me now, and I couldn't believe Sander had not figured this out. "Brad, did you tell him exactly where you found the knife?"

"No, I said it was on the floor. I never touched it."

"Detective, I'm sure you've already thought of this." I rather doubted he had. "When Brad showed me the room where Steven was attacked, he said he heard something scrape against the floor when he pushed open the door. It had to be the knife."

Brad and Sander seemed to be waiting for more. Mr. Sherman was deeply absorbed with the entire discussion.

"If someone had attacked him," I said, "that person couldn't have dropped the knife so close to the inside of the door when he left the room."

Sander turned toward us and in the decisive manner of Sherlock Holmes, said, "The only person in the lounge was Drake, himself. Hunter, why didn't you tell me about the knife?"

"You never asked and I didn't think of it at the time. Lisa's persistence caused me to remember, but I didn't make the connection."

The detective seemed perplexed. "So, Drake used a paper towel to wipe off the fingerprints. Then he flushed it."

"Yes," I said, "He dropped the knife without thinking where it landed. It probably slid on the tile. He lay down and waited for someone to find him, never thinking he might bleed to death in the meantime." It was so simple when I heard myself say it aloud.

"It could have happened that way," Sander said, "but a thief was my first choice. Of course, Drake was lucky the wound wasn't fatal, since he screwed it up. I'll think on it. Yes, I certainly will."

"What's to think about? He confessed!" *How much proof did this man need?*

"This is incredible," Mr. Sherman said. "I would never have suspected Drake."

Brad shook his head. "Lisa, is that why you were so inquisitive about where I found him?"

"I didn't know why its importance kept bothering me. But now it all comes together."

"I'm not sure what you mean by *it*," Sander said. "However, since we have Mr. Drake taken care of, I believe you have some proof for me?"

"Yes, I do." I took the package from my bag and handed it to him.

"And this is?"

"It needs a little explaining."

Sander raised his left eyebrow. "Why doesn't that surprise me?" he asked.

"Dulce's death didn't make sense, and even less after her ex-husband told me she had no medical problems. How many young women with perfect health have heart attacks?"

"Not many, I'd guess. But I'm sure you have an answer."

"You know, Dulce's death already brought unanswered questions, but not for long as far as you were concerned. The fact Steven told me she had blue eyes but wore brown contacts wasn't in itself so suspicious. It kept lingering in my thoughts. Something in an old *National Geographic* kept cropping up in my memory. That's when I began researching poisons. I know it sounded a little far-fetched, but I couldn't nudge it out of my mind."

"This may be well and good, but can you get to the point?" Sander asked.

"Steven must have destroyed Dulce's second pair of contacts along with any remaining eye drops in her dressing room. I found a bottle of drops and the other pair of lenses in her locker."

So far, Sander hadn't asked what Dulce's lenses had to do with her death. He gave a wary nod, as if trying to grasp the logic. "Miss Warren, would you please tell me this? What did Miss Carter's contacts have to do with her death?"

Talk about a cue. The man stepped on my line. "You see, Steven began by putting small increments of refined curare in Dulce's lens wash. If her sight was only a little blurred, she possibly thought she needed a new prescription. Later, he put the poison into her eye drops."

"And that small amount killed her?"

"More drops than before, but it didn't take much. The last time she used them could have relaxed her into an eternal nap right on the spot if the cleaning woman hadn't found her when she did. Dulce absorbed enough poison to make her stop breathing. She might have been saved, but at the time, who would've suspected?" I shuddered. "I wonder what Dulce thought was happening to her, or even if she had time to think."

Detective Sander opened the box and removed the bottle. "This is news to me. But how did you know all this?"

I stood, thinking it would give more emphasis to my explanation. I wanted to keep his attention before he changed his mind about hearing me out. Perhaps he'll listen to me now.

"Donna Springston's father is an ophthalmologist. During eye surgery, they often use a minute bit of curare to make the eye immobile. Dr. Springston verified that enough of those minuscules could cause death. So I mailed Dulce's lenses and eyewash to Uncle Hamp in Dallas. He had his toxicologist check it out."

The detective held the bottle up to the light and studied the liquid as though he could determine its contents. He set it on the desk and unfolded the accompanying report. After reading it, he handed the paper to Mr. Sherman.

"Brad, I remember now you once told me Dulce had beautiful brown eyes, so you didn't know what color they really were."

"That's right, no hint at all."

"You recall when someone ransacked my room? It was Steven, searching for a card that came with Dulce's thirteen roses. I never knew all its contents, but it had to be incriminating. Apparently, no one knew of their affair. And, now, I know he signed your name when he purchased my thirteen roses."

I explained to them what Steven told me about him and Dulce being lovers and of Gregory blackmailing him. "Of course, Detective, you had no way of knowing that."

"If he hadn't confessed to you," he said, "we would have had a hard time pinning Hardin's murder on him."

"Maybe not too difficult, not after I went through the pictures I took of the Long Island cast party." I told them about Steven's scarf and how I had pulled it from him.

Sander sighed. "This does give us something to work on. I'll say this, if you ever give up acting, I'll put in a good word for you at the N.Y.P.D."

"She better not give up acting," Sherman exclaimed, "not if I have anything to do with it."

I must have smiled, but I suddenly felt weak. I entertained the idea of fainting but then thought better of it. I drifted back to when Steven and I first met. He was thrilled when Nate and Mel offered me the contract.

I became aware of tears escaping down my face... for the man I thought I knew.

"Miss Warren... Miss Warren?" Sander's voice held a touch of sympathy. "We'll get back with you. I know you have a show to do tonight. I'll drive you to the theater now."

Nate Sherman interrupted. "That won't be necessary. I'll take care of it." He turned to me. "Lisa, we can use a kinescope repeat, or perhaps Cassie can fill in for you."

I brought myself to the present and threw a sharp look at our producer. "Only if I actually broke my leg!" I smiled and added, "I need to get my dance shoes from my dressing room. Won't take a minute."

"We'll be waiting," Brad said.

How often have I opened this door and walked right in? But this time, a sensation I couldn't explain overwhelmed me. The room was not cold as before. I heard a faint swooshing sound, like a breeze floating through my grandmother's lace-curtained windows.

I know I heard someone say, "Thank you." Then, an image became visible in the large wall mirror. Dulce Carter gazed at me with a pleased smile, her eyes devoid of tears. I spun around to see from where the reflection came. Nothing. She was only in the mirror. When I turned back, she had disappeared. Did I imagine she spoke? An immediate feeling of warmth and comfort took over. The sweet fragrance of roses filled the room.

I grabbed my dance shoes and rejoined Brad and Mr. Sherman. At the theater, I managed to get to the costume room without anyone seeing me. I wanted only to concentrate on the show.

Donna, already in dress, greeted me with a hug. "Lisa, I'm so sorry. Everybody's heard. It must have been horrible for you."

"Good adjective. It may have been one of my better performances. I still find it hard to believe."

"I know," she said. "People say it takes time to overcome bad memories."

How much time, I wondered. But I still have to get over it myself. "Thanks, friend. We'd best report for rehearsal."

"I'll see you in a few minutes."

As soon as Donna left, a light tap sounded on my door. "Lisa, may I talk to you?"

I opened the door to see Raymond. His face flushed. "Brad told me what happened. God, I'm glad you're safe." He put his arms around me and planted a big kiss on my forehead. "There, that's for your pretty head. Now go out there tonight and knock 'em dead. Uh, poor choice of words, but you know what I mean."

"Thanks, Raymond. I needed a pep talk."

He turned to leave. "Wait... I think I'll do that again, for good luck, of course."

What could I say after a day like this? At least I kept my sanity. With nerve endings quivering, I finished the show. So what if I did make up a few words in the ocean scene? Maybe the viewers thought I'd swallowed a fish.

Brad had asked me to wait for him. This part of the day was entirely yare, meaning bright and nothing to do with boats. I changed clothes and walked to the front of the theater. Brad stood there, waiting.

I said, "Hi." It sounded a little monosyllabic for all I really felt like saying, including an apology for suspecting him of murder.

"Lisa, if you feel up to it, how about going over to the Grill. I'll take you home afterward."

He linked his arm in mine and we walked around the corner.

Once we entered the Grill, Cassie stopped us. "Lisa, I'm really glad you're all right. You gave a great performance tonight."

"Thank you, Cassie. I appreciate it." She finally sounded sincere.

When I stopped to sign a few autographs, I heard Vince call my name. We sat next to him with the rest of the group at our choice roundtable. He pulled out his envelope of the cast party pictures. "Lisa, I went through snapshots and you won't believe what I—"

"Yes, I do believe. It's the scarf. I would never have remembered had it not been for the picture. Now that you know, if Steven had succeeded with the sash around my neck, the scarf around his might have helped convict him."

"I'll testify if necessary, although it may not come to that."

"You know what else, Vince? Audrey wore a white bathing suit on the yacht. I told Donna I saw a flash of white just before I went overboard. Audrey was so jealous of Nate, and don't you dare repeat this, I thought for a moment she had pushed me. Or, on second thought, maybe..."

"Steven's white pullover," Vince said. "I wouldn't want anyone to be that much in love with me."

"Now that you've brought up the subject of love, why don't you ask Jenni out again? I have a strong feeling she'll accept." Three words described this Italian. Neat, talented, wonderful. Whoever landed him would be one lucky girl. She might even be Jenni.

"I think I'll do that," he said. "You know, I really like her."

Suddenly, hunger pangs struck. After all, I caught a murderer and did an entire show on only a couple of chocolate lattices. Well, so maybe I wasn't really famished. I'd settle for a Caesar salad without anchovies. And come to think of it, my nerves would appreciate a glass of wine. White wine. I'd already had one headache.

No one else mentioned my traumatic afternoon at the Costume Company. I think Brad understood I wanted to put it out of my mind for the present, forever, if possible. We discussed his future as a director and my dream of Broadway and opera. He believed someone from one, or both, would call me. The possibility of television shows no longer being live, but filmed, came up. Would they ever be, we wondered. "Nah, never happen."

I gazed into Brad's sapphire-blue eyes, their natural color, not contacts.

He gazed back. "Lisa, do you suppose I could interest you in a *real* date tomorrow evening, just the two of us?..." Definitely a warm demeanor.

www.ingramcontent.com/pod-product-compliance
Lightning Source LLC
Chambersburg PA
CBHW031426250626
47155CB00004B/1639

* 9 7 8 0 9 3 7 6 6 0 7 0 6 *